Tales

from

Below the Frost Line

The Anrald Writers

Editors: Julie Malear & Monika Conroy

Anrald Press
Boynton Beach, Florida
A rare collection of short stories from South Florida Writers

This is a work of fiction. Names, characters, places and incidents are either the product of the author's imagination, or are used fictitiously and any resemblance to actual persons, living or dead, businesses, companies, events, or locales is entirely coincidental.

Anrald Press
P.O. Box 233
Boynton Beach, FL 33425

Editors: Julie Malear & Monika Conroy
Tales from Below the Frost Line

Cover Design: ©Julie Malear
Cover Layout: Monika Conroy

Library of Congress Control Number: 2004114574
ISBN: 0-9760826-1-6
Anrald Press

Printed in the United States by Morris Publishing
3212 East Highway 30
Kearney, NE 68847
1-800-650-7888

CONTENTS

Writers are listed in alphabetical order.

INTRODUCTION
of our Authors

When **ANRALD PRESS**, located in Boynton Beach, Florida began this compilation of short stories from "below the frost line"—ie.: South Florida—the editors wanted writers with imagination and creativity who could tell tales of relationships in their own unique style that exhibits the influence of the Sunshine State. Many of these stories have won awards. During the creation of *Tales*, ANRALD PRESS and its writers were besieged by problems arising from the quadruple hit of Hurricanes Charley, Frances, Ivan and Jeanne. In spite of the winds, high water and downed computers, these writers pursued their love for writing. Thus *"Tales from Below the Frost Line"* was born.

Below are brief bios of the writers:

Millicent Brady joined Anrald in 1989. She enjoys writing short stories, mostly Science Fiction and Fantasy. She entered two of her short stories, *Tell Val* and *Beyond Beta*, in the Andre Norton Category of the Florida State Writing Competition in 1990. *Tell Val* took second place and *Beyond Beta* received an honorable mention. *Tell Val* was later published in *The Cosmic Unicorn*, winter 1994. Although she favors science fiction, she is very versatile in her choices of subject matter. She has coauthored a novel with John Vignari, entitled *Mafia Born*, published by 1st Books Library. The book explores what it is like to grow up in a Mafia family.

Tom Collins. I attended my first writing course when I retired at age 64. I stumbled into a most patient and knowledgeable teacher, Ms. L. A. Justice. With her guidance, I had an article published on the front page of *The Boca Raton News* in five weeks. Then, I was bitten by the fiction bug and attended more classes. I've been published many times in magazines such as, *Storyteller, Reminisce, Grit* and *Dog & Kennel*. I won first prize in a fiction contest sponsored by *The Storyteller Magazine*. My humor column, *Tomfoolery*, has been published for eight years now and is still getting laughs. (At least from my wife.) Not bad, for a guy with only a diploma from Merrillville High School in Indiana.

Monika Conroy, is a winner of seven literary awards for writing short stories published in literary magazines. In the early seventies, her interest in writing became more serious with the publication of her first written work. She holds degrees in Linguistics and Language as well as being a certified Florida Supreme Court mediator and has focused on her writing skills through numerous writing classes, writer's conferences and workshops. Her writing interest, however, takes a very different path. "I enjoy creating whole new civilizations, cultures and complex characters." She is currently working on the fictionalized origin of the Tarot Cards, *The Dragon and the Artist*, tracing how each card acquired its unique meaning, including the lost card, the key to the interpretation of the tarot.

Ginger Curry is a multi-talented writer specializing in editing, critiquing and rewriting manuscripts, ghost-writing, and creative writing classes. She has extensive suspense fiction experience. Published works include columns, over 100 short stories and articles plus a book, *The Name Dropper: From Rolling Wheel to Yachts,* (Frank Neal with Ginger Curry.) She is published in numerous periodicals, such as *Tampa Tribune, Woman's World, Tales of the Witch World #2, etc.* She was Fiction Chair for FFWA 13 years where she critiqued and judged thousands of manuscripts. Listed in a number of *Who's Who* and other autobiographical books, she has won over 100 prizes for her writing--most recent: First Prize in NLAPW competition for her novel *Sea Eye.*

Diane Duritt, under a nom de plume, introduces her protagonist, Leann Regent, Ph.D. in a first novel, *In Confidence.* Currently in revision, this Fort Lauderdale based novel follows Dr. Regent, Clinical Psychologist, as she faces the fallout of a murder that threatens to jeopardize her practice and her life. Diane's career role as a Psychological Examiner has provided insight into the development of personality and human emotion. As an interloper into the inner psyche, she has met with the dark side of the human mind. Diane applies her education and knowledge to her writing. She is an affiliate of the Mystery Writers of America. Diane lives in South Florida with her husband and felines, Clara and Cozette.

Rayna Harris earned a Master of Arts degree in Hebrew Literature and Education from the Hebrew University of Jerusalem and Hunter College. She taught English as a Foreign Language at the Hebrew University in Jerusalem and taught English and Hebrew in New York and Florida high schools. She is a recent recipient of a Munzer Scholarship in creative writing. Her stories have been published in *Coastlines,* and *Jewish Heritage.* She is currently working on a novel set in Jerusalem during the Six Day War.

Robert Kerpel's tightly drawn fiction blends hard reality with unique imagination. When he left the streets of New York and moved to Florida, he brought his street-smarts, the adventures he experienced, and his astute observations of human nature, all of which color his writing today. Although currently working on two books—one on slavery in the Amazon; the other a serio-comic novel on man's responsibility for the sexual seeds he sows--Bob still has time to teach poetry, short-shorts, novels, novellas and short stories, one of which won first prize in Florida Freelance Writers' Association competition. Educated at Peekskill Military Academy and Columbia University, he is not only an avid reader and prolific and imaginative writer, but works out to keep himself in top shape physically.

Janet Le Clair, a freelance writer and photographer for *The Original Irregular,* a newspaper covering the western mountains of Maine. Her short stories have appeared in *KMR Publications, Kaleidoscope* and *Methodist Publishing Company* and her articles appeared in *Gold Coast Life* and *Palm Beach Post.* Janet won Florida Freelance Writers awards for a short story and was a judge for the FFWA State Short Story. Janet served as president and vice-president of this club for several years. Her novel, *Double Image,* a supernatural suspense, won a top ten award from the National Writer's Club and she is currently working on a second book, an historical novel dealing with the expulsion of the Acadians from Nova Scotia in 1755, of which Janet is a descendent.

Julie Malear, previously a working artist, launched her writing career in newspapers with columns, features, hard news, cartoons, layouts, editing and complete sections. She co-wrote *Love Story of Boldt Castle*, a paperback, and appeared regularly in colorful, local magazines: *Fiesta, Boca Raton, SunGuide* and others. After writing countless stories for national detective magazines and 14 profiles for a glossy crime encyclopedia, her stories went to paper-backs. One book, purchased for a movie, won state and national awards as did several of her short stories. She's in two Who's Who books. Her hardback, *Shattered Bonds,* about Cindy Band's tragedy, is still "on tour" with signings, TV and radio. Julie currently edits, creates a newsletter and is working on five new books, three of them fiction.

Mary Thurman Yuhas, a freelance writer who writes for the *Sun-Sentinel* newspaper and for a number of magazines, has in-depth experience writing biographies and profiles. Mary is writing her first book a personal memoir *Growing Up Crazy.* It is her story of growing up with a mother who suffers from paranoid schizophrenia. She says, "Writing is a passion. I love people and love to write about their lives. Nothing is more rewarding to me than interviewing someone and afterwards writing an article that not only tells the story but also leaves the reader feeling that he or she knows the person. I cannot imagine doing anything other than exactly what I do."

TELL VAL

My first day back from vacation was one of those hot South Florida days that the Snowbirds migrate north to escape. There wasn't the slightest hint of the kind of weather that lent credibility to Cory's standard morning greeting, "Beautiful day in the Palm Beaches."

"It'll be a beautiful day when I get my route cut," I replied as we joined the carriers waiting to clock in at eight. Around us, zombie-like clerks from the graveyard shift went about their work, pushing gurneys and crab cages loaded with mail.

I clocked in and spotted Jay Wilson, our balding supervisor.

"Hey, Jay, what's the word on my route check?" I asked.

"Had to postpone it," he said, pausing momentarily, on his way outside to smoke a cigarette. "I'll let you know when it's rescheduled."

Jay knew it was useless to inspect a seasonal route like mine during the off-season. "That's the third postponement, Jay. If you wait much longer you might as well forget it until fall."

Jay mumbled something about how it wasn't his fault, then scurried away and almost bumped into Cory.

"Spoken like a true supervisor," Cory taunted.

Angrily, I began sorting mail and turned my attention to the workroom chatter. As usual, the noise level was high. This morning Jim Buglione gushed with chatter. He was elaborating on the continuing escapades of Candi, a dumb broad type, promiscuous female who obviously existed only in the warped corridors of his mind.

"Hey, Bug," called Phil as he entered the zone, "ain't you got nothing to say?"

Phil sorted mail between Jim and me and this was his "I'm here" announcement as he sauntered past Jim each morning.

Ignoring Phil, Jim continued with his story. I'd heard enough and tuned him out, letting the usual assortment of one liners and pet phrases slide over me. I was glad to see that my route had been well taken care of in my absence. I'd expected to find a pile of undeliverable mail but the "no such numbers" and the "moved left no forwards" had all been taken care of.

I asked Phil who ran my route while I was on vacation.

"Valerie Simmons," he responded. "Kept it up good too," and without overtime."

"You trying to say I'm a slacker?"

"Nope. Just letting you know how things went with your route."

"I don't know how the hell she did that unless she raced right through without stopping for lunch or breaks. I'm no slouch, you know, and I sure as hell can't keep it up without going into overtime most days."

"Come on now, Beverly. You know how eager new carriers are to please. With Valerie, you got the added benefit of competence."

Valerie, a dark-haired young beauty, had come on board about a month before I left. I learned from Phil that she would be back in our zone the next day.

On the street, the route was as clean as it had been in the office. I found no misdeliveries waiting in boxes to be picked up. If only I could get my route inspection done. I knew exactly what should be cut from the route – Springbrook Pines, a new development in the final phase of construction. Upon completion, Springbrook would add fifty-three addresses to my route.

The first thing I noticed after turning into Springbrook was the absence of construction crews. While making my deliveries to curbside boxes, all of which were of uniform height and size, I slowly realized that something else was strange. Judging from the cars in driveways, everyone was home, yet this was a community of working people – not retirees. And, another thing . . . something I couldn't quite focus on . . . or wouldn't. Haunted me the rest of the day, then, as I was lying in bed at night, it hit me. I hadn't seen a single person in the entire ninety minutes I'd been in the development. All those cars in driveways and no people about. Children should have been coming home from school, yet I had seen no school busses or children. Where was ten-year-old Chris Randall with his skateboard? And the Cook children, asking for rubber bands . . . where had they been today?

I was sure there had to be a logical reason for all this. It reminded me of the time I'd seen the yellow sediment in dried up puddles following a heavy rainfall. That was neither acid rain nor germ warfare; merely pollen from the giant pine trees bordering the development. On that sobering note, I put the matter to rest and went to sleep.

Tuesday morning at the office, Valerie came over to me and said she hoped I found everything all right with the route. It was strange the way I felt while she stood there. I'm not sure I can explain it except to say that it was a tranquil feeling where nothing mattered. I sensed no need to thank her for taking care of my route and no reason to be upset because she had worked nonstop, which, at least on paper, made me look bad by comparison. It was not until she walked away that I remembered I'd intended to ask her if she'd noticed anything out of the ordinary in Springbrook.

That morning the office chatter took on a slightly different air. A new phrase had found its way into the morning jargon during my absence. "Tell Val" now seemed the favored response following all complaints. Valerie was filling in for Linda, who'd called in sick. I didn't understand the nature of the comment, but I'd been at the P.O. long enough to know that being away for a week or two was like missing a few episodes of a soap opera. You catch up fast enough.

That afternoon when maneuvering my jeep through Springbrook, I noticed the cars were still there and the construction crews were not. But, it was something else that destroyed my logical explanation theory. I know this sounds insane, but all the mailboxes seemed about six inches lower. Crazy, huh? But I've been putting mail into those boxes long enough to know when something is different.

Everything was wrong. The roads were all too narrow. Places where I'd normally hang a U-ee, I couldn't . . . not without running off the pavement. And, check this out: it was trash day and there were no garbage cans strewn in my path. The previous night's resolve was evaporating like puddles of water on a hot summer day.

Whatever was happening was getting progressively worse. Next day the boxes were another six inches lower and my jeep seemed huge and awkward on the constricted streets. Houses and cars even seemed smaller.

I remembered something Cory said before I went on vacation. He was talking about this house that vanished from his route. Like The Bug and his infamous Candi, nobody took Cory's shrinking house seriously. He used to complain all the time about the couple in six-o-one, the vanished house. The last time Cory mentioned the disappearance, Linda lit into him. "Tell me something, Cory," she'd said. "Why do we have to share in your fantasy?"

Thing was, Cory said the house shrank until it disappeared. Well, Springbrook Pines was shrinking or I was crazy. When I returned off the route, late as usual, Cory had already gone home.

Thursday morning a certified letter came for Mr. Randall. I had trouble getting mail into some of the miniaturized boxes, now little more than a foot off the ground. All still contained yesterday's mail, which had shrunk. I parked my jeep and sat looking at the Randall house. In a different setting, it could have been a grandiose playhouse for an overindulged child. The Camaro in the driveway resembled a kiddy car. Much as I dreaded walking up to that door, the thought of yesterday's shrunken mail made the act of lingering even less appealing. Reluctantly, I started up the narrow walk. A dog barked. Could it be Mitzi, the Randall's big black shaggy mutt? "Here Mitzi. Here girl." My voice came out all squeaky, sounding eerily hollow in the unnatural quiet.

When Mitzi rounded the corner it took all I could do not to bolt and run. She was the size of a fat tomcat. Mitzi growled as though she didn't know me. I hadn't changed. She had. Did her world appear normal to her? Did she think I'd become a giant? With thundering heart, I took a deep breath and rang the minuscule bell and thought about all the scary movies I'd ever seen. I invariably thought the people in those movies pretty stupid for sticking around. "Not me," I'd say. Well, there I was . .. ringing the stupid bell, inviting confrontation with whatever horror lay beyond that miniature door.

No one answered and I hurried back to my jeep, scrambling in so fast I banged my knee on the doorframe. Searing pain. *Jesus, how did I do that? Did the jeep shrink?* Almost lost it that time. . .but then, everything seemed normal . . same amount of leg room, same fit in the seat, same distance from the ground . . . but wait . . . Mitzi thinks everything's normal too. She thinks I'm different. Look at her sitting there growling. "Calm down," I told myself out loud. "Calm down and split this place." I tossed the notice left slip in the mailbox and raced through the remaining Springbrook stops clinging to the thought that tomorrow begins my long weekend.

That night I phoned Cory. I told him everything that had been happening on my route.

"Take my advice and keep quiet," he said. "It'll take care of itself."

"What does that mean?" I asked.

"After the Conklin house vanished, the number disappeared from my letter case. They got no more mail. Like the house and the people never existed."

"How long did it all take?"

"Well, let's see. It started right after I was out with the flu . . ."

"Hold it Cory . . . did you talk to whoever ran your route while you were out?"

"What for? She knows."

"She who?"

"Val . . . Valerie Simmons." There was a pause on the other end of the phone. "Don't you know what the `Tell Val' business is all about?" Cory asked.

"Haven't given it much thought."

"It's Springbrook Pines that's disappearing, isn't it?"

"Yeah. How'd you know?"

"It's Valerie. She ran your route while you were on leave, you know."

"I know that, but I don't follow you."

"You gotta be careful what you say around her. Everybody knows she can make things like headaches and warts go away, but that's just the tip of the iceberg. She must have heard me gripe about the Conklins. Lord knows I bitched enough. She was in our zone the week before you left on vacation and all you talked about was . . ."

". . . was the route cut I wanted," I said, finishing the sentence for him.

"They all think she's some kind of healer,' Cory said, "but she's a witch."

I spent my three-day weekend with my son at Disney World trying to forget Springbrook, Valerie and the post office. On Monday, there was no mail for Springbrook. Valerie was busy sorting mail next to me on Phil's route. Once our eyes met and her smile seemed to say, "I trust you are satisfied with your route cut."

Jim waved a piece of mystery mail.

"Can you believe this," he exclaimed. "No street number. . . just `postman, it's the house with the purple trim, five utility poles past Second Avenue.' "

"Do you know where it goes?" Asked Cory.

"Yeah, that's the Johnson house."

"Then deliver it, Sherlock."

It was business as usual. I heard Steve bitching about Sally's Place, a bar and grill on his route. He hated going there because it was a hangout for pushers and addicts. "My route wouldn't be half bad if I could get rid of that place," he said.

"Tell Val," I said. "Tell Val all about it."

In my father's house are many mansions
If it were not so, I would have told you
I go to prepare a place for you.
John 14:2

CAN WE TALK

"Is it ready yet?"

"No. It's still too cold."

"Can't we speed it up?"

These last few months, the voices were growing more persistent. I heard the phone ringing as I approached the house. Something to concentrate on . . . the voices ceased. I never could stand it when they hang up before I reach the phone. Thank goodness for caller ID these days. I hurried inside and grabbed the phone on the fifth ring. It was Jewel.

"Hi, Gail, I'm so glad I caught you home."

I stepped out of my shoes and tried to conceal my disappointment. "I just walked in," I replied. Jewel called once or twice a week to talk. These calls always lasted at least an hour. It was her therapy and I'd fallen into the role of therapist. It was therapeutic for us both. My kids were outgrowing their dependency and Jewel needed a sounding board. I geared up for the ordeal.

"Did I tell you about the new guy I met? No? I guess not. I haven't talked to you in a while."

Jewel seldom waited for response from me. She just kept right on talking.

"He's the most interesting person. You'll have to meet him. You two have a lot in common you know."

Jewel is about the most trusting person I know. *Another Mr. Right, I thought.* Incredibly beautiful with flawless features, she possessed the kind of golden, radiant beauty that inspires poets and once sparked envy among the old gods.

"Really? I asked. I laid the phone down and pulled off my sweater – put my ear to the receiver to verify she was still talking and put on water for coffee. I picked up the phone again just in time to hear her ask, "Isn't this a screwed up world? What do you think of that?"

"It's terrible," I said. It didn't matter what details I'd missed. I was certain to hear them again.

Jewel talked about her new boyfriend's interest in psychic phenomena. "He said we're soul mates and that it was our destiny to meet. You know, Gail, when I first laid eyes on him, I knew he was special. I could feel it."

What a pity Jewel's intelligence couldn't match her looks. The water came to a boil and I eased the receiver down on the counter and got the instant coffee from the cabinet. I knew from experience, Jewel would be rattling on about what's-his-name. I was never quite sure how I became the person of choice for these downloadings, except that she had no other female friends. Understandable, most women were inclined to keep a safe distance between Jewel and their husbands or boyfriends. I had neither.

Still stirring my coffee, I picked up the phone.

"It just makes so much sense, you know. I mean, they don't tell us everything . . ."

"They certainly don't," I said.

She continued, "I don't trust this government. Do you?" As usual, she expected no reply. "He could be right you know."

Well, by that time I still had no idea what she was talking about.

"You think about it," she said.

"What's to think about," I asked, fishing for clues.

"Well, how about all those strange circles and stuff appearing in corn fields in England and Canada?"

I was beginning to get the picture. "I suppose you think that's the work of aliens."

"Makes more sense than people running around in the middle of the night doing it."

I thought it awfully ironic that Jewel should think people always made sense when she was being so irrational. "How does it make sense for aliens to come here and mess around in cornfields? I'd think they'd have better things to do," I said.

"Zelix says it's how they send messages to other aliens."

"Seems awful primitive for space travelers."

"Well, maybe they have a sense of humor and want to keep us confused."

I was flabbergasted.

"And you know," she went on, they say the military found a crashed saucer with dead aliens and hid them away in a hangar somewhere."

"That was New Mexico."

"Yeah, they even autopsied one of the aliens."

"Jewel, what's this guy been telling you?"

"Not just me. He tells everybody who comes. Gail . . . this channeller's good."

"Who's good?"

"The channeller we went to see. Haven't you been listening? They go into trance, you know, and the spirits speak through them − only Zelix is not a spirit. He's one of them."

And I'd been thinking Zelix was her new boyfriend. At least this hour promised not to be dull. "Tell me again, I prodded, "I'm not sure I heard you right. What did the spirits . . ., I mean what did Zelix say?"

"Oh Gail, I wish you could've been there. He said everything's coming together on the earth plane. That we're moving toward some kind of new order. But that part about the children. . ., it's so sad."

"About what children, Jewel?"

"Missing children. He said there are aliens living among us and our government knows all about it. He said the government gets things from them, like some of these new technologies. Gail," she lowered her voice, "you know all the missing kids? He says the government lets them have the children to experiment with in exchange for information."

"That's crazy, Jewel. You can't believe that crap."

"But I was there, Gail. I heard his voice change from ordinary like us to thick Irish brogue."

"So what. It means nothing. Actors do it all the time. And, how do you explain aliens that speak in Irish Brogue?"

"He was speaking to us from Ireland. That's where he lives."

"I see." I was tired of trying to reason with her. If Jewel wanted to believe that crap, why should I argue with her?

"He's been right about other things," she volunteered.

"Like what?" Jewel had innocently unleashed confused memories from my childhood. I'd momentarily recalled wandering around in my father's orange grove so long ago, when three days of my own life had been spent as a missing child."

"He predicted the San Francisco earthquake," Jewel said.

"I could have predicted that. The whole world knows San Francisco sits on a major fault. What else did he predict?"

"Lots of things. You remember Cathy, don't you?"

I knew right away where this was headed and I didn't like it. Didn't like being reminded of those three days. Cathy Taylor, my next-door neighbor's little eight-year-old had disappeared five years ago from this very neighborhood. "Of course, I remember," I said.

"Well, how else could she disappear between the store and home? The store's right around the corner, and you know it was the middle of the day. Like she just stepped right off the earth, you know."

The whole neighborhood had searched for Cathy.

The police suspected, with good reason, that the mother's boyfriend was involved but was never able to prove anything or find a body. Her disappearance is still a cold case file. As recent as last year police were poking around her house looking for buried remains.

"Some of those disappearances have been explained."

"Not all of them are kidnapped by aliens, but Cathy could have been. Sometimes the aliens send them back but they don't remember anything. Some of them have even been returned with their genes altered."

I wished I could alter Jewel's genes. This was getting nowhere.

The first time I saw the lights, was in the summer of 1954 when I was six years old. We were sitting on our front porch, Mom and Dad and Phyllis and me. Phyllis was ten that summer.

Mom was first to point them out. "Look," she said, "there it is." As we watched, a bright orange glow seemed to rise up from the earth, about a quarter of a mile away in the orange grove across the street.

"Same as last time," Dad remarked. "It always appears the same way." Looking like a big ball of fire, it rose until it reached a height of about twenty feet above the trees.

"It's stopped!" Phyllis declared. Then the big fireball kind of bounced across the treetops for a while and I watched in a state of hypnotic amazement. Suddenly, it stopped.

"Now watch," Dad said, and the glowing ball soon divided into two smaller fireballs. Both zoomed off at warp speed. "They always do that," he said.

"What are these things that are coming together?" I asked.

"Zelix says all the interest in space travel and movies like Close Encounters and ET is part of a plan to get the public ready for the New Age. They're here already, but the government conceals their presence. That's all going to change and this is to prepare us."

"That's absurd."

"No it isn't. You remember that movie, Alien Nation?"

"You're going to tell me real aliens played in that movie, right?"

"No, they were consultants."

"And you believe all this?"

"Yes, I do," she responded defensively. "Zelix says the reason it's so easy for them to blend in here is because earth people are so naïve that they think theirs is the only intelligent life form in the universe."

Jamie, my oldest son had entered the house during this conversation. I sensed his presence without having seen or heard him. This telepathy between my children and me had always been present . . . something I took for granted and instinctively kept quiet about.

"Jewel," I asked, "what if what you're saying is true? How can we know these aliens?"

"It's not like that science fiction stuff at all. They can't live here in their normal form yet. The genetically altered children grow up and have children. The aliens reincarnate into these human forms. These children are different in ways you can't see."

How convenient, I thought.

"They have special talents . . . talents that are important to the new order . . ."

"Talents like telepathy?" I asked.

"Yes, like that, but more. They're the smart kids, making the best grades in school. They're tomorrow's leaders and they have a mission. "

"So, if I were to undertake an investigation, to look into the background of students in the gifted programs. . ., I should find a higher percentage of students whose parents could've been kidnapped by aliens?"

"Yes, but don't expect the parents to be aware of anything much out of the ordinary. Even the alien kids don't know they're aliens."

"I think if my own kids were aliens, I'd know something."

Oh, Gail, I'm not talking about your kids. Just because they're both in gifted programs doesn't mean they're aliens. The aliens would've had to kidnap you or Dave for that to happen. I just meant . . . well, you know that saying about the parents being the last to know."

Jamie entered the room. "Hold on a moment, Jewel, Jamie wants to tell me something."

"Hi, Mom. Chris is at the library. He wants you to pick him up around six, okay."

"Okay, what's he up to?"

"Science project research."

I should have known. Chris was real excited about his science project this year. He was putting together a model demonstrating the greenhouse effect with projections for the future. It was quite impressive, but then so were all of his projects. "I thought he'd checked everything the library had on the subject of global warming," I remarked.

"Some new periodicals came in this week and he found something interesting in one of them. Seems new research shows that humans are showing evidence of mutations that suggest people are adapting to the greenhouse effect."

The jolt produced a physical sensation, as though someone had slapped me in the face.

"Mom, are you alright? You look a little pale."

"I'm okay, Jamie. Look, I've got Jewel waiting on the phone."

"Sure Mom. Don't forget to pick Chris up."

That was fifteen years ago. Jewel married someone else and I never heard anything more of Zelix and his predictions. Turned out the police were right all along about Cathy's mother's boyfriend. He confessed after skeletal remains found under her mother's home were identified as Cathy's. Jamie is now a chemist working for a major drug company and Chris is a NASA scientist. I have two beautiful granddaughters and a brand new grandson. He's a beautiful baby but they keep him bundled up all the time. My daughter-in-law says all the children have "thin blood." I get chills just thinking about him all bundled up. Must be a family trait.

THE CRYSTAL HEX

The holiday hype that begins the week before Thanksgiving and ends on December 24th was well under way back in 1989 when Crystal first reported for work at the post office. Numerous trays of cards and mountainous stacks of parcels created an illusion of good will and hinted at the lost magic of Christmas. But the overwhelming seasonal workload meant Christmas time was just as likely to be depressing, as it was to be exhilarating.

Christmas of 1989, rapidly approaching, promised only cruelty for Peg Johnson. We were all working under stress but it was an especially bad time for Peg, whose marriage was about to be dissolved. Now in retrospect, it seems incredible that no one realized just how unstable Peg had become. Preoccupied in our own worlds, we managed not to notice that Peg appeared to be drinking a bit more of late and that the circles beneath her eyes grew deeper and darker.

Crystal's first day on the job, was wet and chilly. It had been raining all morning – the kind of light drizzle that made you wish for a downpour to be done with the whole mess.

Inside was cramped and noisy. Clerks moved among the carriers distributing mail order catalogs from companies making their final appeal for Christmas dollars. Overflowing hampers of parcels cluttered the workroom floor. Amidst the din, a voice rang out, "hey, goddamnit, listen up."

Everyone turned to see Peg standing amid the parcels, waving that awful gun –"goddamn sons of bitches," she muttered, "I'll show 'em!"

Before we could say or do anything, she put the gun to her head and pulled the trigger. Time ceased, leaving bits of brain, blood and bone suspended in air and permanently etched upon our minds.

Crystal's first day at work became interwoven in our collective memory with Peg's dramatic exit. Why she ever stayed on a temporary job that started with such a bang, I couldn't imagine. From the beginning, it was apparent there was something different about Crystal . . . a difference that went beyond her being Haitian/American . . . beyond the tough exterior of a person determined to escape the limitations of her environment.

She was actually rather ordinary in appearance, attractive in a strange, dark and haunting sort of way. Smooth mahogany skin, tight and blemish free, a tall, big boned young woman barely twenty years old. Yet, there was something more to Crystal . . . something alluded to in the dark wide eyes that drew you in but stopped just short of identifying the thing that set her apart. Everybody sensed it—this something discernible but not knowable—and everyone left her alone, keeping a polite distance.

Everyone that is except Bert, perennial friend of the downtrodden and the rejected.

Crystal's entry into the swing room during our morning breaks was always accompanied by a noticeable decrease in noise . . . like we were holding our breath, hoping she would sit somewhere else.

Bert was standing at the Coke machine when he first met Crystal. "Hi," he said. "You must be Crystal. How you doing?"

"In which world?" she responded, looking him directly in the eye. That Crystal was not always in this world was obvious. Still, it was startling to hear her say so.

The silence deepened... Bert paused momentarily, rubbed the bald spot on top of his head and replied, "In this world

. . . the one I'm in." Bert looked pleased, as though he had solved a tough problem.

Crystal might have finished out her temporary stay in our office without incident; after all, she was not the first weirdo to come through our zone. But, it was Christmas time, we were operating under stress and, of course, Peg's route was down.

As the holiday drew closer and we became more involved in the rush to deliver cards and parcels, Crystal slipped into the background. Heads turned, but no one even bothered with whispered asides the day she came to work bald. Only Bert had nerve enough to comment. "Hey, Crystal," he called out to her across the parking lot that morning. "Wait up."

We were walking together, and I could have killed him. "What did you do that for?" I whispered. Walking with Crystal was about the last thing I wanted to do. I felt uncomfortable in her presence without knowing why. She lit a cigarette while waiting for us to catch up and I reflected that I'd never seen a Haitian woman smoke before. I watched swirls of smoke curl above her shaved head and thought of how much had changed since I first came to the P.O.

I'd been among the first women carriers hired when quotas needed to be met. Quotas were a lot more important then than they are now and being female and black to boot, I'd helped them fill both. Though women, in 1989, represented roughly a third of the work force, I still got an occasional "Here comes the U.S. female," or "It's the lady postman." In the office, though, I'd eventually become accepted, to a point at least.

"Don't be so mean," Bert chided. "Why is everybody so distant with her?

I was certain he thought I, of all people, should be sympathetic. "She's the one that's distant." I said. Crystal was too close now for any response from Bert, but I sensed a strong disapproval.

"Hi, Crystal," I said, remembering her swing room reply to Bert's "how you doing?"

"I almost didn't recognize you, Crystal," Bert said. "Why'd you shave your head? You protesting something?"

"Time for a change," she said, exhaling smoke. Crystal was at least three inches taller than Bert's five eight. In the drab surroundings of the P.O. she projected an imposing presence.

"What do you think of the Postal Service so far?" Bert inquired.

That comment left me wondering what the hell he expected her to think of the P.O. after the events of her first day here. "It sucks," was her reply.

Christmas had come and gone and Crystal finished the first month of her ninety-day appointment. I reminded her that in two months she could kiss the post office goodbye. "Consider it a learning experience," I suggested, "like a tour in the military – only shorter."

We had reached the employees' entrance to the building and paused for Crystal to finish her cigarette. "You don't want me here, do you?" she asked.

"I only meant . . . well most of us are stuck here - started right out of high school and got comfortable when this was considered a good job. You can take control of your life. Not get stuck in a job you hate."

Bert changed the subject. I said, "Check you later." And went inside.

Reluctantly, I considered my feelings about Crystal. Was I jealous? Didn't I wish I could be a little less concerned about what people thought of me? While being accepted was important to me, it was clear Crystal didn't give a damn.

Another week went by and while Crystal remained a source of swing room gossip, she had ceased to be the main focus of attention. It was not out of prejudice or superstition that Crystal was shunned. Although no one would ever admit it, the reason was fear. We were cautious because the massacre in the Oklahoma post office was all too recent. In those days, we were all a bit paranoid, constantly accessing and re-accessing coworker's potential for violence. Crystal was not the only one given a wide berth, just the most recent. True, we had no real indication that Crystal was capable of violence, but you could never be too sure. Look how we'd misjudged Peg. Avoiding Crystal was, in our way of thinking, a form of insurance.

Christmas was two weeks past when Frank got the parcel for a Haitian family on his route. It had no return address. What got Frank's attention was the strange drawings on the outer wrapper. Now either Frank had totally forgotten Crystal was in earshot or he no longer cared.

"Hey, look at this!" He announced, holding the parcel out. "A hexed Christmas gift and it's late. Wonder what it is." He shook the parcel. "I better be careful or this hex might jump on me." He laughed. "Can voodoo do that?"

"Voodoo can do anything."

All eyes turned toward Crystal, who now faced the room, her back to her workstation. You could almost hear the mental gears cranking. Had anyone else said that, we'd have jumped all over it . . . but Crystal had said it, so we were holding back. The silent moment stretched toward infinity before Frank spoke.

"If it can do anything, why doesn't it solve some of the political and economic problems in Haiti?" He had spoken while still casing mail, his tall, lean frame turned away from the room so he never saw the look Crystal gave him.

"Voodoo is the problem in Haiti."

Frank peered over his shoulder at her.

Crystal looked at Frank as though he must be the most stupid human being on earth. "Do you not see?" She said. "It's spell and counter spell."

"So," Frank said, returning to sorting mail. "The one with the most spells wins."

Crystal favored him with another how-stupid-can-you-get look and replied that anybody could purchase a spell. By this time we could see that Frank was thinking maybe he'd gone too far already. It was equally obvious he was having a hard time stopping. He stroked the full dark beard that had earned him the nickname, Abe. "Humm…." he said, "I really can't believe you believe that…"

"Doesn't matter what you or I believe. Enough believe to make it so." She turned back to face the letter case, dismissing him.

That was the germ that planted the seed in Frank's mind. So Crystal wasn't so mysterious after all. Oh she was weird . . . but there was nothing strange about a Haitian woman believing in voodoo.

Frank decided to test Crystal's belief. He concluded that if everybody, or almost everybody in the office, believed Crystal had been hexed, then she'd believe it. "We'll set the stage and see what develops," he said.

Looking back, I can hardly believe I participated in what happened. I know first hand that people are capable of behavior within a group that they would never consider alone. Crystal had begun delivering mail. First we arranged for her to have a flat tire while delivering Peg Johnson's route. A friend of Frank's in vehicle maintenance switched a good tire on Crystal's vehicle with one that had a slow leak. It was guaranteed to go flat during the day.

While we sorted mail that morning, Bert, one of the few who knew nothing of the plot we'd hatched, asked Crystal if she thought she'd be all right her first day on the route.

Crystal replied that of course she would. "What could possibly go wrong?"

"There's no telling what can go wrong when you're driving old six-six-six," said Frank.

That was the first time any of us had heard Peg's Jeep referred to as "old six-six-six," but we understood the reference came from the last three digits of the vehicle number.

"What does that mean?" Crystal asked.

"I guess she hasn't heard about Peg's Jeep," Delores cut in, picking up on Frank's cue. "Tell her about 'old six-six-six,' Frank.

It's just the number of the jeep. Doesn't mean anything, so pay no attention to them," Bert told Crystal.

"Well, all I know is Peg had a lot of trouble delivering city route sixty-six-o-six out of old six-six-six, Frank said.

Crystal reiterated that she would be all right.

Knowing glances traveled around the room like electricity cackling through high voltage wires. We didn't know if Crystal understood any of the six-six-six stuff. What we did know was that she was going to have a flat tire before finishing the route.

Our favorite pastime became arranging jinxes for Crystal. We spent our mornings talking about all the strange things, both real and imagined that ever happened in the post office and managed to assign them all to Peg's route. In the afternoons we'd watch for Crystal's reaction to whatever new jinx we'd arranged.

Frank's friend in vehicle maintenance rigged her horn so the first time she honked, it would stick and not shut off. Crystal seemed undaunted by it all.

Just when we were beginning to think we would run out of tricks before Crystal ran out of patience, the lock to the back door of her jeep malfunctioned without help from us. The door flew open in traffic and a tray of mail overturned in the middle of the northbound lane on Lake Avenue. I guess that's what did it for Crystal. In her mind the hex was as much a reality as the mail she delivered.

Even Bert, having no idea of what the rest of us were up to was heard speculating on the possibility of a curse. Some of us, myself included, felt the situation was getting out of hand — that having a little fun at Crystal's expense was not so innocent after all. Some of us had even begun to like her in spite of her unwillingness to fit in. We were ready to back off, but Frank was in high gear.

"This is working out better than I hoped," he boasted. "How 'bout that door flying open? We couldn't have planned it better if we'd tried."

We were sitting in the swing room having coffee and as I studied Frank's face all aglow with what I belatedly considered perverse excitement, I was overcome with a feeling of disgust.

Frank continued, "Wait 'til you see what I've got planned next." He walked over to the refrigerator, retrieved a small box and flashed a mischievous grin.

"Well, come on. Don't keep us in suspense," Delores demanded.

He removed the lid, reached in and pulled out a small plastic bag.

"Yuk! What the hell is that?" She asked.

"Brains."

"Brains?"

"The eat market variety," Frank replied. As I looked from the pale grayish, twisted contents of the plastic bag to the unrestrained delight in Frank's grinning face, I was appalled.

The image of Peg staring blankly out of ice blue eyes just before pulling the trigger had burned itself into my memory and now Frank wanted us to make up nightmares about her suicide for the morning's conversation. I could hardly believe I'd participated in such sick sport. "Count me out," I said, pushing my chair back from the table.

It turned out nobody wanted to know what Frank had planned for the cow brains and he was forced to scrap the idea after finding no collaborators.

It was around this time that other things started happening . . . small things at first. I ran out of gas, forgot to get a signed receipt for a certified letter and even got confused once about the time one day. I rushed like a maniac thinking I was running an hour behind only to get done an hour early. I chalked it up to preoccupation with Frank's games—I'd always thought of our pranks as Frank's games – talk about deception. Then, I found out similar things were happening to others in our zone and, everybody was losing interest in what came to be known as The Crystal Hex.

A run of bad luck, accompanied by an aura of depression besieged our zone. In one week, two carriers sustained back injuries, Delores had a vehicle accident and Frank was fined one hundred dollars for parking his jeep in a handicap parking space. "Five years on this cruddy route," he lamented, "and some asshole writes me a goddamn ticket."

"Why'd you park there?" Asked Bert.

"I always park there when there's no other space nearby. How am I supposed to deliver the mail if there's no place to park? Three vacant handicap spaces and I'm only in there a couple of minutes."

"That cop must have the fastest pen in the city," Delores said.

"Yeah, well nobody ever wrote me a ticket before. I'll find out who the bastard is. I'll teach him to muck around with me. I'll fix that asshole."

Frank was racking up lots of experience fixing people lately. The Crystal Hex seemed to be taking on new dimension as Crystal and Bert might well have been the only people in our zone not currently jinxed. I listened to Frank blowing off steam about this bit of misfortune and something just clicked in my mind. "Crystal," I said, "How are things going with you? You doing okay with that route now?"

"Doing fine."

"No more problems with the jeep?"

"Oh," she said, "I got rid of that jinx for you."

By this point, everyone was listening.

"How'd you do that?"

She stopped sorting mail and turned to look at me. With a new growth of wavy black hair close to her head, she would have looked masculine except for the large loop earrings and ample breasts.

"What jinx?" Asked Bert.

"The Hex," said Crystal. "I sent it back where it came from."

Funny how you don't ordinarily notice things like the air conditioner humming or sounds drifting in from other sectors. Beyond the partition that separated our zone from the main lobby, a baby wailed. I tried to visualize a restless toddler and a long line of customers, but I could see only Crystal, saying ". . . it's spell and counter spell . . . doesn't matter what you think. . ."

PUPPY LOVE

Missy, a handsome black and white English Setter, was the only dog allowed in our house. The rest of the pack lived in the fenced-in kennel out back. My Dad raised, trained and sold English Setters for bird hunting. He considered them the best of the field dogs for pheasant and quail.

English Setters have the gentle disposition dog lovers admire. They are easily trained, as most of what is expected of them is inborn. Setters love the hunt and Missy was a tireless hunter. She worked the fields with her nose close to the ground, occasionally lifting her head high sniffing for a scent to chase. Dad seldom came home from a hunting trip empty handed.

Mostly, Missy was a loving dog; at home, she followed my mother's every step. With our nearest neighbor a mile away, she was a satisfying source of security, barking when anyone came near the house.

At age sixteen, I had a Model A Ford and a rigid curfew. My parking place, under my parents bedroom window, made it difficult to sneak in after hours. One cool spring night I was running an hour late. At the entrance to our driveway I shut off the car's lights and motor and coasted silently to my parking spot. Not wanting to make an extra sound, I left the car door hanging open.

The next morning Mom asked me to drive to the dairy farm for a gallon of milk. When I arrived at the car door I had left ajar, I saw, curled up on the front seat, a little ball of white fur decorated with brown trim around the face. Wearing no collar, I figured she had been "dropped off in the country" and had climbed in through the open car door. The dog looked up at me with eager brown eyes . . . tough to resist.

The morning air had a chill to it and the little dog snuggled close to me on the ride to the farm. At the dairy, I left the door open, hoping she would jump out and be gone when I came out of the milk house. But no, she was waiting, standing on the car seat wagging her stump of a tail.

We had eight purebred English setters in the kennel at the back of the house. Asking my dad to let me keep this little mutt was out of the question. Besides, we were dog snobs. Every one of our dogs had a pedigree as long as my arm. No way my pop was going to allow this mongrel to stay. Except for Missy, our dogs were not pets. They were hunters. I left the little dog in the car when I brought the milk into the house.

Dad went to work and I took Mom out to see the furry, white ball on my car seat. Mom fell in love, in love with a dog so small she could hold it in her arms and spoil it. None of dad's arguments would hold water against that. Mom cuddled the pup and named her Foxy, we guessed she was a Fox Terrier.

Dad didn't put up a fight about keeping the little dog. When he got home from work that evening, Mom was standing in the doorway with a freshly bathed Foxy in her arms. End of discussion.

Missy took that pup for her own and they had the run of the house. During that summer, Foxy became a part of the family. She shared ice cream cones with me and sometimes with unsuspecting friends who let her get too close. That autumn, the two dogs would sit in the driveway waiting for me to get home from school. We would roughhouse and I'd throw sticks for them to fetch. Foxy's little legs went as fast as they could, but Missy always returned the stick with Foxy snapping and growling at it. At night Missy let Foxy share her bed; they slept curled up together. They became inseparable.

The hunting season was right around the corner and Dad began retraining the setters, taking them out to the fields and farms that surrounded our place. Foxy had been with Missy so long she thought she was a hunter and dad had to lock her in the house to keep her home.

On a cold morning, during the bird season, Dad and two of his friends had taken four of the setters, including Missy, hunting. When they returned, the men divided up the catch and Dad and Missy came into the house. Now came the only part of having a long haired hunting dog that I didn't like.

We would spread newspapers on the floor and Missy would lie down; I would start picking and combing burrs out of that long hair. Burrs, hundreds of burrs and an occasional tick.
Later that fall, after a hunt, Dad got home before I did. He put the papers down on the wood floor and Missy lay down exhausted. After he showered, Dad came downstairs and there on the papers sat Foxy picking burrs out of Missy with her sharp little teeth. Dad sat there watching and laughing. When I got home Dad wanted to know if I'd taught her to de-burr Missy so I wouldn't have to do it. Those terriers are smart dogs, I told him. Foxy was earning her keep.

This was during World War II. My dad worked in the steel mills in Gary, Indiana, and had to take his turn working the four to midnight shift. On a dark, moonless, rainy night, dad was coming home after working until midnight. The man driving the car pool that week, told my dad he thought he saw one of our dogs sitting along side of the road.

As soon as he got home, Dad got a flashlight out of his car and ran out to the kennels. All the dogs were there. Must have been a mistake. He came back in the house and there was no greeting from the house dogs. Dad searched upstairs and in the basement, no dogs. Then he woke me and asked me to ride with him to try and find our pets. Putting on our rain gear, we took the flashlights, hopped into his car and headed back up the road. Sure enough, there sat Missy in the teeming rain. I opened the car door and we both called her name. Missy turned her head and looked at us and then turned away again. Figuring she was hurt, we got out of the car and went to her. The flashlights illuminated a touching sight. Lying rain-soaked at Missy's feet was her little sidekick, Foxy. Dad saw the pup wasn't breathing. He felt her heart, then looked up at me and slowly shook his head. Lying so close to the side of the road, we figured she had been hit by a car and killed. Missy would not give up her vigil until I carried Foxy to the car. Only then did Missy climb into the back seat.

I buried my little buddy, Foxy, under a mulberry tree in the back yard. That spot turned out to be Missy's favorite place to take her nap.

THE ROSEWOOD CASKET

On a cold, windy afternoon Denny walked out of the grimy steel mill and drove home for the last time. He had worked on the swing shift there for forty-three years and his muscular six-foot plus frame seemed none the worse for wear.

The next morning, as the gray streaks of dawn muscled through the frigid Chicago darkness, he climbed into his SUV and started the engine. He heard the thin coating of ice crackle as he lowered the side window to take a last heart-tugging look at the house that had been his home for more than thirty years. He squeezed his eyes shut on a tear. Then he began the twelve hundred-mile drive to Florida . . . alone, sure he would never be happy again. No one said good-bye to him, Bernice had locked her bedroom door and Lewis, their only child, had moved away.

During the lonely drive, his mind kept racing back to the events that sent him to Florida. *I should have seen this coming,* he thought. Bernice's response to his kiss had become as indifferent as to his handshake.

He was proud to see his son, Lewis, grow up and go off to college, a trip he had never made. As his car passed over the state line into Missouri, he thought of the weekend he and his son spent in Saint Louis watching the Cardinals and Cubs play. He recalled it was the only time they were away by themselves. Bernice, his wife, kept Lewis close by her side; she coaxed, prodded and rewarded him all through school to make sure he would strive for a college degree. She constantly demeaned

Denny to his son with remarks like, "I want you to amount to something more than a steel mill laborer." Bernice lavished Lewis with cash for A's on his report card, pointing out the money came from her job, not Denny's.

After high school, Lewis went to New Orleans and attended Loyola University. He graduated, married a girl he met at college and never returned to Chicago, or thanked the old steelworker whose hard work made it all possible.

Denny learned to live with Bernice's constant barbs. During every discussion concerning money, she threw her high paying paralegal job into Denny's blue-collar face. Arriving home from yet another night shift, Bernice greeted him with: "I've filed for a divorce! Don't try to talk me out of it. I've made up my mind. I've changed, improved myself, and you, you're the same steel mill laborer you were when we married. I'll keep our Chicago house, and you can have our place in Florida. You always said how you like it down there . . . with the fishermen and all."

A lawyer from the firm where she worked represented Bernice; Denny's lawyer was the young son of a fellow Elks Lodge member. Denny's eager new lawyer pointed out to the judge that the Chicago house was valued at four times what their little Florida home was worth. The judge checked the numbers and awarded Denny seventy-five percent of the cash in their joint bank account.

The straight-through drive to Clearwater, with catnaps in MacDonald parking lots in Tennessee and Georgia, put him in the driveway of his Florida home at Gulf Side Palms just before noon the next day.

Now he was . . . *with the fishermen and all*, and on his first sun drenched morning he watched pelicans glide overhead as he finished unloading his SUV. Then he drove into town for breakfast and to stock up on groceries. As he sat by himself devouring his ham and eggs, he thought, *That damn caller ID*, it allowed Bernice to avoid his attempts to reach her. As he mopped up the last of egg yolk with a piece of toast, he thought, *has it been only three days* since *I packed the SUV?*

Alone in Florida, Denny did some fishing, painted the outside of his little house and stopped in at the Elk's lodge for a beer on occasion. But staying busy didn't stop the thoughts that made him fall victim to a brooding heart.

His hellhounds brought recurring thoughts of nothing to live for. Why? Why did he still feel this way? He remembered a fellow steel mill worker, Joe Jennings, telling him he had his divorce decree at three-thirty and was in time for happy-hour at the Singles Swing Saloon, wearing a new royal blue Hawaiian shirt, splashed with yellow parrots. *Why was Joe happy and not me?*

A week after his return to the Sunshine State, Denny was *stuck in a traffic jam*; waiting for a funeral procession to pass. As the hearse, bearing the coffin, slowly rolled by, it triggered a thought; he decided to start a project. He was going to build his own casket . . . and, maybe, provide the means and time of his own death. Thoughts like these were Alpo for his hellhounds.

He continued brooding and loafing around the house, going nowhere without a beer in his hand. Then, on impulse, he drove to Big Bay Lumber and Supplies and purchased the wood necessary for the frame of his casket. While he was there he had them order the rosewood he would need.

After two days of measuring, sawing and fitting pieces together, the frame was nearly finished. His doldrums lifted a little while he worked with the wood. As he swept up the sawdust that piled up under the miter saw, he heard his neighbor's voice.

"Hello, Sullivan, I'm back from Ohio."

"Hi, Arnie, come on in."

It made Denny feel relaxed having Arnie to chat with. They were both mid-westerners and long time fishing buddies.

"Your missus over at the pool?" asked Arnie.

"She won't be coming down. We called it quits."

Arnie pushed his glasses back up on his nose and said, "Aw, that's too bad. Well, I'm right next door if you need anything."

Need anything? Denny thought. *I need someone to put her arms around me and tell me she loves me. Someone I can hug and spend time with.*

Denny did his grocery shopping, cooking and housekeeping and kept working at his project. Late afternoons he headed out to the beach to watch the sunset. On a clear afternoon, his heart heavier than an anchor, he watched the fishing boats come in and tie off at the pier. After the orange sun melted into the Gulf of Mexico, he walked across Mandalay Avenue to The SlipKnot Bar and Grill. For tables, the 1930s building used painted hatch covers from ancient boats, scarred with cigarette burns. Few of the chairs and bar stools matched, and most wobbled when sat on. The walls were papered with pictures of show-off fish catches: grouper, king, red and a couple of long-billed sails.

Denny sat at the bar and asked for a draft beer. He ordered dinner from a menu that consisted of one item, catch of the day sandwiches and cold slaw.

As he sipped his beer he looked around the room. "Good grief," he said to the bar maid, "a man could buy a 36-foot Hatteras for less than it would cost to bring this joint up to run of the mill."

This hot day, as usual, the bar's ancient air-conditioner was losing the afternoon battle to the Florida heat and the sun-baked fishermen. Denny bit into the best grouper sandwich he had ever eaten. He had another beer, finished his sandwich, listened to a conversation regarding the Cubs' chances next season, and headed home.

The next morning after coffee, he finished hand sanding the framework of the casket. He ran his hand over the smooth—as—glass wood and was proud to see he still had his carpenter's touch. Denny stepped back and admired the precision work he had done on the corners. Then it happened, he saw himself laid out in the finished rosewood coffin. His hellhounds were winning the war going on in his head.

Later that morning, Arnie, dressed in his jogging gear and puffing, walked into the open garage and asked, "Whatcha making?"

"I, uh, I'm building a fancy storage cabinet."

"Speaking of cabinets, and that's why I'm here, Meg Carson, one street over, had one of her kitchen cabinets come loose. Being a live-alone widow she could use some help. What do ya say?"

"I guess I could take a look." Denny picked up his tape measure and tool belt.

"Come on, I'll introduce you. You'll like her. She loves to smile."

A woman that loved to smile would be a change, Denny thought.

They walked to the street behind them and down the block to Meg's house.

Meg answered Arnie's knock, and she *was* smiling.

"Well, what do you know," said Denny, as he looked into a round face with bright green eyes. "You served me a beer or two at The SlipKnot,"

"Hi, Chicago," she said, "maybe now I can learn your real name."

"Denny this is Meg, Meg, this is Denny," said Arnie.

They shook hands and Meg asked the two friends to come in.

"Okay, let's take a look at the problem." Denny said smiling at Meg.

She headed toward the kitchen. Denny followed watching the swoosh of her orange mau-mau. The cabinet, propped up on the floor beneath huge ragged holes, was empty, its dishes were piled in a corner of the room.

"The home repair guy said he had to break out most of the wall and reinforce some studs or something. I know it's going to be costly."

As she jabbered on, Arnie held the end of the tape for Denny while he jotted down measurements. He made a note of the material he would need.

"It won't cost much. I'll pick the stuff up at the lumber yard tomorrow."

"Can I ride along with you? That way I can pay for it with my credit card."

He nodded. "I'll pick you up tomorrow morning at 8:30. I'll drive, if you bring coffee."

The next morning's ride was pleasant; Meg was gabby and cheerful and her coffee smelled and tasted great.

With the material loaded in his SUV Denny drove back to Meg's and was tearing out the damaged wall by ten o'clock. Meg made fresh coffee to go along with her continuous chatter about The SlipKnot and life at Gulf Side Palms.

Denny couldn't help but compare her with his ex-wife, who controlled her figure by constant dieting and three visits a week to a gym with her personal trainer. Bernice was the picture of business chic; tall and palm-tree thin, always dressed in the latest style, size four, mostly from Marshall Field's. Weekly visits to a salon kept her coif the perfect shade and stylishly cut.

Meg, on the other hand, was round and brown, and Denny compared the green of her eyes to the color of the Gulf. She worked three days a week as the barmaid at The SlipKnot and spent her leisure time on a lounge chair at the pool. But even with her chopped short home hairdo, size ten filled to the limit, with that smile she looked great to Denny.

Over Meg's protests, Denny drove home and fixed his own lunch. It gave him a chance to check his answer machine and mailbox; as usual, nothing from Chicago. Back on the job, he had the cabinet hung and the wall plastered by 5:30.

Denny stepped back and admired his work. Gathering up his tools he said, "I'll paint tomorrow. You won't be able to tell it was ever repaired."

"That looks terrific." Meg gave Denny her big smile. "This time, I won't take no for an answer. Go home and clean up and get yourself back here for dinner around seven. I've got plenty of cold beer in the fridge."

It began as easily as that, and over the ensuing months their time together took them on two and three day trips, deep-sea fishing in the Gulf of Mexico, shelling at Sanibel Island and listening to jazz at the Eddy Condon room in Goodland.

Through it all Denny finished his project, a gnawing in the back of his mind wouldn't let him stop. The rosewood joints were mitered and sanded to perfection. The brass handles gleamed and the last step, a coat of clear polyurethane sprayed on, accentuated the grain of the rosewood. The finished product was the best work he had ever done: smooth and shiny with delicate curves.

Denny sat on a stool and opened a cold beer. He looked with satisfaction at what he had accomplished. He was happy, but something was missing, a niggling he couldn't put his finger on. When he finished the beer, he covered the casket and his hellhounds with a tarp. They sat in a corner of his garage, a glum reminder of cheerless days in Chicago.

That evening as she and Denny were eating dinner she said, "I've got something to tell you. Howie is going to sell The SlipKnot. The busy Labor Day weekend was too much for him. We ran out of fish at 1:30 and Howie said, 'after thirty years I'm gettin' too old to fight another season, too damn many snow birds and tourists crowding in here now.'"

Denny swallowed and stared at her.

"It's not like working when I'm behind the bar kidding with the patrons. I really love that place."

Silent, Denny ran his hand over his hair to smooth it down. He thought back to the 43 years he had worked in the mills: day in, day out, always concerned about payday. Denny had been sensible all his life and what had it gotten him? He set his fork down, stared hard at Meg, then blurted out, "Meg, let's buy the joint."

She jumped up, rushed around the table, squeezed his neck and gave him a big smooch. "Let me talk to Howie, see what we can work out."

Between them they had more than enough to swing the deal. The legal work started, they made plans.

"Let's keep it just like it is for the coming season, okay?" said Meg.

Grinning, Denny said, "Well, maybe a new and bigger air conditioner."

That night, walking home from Meg's, he looked up at the moon balanced over the top of the palm trees and said, "I don't miss that damn dirty Chicago at all."

As he did most every night, he dialed Lewis' cell phone number. Denny didn't expect an answer, Lewis would check his caller ID and not pick up, but he had to try. Denny gasped when Lewis, answered with a cheerful, "Hi Dad."

When Denny caught his breath he said, "Is it really you, Lewis?"

"It's me, Dad, and can you ever forgive me for being such a jerk?"

" Forgiven and forgotten," Denny said from his heart.

"I didn't realize what Mom had done until she started the same thing with Annie, and she's the best wife a guy could have. Annie and I are truly happy, Dad.

"But I'm in Chicago now. I just returned from the hospital, Mom had a stroke. She'll be released in two or three days and move in with her sister. I'll fly back home, then I'm driving over to Florida for a visit." Lewis faltered, "I uh, I want you to get to know your grandson."

Again Denny swallowed hard before he said, "Do you remember how to get here?"

"See you in a week or so . . . Dad."

The next day Denny and Meg signed the final papers and took possession of The SlipKnot. They celebrated with free beer for all.

Two mornings later as Denny went out to retrieve his newspaper, Arnie was watering his roses.

"Arnie," Denny called. "Got a few minutes you can spare to give me a hand?"

"Sure thing neighbor, let me turn off the hose."

Denny led him into the garage and peeled the tarp away from the rosewood casket.

Arnie whistled. "Don't that beat all."

"I need to get this up into the attic. I promise I'll explain the whole thing to you over lunch at The SlipKnot later."

Denny unhinged the lid and they grunted the casket up into the attic in two trips.

"Thanks, Arnie, you're the kind of neighbor everyone wants."

Inside the house, a while later, Denny prepared his bank deposit. He dropped it off at the drive-in window and headed for the beach area and his new business. He made one stop along the way, The Gulf Surf Shop.

After the clerk handed him his change and his purchase, Denny asked, "Do you have a place I can change?"

"Sure thing, sir. Right down that hallway."

Minutes later Denny stepped out of the store into the brilliant Florida sun wearing a royal blue Hawaiian shirt splashed with yellow parrots.

THE FAMILY

Bob Monroe's old Plymouth chugged to a stop alongside his mobile home. He parked under the stand of live oak trees that he and his wife had planted 18 years earlier when they first moved into the park. They had set the seedlings around their lot so that as they grew, the trees would shield their little home from the torrid South Florida sun. Before he turned off the car's lights, Bob noticed the grass needed cutting again and the shrubs were overgrown.

He would have to spend most of Sunday, his one day off at the Citrus Tree Nursery, mowing and trimming before he could drive out to the cemetery. He looked forward to visiting his wife's grave. He would tidy up the area and put fresh flowers on the small rise as he talked to her, positive she heard every word. On this early evening, as the darkness of day's end spread across the Atlantic Breeze Mobile Home Park, he got out of his car, stepped over tire ruts and walked through the ankle-deep grass.

He carefully climbed the three rickety stairs leading to the side door and forced the key into a lock that had become stubborn from being twisted and turned for too many years. Inside, he tossed his keys and sweat-streaked cap onto a chipped Formica counter and switched on the lamp hanging above the kitchen table. He craned his skinny neck to look into the front room, and as usual, there was no mail on the floor under the slot. Just as well, he thought, no bills. After a steamy shower to clean off the day and ease his aching muscles, he donned fresh clothes and headed for the kitchen where he took a TV dinner from the near-empty freezer and shoved it into the microwave. Pulling a cold beer from the refrigerator he walked into the darkened living room and eased his overworked muscles into a threadbare recliner.

Bob's parents had brought him to his new home in Pompano Beach from southern Indiana as a kid. He had never been farther from his new home than Miami one way and West Palm Beach the other. With few friends, no one other than himself had been inside his mobile home during the last year, except the refrigerator repairman. Dozing, trying not to think about his loneliness, he watched the rays from the street light slice through the blinds, and provide a spotlight for the dust motes that danced around the room. Bob sat there, his balding head nodding, until the microwave called him to dinner. After eating, he cleaned up the kitchen.

He liked to keep the place tidy, the way his wife did. Back in the living room he switched on the TV and laboriously lowered himself again into his recliner. He carefully pulled the lever to raise the footrest. He had repaired it once and it sounded like it was ready to go again. He couldn't afford a new one, since his job paid little more than minimum wage. The pay from a tough week's work barely covered his living expenses. He was never late paying his lot rent and utility bill. He remembered, as a kid, having the electric power shut off when they couldn't pay the bill, and moving in the dark of night to avoid paying the last month's rent. Though he understood his dad, a tenant farmer, couldn't help it, he vowed it would never be without a job and he would never be late paying a bill. This night, sitting in the flickering light from the TV, feeling drowsy, he mentally counted the meager amount of money he had been able to set aside for his wife's headstone.

The amount grew slowly, just a dollar or two at a time. Dreamily thinking about his wife and their times together, his eyes fluttered and closed. The phone's sharp jangle snapped him out of his reverie and echoed through the sparsely furnished trailer. Instead of reaching for the phone, Bob picked up his half-empty can of beer and took a long pull. Setting the beer down, he lifted the insistent, clanging phone. Before he could say hello, an excited voice he hadn't heard in over a year said, "Yo, Dad, it's me, Ralph." Bob's heart sank. "How's it going, Dad? What time is it there? I can't get this damn time difference straight. In fact, I don't know why I ever came to California." The voice talked fast and nonstop. The old man spent too much time alone since his wife died and his mind had clouded, but he knew why his son was in California. Bob had thrown Ralph out of the house and told him not to come back. It wasn't that his only son admitted selling Bob's shot gun and furniture to buy dope, nor the money pilfered from pants' pockets while he slept.

It wasn't about the morning Bob stepped out on the side porch to get the newspaper and saw Ralph sprawled on the driveway, passed out, the neighbors gawking. These things broke his heart over and over, but Ralph was his son and he made allowances. The breaking point came when Ralph stole the money Bob had been stashing away for his wife's headstone. The rising voice on the phone pleaded, "Dad, I've changed, man; I'm clean, I want to come home and be with you." Bob, as lonely as he was, didn't reply, his mind was on his beloved wife in an unmarked grave. All he heard were irritating noises coming from the phone. "You'll see, Dad. You'll be proud of me. I'll get me a job and help you out with money. I'll even paint the trailer for ya and cut the grass."

The pain was deep and real for the old man. His son, his only child, was at the other end of the line and . . . he didn't care. He knew he should care, but he just didn't. Ralph had lied and stolen from him once too often. "What do you think, Dad? Me and you, we're family. I know you want your only son with ya. You don't wanna be stayin' alone. Just send me four-hundred dollars for fare back home and we'll be together again." The old man's mind drifted to happier days, when they had been a family. The good times the three of them had spent together at the beach and Little League games. He sorely missed those times, but those days, like his wife, were gone forever. But . . . Ralph was his son.

Thoughts of having someone to talk to at dinner . . . help keeping the place looking good . . . his son and he a family again. Not coming home to an empty house would feel good. He was weakening and he didn't want to think about Ralph's underhanded ways of getting the things he wanted. This night Ralph sounded honest in his approach for money to come home on. The voice had paused and Bob heard a deep breath come through the phone. Then the voice continued, this time slowly, softly. "Please Dad ... for Mom's sake. Honest Dad, if you'll just send the money, you won't be sorry," were the last words Bob heard as he hung up the phone.

Notes:

Puppy Love. I was in a mind-dead mode, searching for a topic to write about when my wife read a touching story to me from a dog magazine. It was about a family that fell in love with a puppy they had adopted but which only lived a short 18 months. At that time we had a beautiful, four-year-old Airedale Terrier named *Maggie.* My wife commented how lucky we were to have a healthy dog and that we would probably be able to have her into her old age. The story of the puppy dying young brought to mind an incident from my youth.

The Rosewood Casket is a composite of men I've met that came to Florida to get away from heartaches and problems that had developed in their hometown. For many, it was the first time they were separated from loved ones and they had trouble adjusting. Most of them thought they would never find peace of mind and happiness again, and some didn't. Then there were those that not only found happiness, but found a life that was much more rewarding than anything they had known before.

The Family. We were having a live oak tree, purchased at a nursery, delivered and planted in our front yard. One of the men doing the planting seemed very quiet and withdrawn. You know the type. I tried to engage him in conversation. Neither his melancholy mood nor his one word answers changed the whole time he worked at planting the tree. I gave up and went indoors, wondering what could have caused this man to pull back to the point that he couldn't converse about a subject he was familiar with—trees. It had to be a deeply personal reason.

THE COLOR OF RAGS

Shuffling steps and grease stained hands dragged the unyielding shopping cart over the cracked, dusty sidewalk. Grime covered the wheels of the rusty cart that squealed with wrenching agony as they turned and turned.

An unforgiving sun and layers of dirt had etched lines into the woman's face that made her older than the actual years of past birthdays. The casual observer would never believe her to be just fifty. A skinny piece of wire, once used to seal a loaf of bread in its bag, was now reduced to tying matted hair together. The many layers of clothes hid the smallness of her body, vaguely hinting of a lumpy shape beneath the tattered rags. Rags whose colors had vanished, leaving behind muted grays, blues and browns. The woman was listening to music that only she heard while the foul stench of despair emanated from her.

Her mind was coming out of her peach-colored haze and her eyes took in the bitter world of reality and colors that only destroyed. The neighborhood bag lady was on her daily rounds.

The occupant of the elegant fifth floor co-op apartment was engrossed in her afternoon ritual. A'cee scanned the street, looking for the B'gee. Long ago the slender woman had baptized the bag lady, 'B'gee, the accent and stress on the first syllable. Perhaps reflecting on her own name, A'cee. The reasons for the contraction in A'cee's name were forgotten or more accurately, brushed aside. Yet, the small remaining memory surfaced unrelentingly every afternoon. The squeaking wheels foretold of the bag woman's arrival before A'cee could see her.

"Must you always watch for her?" The male asked with reproach in his cultured voice.

"Why not? It's a pleasant diversion," she said calmly. "I am seeing private enterprise at its most fundamental, at work." She sipped her martini. "Daily she collects cans, bottles and paper which people discard and brings them to your plant. The money she gets from recycling only ends up in your liquor store. You really don't ever lose, do you?" There was no reproach or condemnation in A'cee's tone, just a matter of fact attitude that struck a nerve in the man.

"This is warped," the man hissed. But recognizing the futility of the outburst, his normal tone returned. "Why do you persist in this? You are elevating a filthy, revolting scum to our social level. Really my dear, your lack of propriety is showing."

The slender woman turned away from her window, her manicured nail swirled the drink in her glass. Her slightly drunken eyes rested themselves on the paunchy, ruddy faced man sitting across the room from her.

"Swine." She gulped her drink down and turned around again, staring out the window.

"Very eloquently put. Now, would you like another martini?" His hand mockingly raised up the empty bottle in a sarcastic salute to her victory. "Remember, we must do our civic duty and support the homeless, disadvantaged people."

Plunk. The bottle sounded dull and noisy as it landed in the waste basket, punctuating the sentence perfectly.

A'cee's eyes followed the bag lady. One of her shoes was missing and the other had been secured around her foot with shoelaces and twine. The woman kept on watching the solitary figure that was lost in her secret world of colors.

B'gee's eyes furtively scanned the dumpster, "*A veritable Mountain of Treasure*," her mind uttered. "*Soon she could be back in the sanctity of her peach heaven.*"

Her hands scrounged, sorted and picked. They found a flask, its torn label reading, 'Gordon's Gin.' B'gee raised the bottle to her lips, her tongue anxiously darting into the slender neck, greedily swallowing the few drops that freed themselves and ran down a thirsty throat. A burp of air accompanied the expression of satisfaction before she stored the bottle in the box marked 'clear glass.' A wrapper holding pieces of a sandwich was the next treasure. B'gee sniffed at it a few times. *"Good"* her mind uttered as her gray fingers ripped the paper away. Her mouth opened and her fingers shoved in the few bits, her hand covering her mouth, nose and part of her face. Gulping the stale bread down, she now licked her hand in search of any missed crumbs. Again she belched with satisfaction.

Her damp hand dried itself on the jacket's sleeve before it searched once more, through the dumpster's contents. Found aluminum cans were dumped into the grubby, huge plastic bag tied to the handles of her shopping cart. Clear glass, colored glass and newspaper were carefully sorted, saved and stacked in the bulging cart in plastic crates. She liked this dumpster, a favorite on her daily round. She always foraged in it after she awoke from her sleep in an unlocked meter room. The first few times, the guard chased her away after he spotted her rummaging in the fancy building's dumpster. But he got used to her. At times he even gave her some of his saved cans and, once, a blanket.

B'gee belched with pleasure as her mind briefly grasped the irony that fashionable recycling was safely in the hands of the dregs. Her wandering, lucid thoughts were chased away as she concentrated on the business at hand. Today she was lucky. Her scrounging had paid off early and she could head directly to the recycling plant, then to the nearby liquor store where she could purchase the many colors of her dreams.

Peach was the best. Followed by green, purple then beige. But when beige came, the world would soon turn to gray. She sighed deeply and saw another tin can in the road. Someone must have thrown it out of a car window. Shuffling steps brought her to the can. Her hand reached out to snatch it up before the sparse afternoon traffic could inflict harm on her. Carefully B'gee placed the down payment on her dreams into the plastic bag.   Soon, Peach—her color, her salvation, her warmth and her heaven—would flood her world, and the many confusing questions rambling unanswered in her head wouldn't matter any more.

Dark-red, velveteen nails tapped impatiently on the marble sill of the den window.   The sea breeze entered the slightly ajar windows ruffling the gauze curtains delicately before exiting though the wide open French doors, leaving behind a scented air that smelled of salt, new mown grass and palm trees.   The afternoon sun illuminated the fifth floor co-op whose expansive view straddled the ocean to the left and the Intra-Coastal to the right.   Sun chased the shadows of discontent into secret closets.   The purple-green art deco martini glass contained the final remnants of its former contents along with a slightly drunken olive.   Dark-red lips matching painted nails parted, but no sound came forth—only breaths that revealed that the martini could not have been the first, but the last of many. Although A'cee had learned that drinking helped to dull the process of remembrance, the pain was constant, and fed itself by the very act of living.

With burning intensity, the woman's eyes followed the rambling gait of the bag lady and unnoticed by A'cee, a tear leaked from her eye, trickling down a smooth cheek.   Her dark-red lips opened, permitting a sound to escape that was lost to all, except herself.   "Mama?"

DEATH WEARS A SMILE

"But Mother, I simply have to leave! I can't help it. Please? Please try to understand." In a conciliatory gesture the daughter's hand reached across a glass table cluttered with tea dishes.

"Clarisse, how can you leave the country? Your home? Your birthplace?" The mother asked, not bothering to conceal the hurt in her gentle voice. The woman's eyes turned away from the daughter's intense stare. In a self-consoling display of emotion, the mother's misty eyes gazed at the sloping hills covered with blossoming cornfields that danced beneath a satiny, gossamer breeze. The Tudor house looming stately behind them was built on a plateau, affording the women a perfect view of the surrounding land. The bleached, white cap on the mother's head covered her titian hair. Unlike her mother, the daughter wore hers loose. The hemp color of the coarse, high-buttoned linen dress showed Thea's rank and place in society—a married woman, who had chosen the country life. The daughter, not yet classified by the government, wore a buttercup print dress with lace at the sleeves and neckline.

"Clarisse," The mother murmured while pouring ginger tea into delicate china cups with shaking hands, "You know the law. I have taught you well! You must know what you have chosen means death." Realizing how harsh a tone she was using, the mother dropped her voice as she softly asked, "Don't you like the country? Look at it," she urged her daughter. Holding the cup and saucer in her left hand, she rested the other on the ornate handle of the copper kettle.

Clarisse, leaning forward, took the offered cup from Thea, blinking back tears as memories of their many afternoon teas surfaced. "Mother, I am of age today and therefore must decide how I want to be classified. I chose the 'City Dweller'." Without realizing it, her toe drew small circles into the soft, warm earth.

Shaking her head, the mother whispered into the delicate fall afternoon, "No one in our family has ever chosen this designation. I don't understand. What does the city have to offer you? Besides lights, long nights and the endless search for the unknown, followed by death. While here, at our home, you have the stillness of the land, the changes of the seasons, and the redundancy of country living." A solitary tear trickled down the woman's cheek and dropped onto her bodice, "Think of what you are saying, daughter!"

"Mother, I'm suffocating here. I have to leave for the city. I have to see the lights."

"Clarisse, the price the lights demand—your life—are they worth it?" the mother interjected haughtily.

Clarisse gazed steadily at her mother and swallowing hard said, "Yes."

The sun wandered down the horizon and orange rays bathed the two women drinking tea in a golden glow. Dogs barked in the distance, their hushed bellows framed the picture of the silent sitting women in their muted sorrow.

"Have you talked to your father about your decision?" The mother asked, breaking the spell of private thoughts.

"No, mother."

Thea, believing she had found a weak spot in her daughter's decision, countered, "Why not? Are you afraid he will try to talk you out of it?"

"No," Clarisse whispered softly. "I'll tell him tonight. After all, he'll drive me to the train station tomorrow," Clarisse answered.

The sharp, piercing whistle of a distant train punctuated the daughter's whispered words.

Frightened by the inevitability of the onrushing train, the mother instinctively raised her hands in horror to her face. As she spoke the pain of Clarisse's decision cracked Thea's voice. "The train station? Your ticket? It is ready? What have you done?" A sigh escaped from Thea as a desperate look settled on the woman's face. She wrung her hands in her lap. "You informed the Regents of your decision already?" Disbelief crept into her husky voice.

"Mother, do you believe that this was a spur of the moment decision?" Clarisse leaned her willowy body towards her mother, a gesture the daughter believed would give emphasis to her words. "No. I thought about this for months, but the city calls me."

"Why didn't you share your thoughts with me or your family before today?" Thea asked stiffly.

"Why? It still comes down to a single question, what is here for me?" Clarisse said solemnly.

"Oh, many things. You can get married and have children. Or build a farm and if that is not to your liking, teach school, work in a store, or run for Regent." A flash of recognition crossed her face as a nebulous thought entered her mind and took hold.

"Child, have I worked you too hard? Are you rebelling against the work I made you do and the ethics I tried to teach you?"

"No mother, that isn't the reason. Work is work. Besides I plan on working once I'm in the city. I am not running away from that."

"Then what else can it be?" The mother's face lit up. "Sex. That's it. All girls your age have those budding feelings and find waiting until marriage too difficult." The woman leaned across the table, her eyes glancing furtively about before they settled on Clarisse. "Daughter, if you are discreet, no one will say anything about it. It is just the wanton display of sexual ardor the way 'City Dwellers' carry on that upsets the Regents and the people."

"No, it isn't sex. Why can't you understand that I have this feeling inside of me that makes me want to go."

"Feelings inside of you." Her head drew sharply back from the daughter. "No! You can't be serious. Freedom. Is that what you are talking about? Come now, it reads well in books, but in reality, no!"

"Yes, freedom. That's the word. The one word everyone is so afraid of." A tiny smile graced the young woman's face as she went on, "The one word that allows you to be yourself."

Thea sat up straight, her bony hands folded themselves in her lap as her verbal attack on the daughter began.

"Freedom! No child! Freedom is in submitting yourself to the law. Freedom is the death of the City Dwellers after their allotted time has run out. Freedom is in following the seasons of the crop, and freedom is obedience to time honored traditions that make our land and government strong."

"Even if the traditions or the law is wrong?" Clarisse whispered.

"Traditions are not wrong and laws borne out of them are for us to obey," Thea said proudly.

"Mother, explain to me how can you defend a tradition, a law that sentences half, half of the population to die so that the other half may live in comfort."

"Clarisse, at your coming of age you decide how you want to be classified. If you choose the land, your life will run its natural course. But you know this." A quizzical look was on her face as she continued, "If you choose the city, you are given ten years. You don't have to work, and everything that you could possibly want or desire will be given to you. At the end of your tenth year, you are given an injection and twenty four hours later you are dead. This is our way to control population. We support the City Dwellers in luxury and they in turn will die for us after ten years. Besides, any children born to women in the city are taken to the land and raised by the community without discrimination of their parentage. What is so terrible about this arrangement?" Her disbelief rang clearly through.

"Population control? Mother, we live on time that does not belong to us."

"Why do you say this, Clarisse?" Concern over the daughter's statement made Thea squirm in her lawn chaise. "Remember, no one is forced to either way of life. It is your choice. We are taught this from childhood on. Clarisse, it is not a secret. It is an alternative life style."

"Alternative life style! Think about what you're saying." The daughter's hands gripped the edge of the glass table, bracing herself as she raised her voice. "And what if one made an error in choosing? Oh mother, the finality of this decision is what makes it so terrible."

Thea looked at her daughter. "You are not the first to question. Even I occasionally wondered. But as I got older, I recognized why traditions and laws are such a great comfort and why they must be obeyed. Your life is planned. Your time is allocated, leaving no room for doubt to enter into your mind. Please? Please, child, rescind your classification."

Clarisse smiled, rose and walked to the edge of the plateau. She glanced around and deeply drank in the musky scent of the country. Her arms reached out, her face turned upward towards a sky drenched in the crimson purple of a waning sun.

"Mother, one more step and I fall."

The girl's arms came down to lift the long skirt of her dress, revealing bare feet. The daughter swayed and slowly started to dance to music only she heard.

Thea watched in silent terror, knowing in her heart that the girl was either mad or would die any moment through a simple misstep. "Sit down and stop this nonsense. It is time for you to come to your senses and start behaving in an acceptable way."

The ground vibrated softly beneath them as the thunderous train on the way to the city crossed the valley.

Happy, with her face flushed and hair damp, the daughter obeyed and sank into the chaise. Clarisse's hand reached across the cluttered table. "Mother, I'm choosing life! Mine!"

THE NATURAL STATE OF BEING

The cream colored, delicately embossed envelope lay innocently enough on the simple white plate, yet the governor's seal in the upper left hand corner hinted at the importance of the message inside. I knew what the envelope contained.

"Do you still persist in believing this nonsense?" Gabriella asked. Voluminous strawberry curls draped her pale face. "What are you waiting for? Or are you afraid to read what's in there?"

"No Gaby. But you're wrong."

She reached out for the object of dispute. "Well, Lucinda, then let me do the honor." And she promptly used her knife to slice open the envelope and, using her thumb and forefinger, deftly removed the invitation. I saw the cruel smile form on her face and for the first time I noticed the age lines on her pale skin as she read the message to herself.

"Read it," Gaby uttered maliciously as she deposited the linen paper in front of me. The black ink glared menacingly back while a tear crept down my cheek.

"In compliance with the Laws of the Sovereign State, you are hereby ordered to attend the execution . . ." I trailed off amid Gabriella's hollow laughter that drowned my voice as the echo of her glee reverberated in the stark room.

"Lucy, can't you see? This proves my point. Good people don't get executed. Only damaged people are."

I stirred the sugar in my cup and the sun broke through the closed window in a myriad of colors that splashed across the gray wall, dousing it in subtle, dainty hues.

"Gabriella, the natural state of being is good. Look at it this way, a well-adjusted person will raise an alike person. A child that is damaged by a parent while being raised will eventually go awry. After all, when we break things, how do we glue them back together so they won't break again?"

The screech of the opening jail door pierced in resonating agony through the silent night. The Guard shuffled softly along the bleak corridor, afraid of waking the single prisoner housed in the Death Row compound. The condemned person's last night was here and a suicide watch had been posted. The Guard was on his way to relieve the mid-night Shift. The soft yellow light illuminated the sleeping area and he saw the rhythmic breathing beneath the blanket and the peaceful, handsomely angelic profile of the sleeper in the night.

"What now, Lucy? You're the bright one with all the answers."

"We have to go, Gaby."

"I've told you the Governor would not grant a pardon."

"Why should he? The crimes were terrible and the public outcry too loud. Remember what we learned during the trial?"

"Yes. Yes. Abuse, mistreatment, drugs, torture as a child, then foster homes, etc., etc. A routine story.

"Gabriella, routine? I don't think so!"

"So what Lucy. Other people survived lives like that."

I looked at Gaby. She seemed innocence personified, but cruelty was her daily bread, and unforgiving her creed to live by. Yet, I loved her. She was part of me, belonged to me, and was spawned by me. But in the last months, our arguments had become worse as the days passed and the execution date neared. For the umpteenth time I would try to convince her that her conclusion was wrong. "Then name me one person that survived?"

Gaby swirled her hair in her hands, forming more and more curls as her hazel eyes, dazed, looked far beyond the window into a distant world only she knew. The cruel smile again formed around her lips. "You, Lucinda."

"I don't count. It's much too easy of an answer."

Thoughts of protest sputtered out. "Well, I don't know other people's lives. They do not tell me what is going on in their heads. So how would I know?"

Bravo Shift came on, relieving the guard from Alpha Shift. "Did the prisoner pick the menu yet?" the relief asked.

"The list of wishes was slipped outside the door."

The guard glanced at the slowly ticking clock posted on the wall. It was a standard, institutional issue and blended in smoothly with its drab surroundings. A white porcelain face, black roman numerals with matching black minute hands, and a red second hand. No gray and no doubts existed here, just starkness, clear-cut. "Well, we better get the show on the road. Three hours pass quickly," he uttered as the red second hand clicked along.

The Guard unlocked the cell door, entered, and tapped the sleeper lightly on the shoulder. Before the condemned prisoner could be strapped into the chair, a whole litany of regulations had to be complied with.

"Your ordered meal will be served shortly. The minister is waiting along with the doctor."

Sleep-filled eyes blinked back momentary disorientation and a yawn was the prisoner's unspoken reply. The guard coughed lightly to hide his discomfort with the silent reply before asking, "Whom would you like to see first?"

"Does it matter?" whispered the prisoner.

"No. I guess I'll bring the doctor in first, seeing that you're not dressed. It would not be right to bring the priest in, with you still . . ." The words trailed off as the guard unlocked the door and re-locked it on his way out.

"Lucy, you should have told them how it all began." Gaby said accusingly as her fork speared the steak and brought the juicy morsel to her lips. "Their bleeding hearts would have understood." Gaby's wide-open mouth revealed perfect teeth that chomped on the meat with gusto.

"Gabriella, remember mother's words? 'Don't air your dirty laundry in public?' I couldn't bring myself to talk about it, besides the doctors, the police and the attorney all did it for me."

"Yeah, but nothing beats hearing it from the mouth of the person who witnessed it. And you were there, there is no way of denying it."

"You're right. I saw it all. This is why I believe that our natural way of being is good."

"No, Lucy, you're wrong. Besides, you're afraid to talk about what happened and what went on. That's why you're using mother's words to hide behind them."

"Gaby, I'm not afraid. Embarrassed, yes!" The hot coffee burnt going down my constricted throat, as the bitter memories of the past welled up in me, creating their own acid taste in my mouth.

"You're remembering, aren't you?"

"Yes. And it was bad."

"You still can't talk about it Lucy, can you?"

I looked at Gaby. She was there when it first happened. She saw it and she could talk about it in her matter of fact way, why not I? "You're right. I'm so sorry." Tears ran down my cheeks. I brought my hands up to my face and resting my elbows on the table, I cried. The pain of what I had known was as ever present as the pale moon against the black sky.

"Lucy stop it. I can't stand it when you get all weepy and sappy," Gaby shouted. "You have to do what I do. Every time the pain comes, I act on it. It's simple and it works."

"Oh child, how I wish it would be this simple. But someone is dying today because of our pain."

"Dying? No, Lucinda. Executed, yes! And all because you did not want to talk!"

"No. I can't." I screamed back at her and blackness engulfed me as the horrid memories of the deeds surfaced. But Gabriella's seductive voice penetrated the fog of pain and the haze of fear in me.

"Get even, Lucy! Get even. That's the secret."

The prisoner shivered lightly as the steel stethoscope touched naked skin. The doctor's examination was thorough. According to the law, the prisoner had to be in perfect health before execution. The irony brought a smile to the condemned person's face as the doctor pronounced, "The prisoner is healthy and ready to be executed."

The doctor placed his hand on the head, "I'm sorry. Please forgive me, but I had no choice."

Hazel eyes looked up at the man, while slender fingers buttoned the shirt and in a hushed tone she whispered. "Yes," came forth. Relieved, the doctor waved at the guard to open the door for him.

The Warden entered the cell. "Do you have any thing to say?"

She looked up, shaking her head in silence.

"You are the third woman in our state's history to be executed. I know you killed all the people, but why do I feel that you don't deserve to die? I have to know for myself: why didn't you talk at your trial?" The hands in his pockets were balled into fists. His jaw was clenched and the sharp pain in his head constricted his eyes. "If you only would have talked, they would have spared your life." He paused lightly before asking, "Are you ready?"

As an answer, the woman stood up, smiled forlornly, and began to lead the way to the chamber with the priest by her side. The clock on the wall ticked and ticked as the woman walked silently toward her death on a plush, red carpet that ended in front of the open door. She knew that the room behind contained the beckoning chair and was encircled with glass walls to allow the invited witnesses to observe the execution.

"Lucy, look around the chamber. Didn't I tell you everyone asked would be here?"

"It's the law, Gaby. Besides, people enjoy sensationalism."

"Did you see her? She looks almost happy. She can't wait until it's all over."

The guard snapped on the restraints and the sharp smell of alcohol permeated the air as he swabbed the marked places on her skin to clean them of body oil. Finished cleaning the exposed areas, he squirted gel from a tube onto the dry skin, assuring a perfect contact for the electrodes. The prisoner was ready! The red second hand of the clock ticked with maddening determination towards the time of execution. The hooded Executioner watched the hand move. It was time.

Gaby panted with fear as recognition surfaced in her. Her hands grabbed my shoulders and the strong hold of her grip belied her fragility. "My God, Lucy, stop her. Don't let her do it. She's killing me. Oh please, stop her."

The prisoner's eyes opened and acceptance was in them. She was all of them—Gabriella, Lucinda and the damaged self.

"Gabriella, we had to stop you, that's why we never spoke."

"You just don't understand, I had the right." Gabriella fought back, her body writhing, trying to escape.

The Executioner yanked the switch down. The light flickered and finally, she was at peace.

THE PRICE OF A PLUM MOON

The woman, and she was one now, wrote her name, Hab-rel, in the yellow silicone sand. Fascinated by the new appearance of her fingers, she stopped writing and began touching herself. Her skin, the palest of white, glared back at her. She watched the life force moving in her as the veins pulsated vigorously. She turned her attention to the huge and slender vat on her right. The narrow object stood silently, a solitary sentinel of things and events to come. Slowly she reached for it. Her hand gently traced the ancient writings on the vessel. She knew that the moment of decision had come. Time, once a gentle lover, was now a bitter master. When daylight came, Hab-rel would have to choose.

Her eyes wandered back to the landscape before her. The pale silver trees were still glowing pink, reflecting the plum moon shining on the land. White rocks, with patches of yellow moss and tufts of coarse, green ground cover, joined in the melody of pink hues as the moon reached its descending path for the night. Dawn with its green suns and luscious, hearty rays would soon greet the world of Tealar.

So she sat. Wrapped only in a light blanket to ward off the chill of the night. She sat quietly with her legs crossed. The man behind her on the ground was sleeping peacefully. His breathing was relaxed and the contented expression on his face revealed that the evening had yielded what he had expected. She turned slightly to look at him. A faint smile appeared on her young face briefly before it vanished into another realm.

Again, she gazed at the silent sentinel. Hab-rel knew that the vat contained a green dye in the same deep shade as the people of her planet who matched the three suns that gave their warmth to Tealar during the day. She was also aware that people had been gathering at the clearing below from where she and her lover were spending the night.

When night had first fallen, Hab-rel had been green like them and graced with flaming red hair and eyes. Now, a few hours later, after having tasted love and gaining knowledge in the ancient tradition, she had turned white. A pale, lovely white. The same startling color of the rocks that littered the world of Tealar. Hab-rel's parents had foreseen that this might happen because their child had always been different. In the custom of their world, they had lovingly provided the vat of dye for their daughter to immerse herself in so she could again match her world and her people. The law was very specific and detailed how a person had to be. Underneath your green skin and a mask to cover your white face, you could feel and think as you pleased, but on the outside, you had to conform. It was an effective law because it had proven repeatedly that what was beneath the covers would mesh eventually with the external world.

Hab-rel recalled the stories she had heard of those who had turned white during the night and had chosen not to obey the law. They also understood that they could not live naturally as white among the green and therefore were banished to Sethor. The inhabitants of Tealar whispered the names of these gifted ones with reverence and awe, but Hab-rel wanted to live and love here, not to be admired from afar. After all, she was made of flesh and her needs were of this world. She wanted to be part of life. She wanted to belong. Overcome with sadness she bowed her head and let her green tears fall on her bare, white legs.

Weary, she wiped her face and looked back at the man. Mautor, who was twice her age, was her teacher and the one who had taken her youth and tasted her innocence. How she loved him! Yet, he was still green. The woman understood. Some men would never pay the price for the knowledge. The cost was just too high for them. In spite of it, she was not angry or bitter. But Hab-rel, last daughter of Vantor and just fifteen, was different. She loved her teacher. Her knowing father, who had so thoughtfully provided the mask as well, understood too. The mask fitted perfectly over her face and the vat of green dye awaited her. Everything was set for her to join the legions of people who had learned to follow orders and compromise. Yet the question that hung in the misty night air troubled her deeply, was she ready for the vat and the obedience it required?

She wondered, did she have the courage to join the other seers that, too, had acquired the gift of knowledge after having tasted sex? She certainly had the gift, as her teacher had discovered. But he had also told her that the journey from here to Sethor where the temple of Refuge and Worship was located, was hard and fraught with difficulties. She wondered, could she withstand its demands? Hab-rel knew if she stayed on Tealar, she would know love and all the other sweet, varied emotions that made life so comfortable and normal. All she would have to do was to wear her mask. Then when the plum moon shone on the silver landscape of Tealar, and she was alone, she could remove the mask and be free again for a short time. And yet, such a choice would guarantee that her gift, her ability, would ultimately disintegrate into the yellow silicone of other lost lives that formed the dust of Tealar.

She woke Mautor with a touch. "My love," she whispered, "I need you."

He reached out, pulling her gently toward him. "Do we have enough time?"

"Yes." Hab-rel said.

His hand stroked her face. "How soft your skin is. What will you do now?" In the past, the two had many intimate talks exploring how each would react should the whiteness happen to them, but Hab-rel had never been definite about it. Her youth craved love and life, but her mind thirsted for knowledge. Mautor, having lived longer, lacked such a dilemma. He would choose to wear the mask, join, and then cry when the plum moon shone.

She smiled at him. "Love me, and maybe in loving you I will find the answer to the puzzle."

After their passion was stilled, they rested. The moon was waning as the green suns ascended. The time was here. Hab-rel parted from her lover's arms reluctantly, rose and picked up the mask.

A huge crowd had assembled. The rites of wisdom were rare now and wondrous to be seen. Hab-rel, following the ancient custom, pulled the blanket around her tightly, making sure her face and body were covered as she walked into the middle of their circle. She stopped when she reached the center. The Elder spoke as he approached her.

"Woman, show us your face so we may know that you still belong to us and that the fruit of knowledge you have tasted in the night has passed by you."

As ordered, Hab-rel pushed the blanket away from her face and revealed her lovely white skin. The crowd gasped and gaped. From the corners of her eyes, Hab-rel could see her mother crying and her father attempting to comfort the distraught woman.

The elder spoke again. "Have you been informed of our laws before you began your night?"

"Yes," she said quietly, "and a vat of dye was provided along with the mask." Her hand let go of the crumpled mask and it fell with a soft thud on the yellow silicone.

"I am required by our laws to ask you a second time before I must render judgment. Hab-rel, you cannot be different from us. A world is only as good as each member and it must be whole to survive. Will you obey? Give me your answer."

"Let it begin." She whispered.

"As you wish." He replied.

The Elder walked away from her, asking himself under his breath, "Why?" He wore the mask; he had adjusted. As he walked back to the edge, he thought repeatedly, such a price! Having reached a safe distance, the Elder bent down and began picking up the white rocks and stuffing them into his coat pockets. This action served as a signal to the people who followed suit. Then the Elder took a deep breath and turned around. He began throwing rocks at the white figure in the circle and the dutiful crowd joined in lustily.

Meanwhile the lone man standing on the cliff pulled his mask over his white face to hide his green tears—tears that were also for Hab-rel whose journey to Sethor had now begun as the first rocks hit her.

A THIRD KIND OF LOVE

Tomorrow there would be a hanging! His hanging! C'est la vie.

Life did not matter anymore, for if the truth were known, Landers had felt dead inside for weeks. The hanging would end the weariness of his body. After all, he had died when she walked in front of the firing squad.

Once, he had been afraid of dying. Now he wondered why, but found no answer forthcoming. In his overt fear, he argued with her, telling her that life and the cost it demanded, betrayal of her friends, were worth it. She just smiled and named no one. He knew now, she had been right! Good Lord, all that was left for him was but the cumbersome act of death itself.

Love, a four letter word whose implication of belonging and responsibilities made him uncomfortable, urged him to run and hide behind his social position and his family name that always had been above reproach. Yet tomorrow, a woman would strip the veneer of respectability away and the love he once feared would reach out and transcend reality. Was she a witch, or did she truly have the gift?

It was an unusually cool morning in the Mississippi Delta when she met her executioners. Before they took her away, she told him, "I wait for you, don't worry." Landers cringed as his memory echoed the other words that seared themselves forever in his mind: Ready! Aim! Fire! And the screaming sounds of the muskets shattered the hushed Delta silence with their violence. Afterward, cradling her bloody body in his arms and whispering his good-byes, he felt the warmth of her life seeping through his fingers into the moist ground of the marsh. He understood then, his rationale was wrong and he had died inside.

She gave her life for his mistake. The question was simple now. How does one exist with all tomorrow erased and only empty days left to occupy a lifetime? A bitter payment for a single night of love! His mind strayed back to that sultry afternoon of their first meeting.

She walked toward him with a basket of laundry on her head just as the Negro women did—yet she was white. At least she appeared to be, and all her features indicated proper breeding. But she walked like a cat on the prowl looking for a mate, and no respectable, southern white woman would ever walk this way. Trash, is what she was. He wondered where she came from and why he had not seen her before. In the small town where he lived, nothing was ever secret. She must have moved here while he was away at school in England.

He returned, gladly interrupting his studies in that cold, stilted country because his father feared an impending blockade and a civil war by the Northerners. Back at home, he spent the first few weeks catching up with local gossip and news. Soon, idle routine took over and boredom set in. Now the threat of war tainted conversations with excitement at the town's daily socials as people stirred with righteous indignation.

Fort St. Philip, a forgotten outpost in the past, was now employed as a temporary shelter for storing a cache of arms. Local men eagerly volunteered to serve as guards until proper distribution of the weapons could be arranged. And he was on his way to the Police Chief carrying next week's duty roster in his pocket.

The young woman who started his train of recollections came closer, and he caught the scent of musk mixed with the clean smell of laundry that lingered behind as she sauntered by. She passed without noticing him.

Slowly, he turned and stared after her and before she could leave, he shouted, "Hey!" She stopped and turned in the direction of his voice. Her questioning gaze fell on the wiry young man, with dark hair and the comeliest blue-gray eyes. A playful smile broke across her face. "I am called Mirrah, not hey," she replied, letting her eyes meet his.

"Mirrah." He let the strangeness of the name roll off his tongue with pleasure and obvious delight. Fascinated by her, he stared unabashedly. She was short, small, and tanned golden with the largest mass of blond curls framing a high cheek-boned face. He held out his hand. "Come with me Mirrah," he told her. "I won't be long. I'll drop of these papers, then I'm free."

"Not now. Tonight. Where will you be?"

"Standing guard at the depot. I can't leave. It's my turn to stand guard." Disappointment rang out.

Mirrah reached out with her free hand to touch his face. "I'll visit with you after dark. What do they call you?"

"Landers."

She pulled his face close to hers and brushed his cheek with her full lips. "Till this night." And smiling, with both hands holding the basket, she ran away and toward a neighborhood, which Landers knew to be the area inhabited by poor trash. He visited the quarters often enough before going to England.

Landers stared until she disappeared from his sight. He knew she had captured him.

The harsh clang of metal doors brought the young man's thoughts back to the present. His father stood before him.

"Son, I tried. But you conspired with a Union sympathizer, and the commander's nephew died in the explosion, this is why the Governor won't commute your sentence. And we are at the dawn of war." The man's eyes looked sadly upon his youngest and favorite son. "Why did you tell your story to the Police Chief? Why did you confess your willingness to leave your post? You were in the clear. The laundress volunteered her complicity. You would have not lost your honor by keeping quiet."

"Father, I loved her."

The man shook his head before he spoke again. His soft, southern voice trembled as he gently rebuked his son. "To love like this is wrong. Have I not taught you that there are only two kinds of women; the kind you marry to bear your children and the other kind you visit when passion runs high in your blood."

Landers turned away from his father and glanced into the starless night. He wondered, would she be waiting for him as promised? But how could she, unless she were the devil's own sister? Yet no creature from the dark could possess such soft forms and eager lips like hers, he thought.

Mirrah did come to the depot that night as promised, shortly after dark. And he, tempted by her sensuous willingness, left his post and wandered off into the silky night with her.

Mirrah's cotton cloak served as the blanket on which they discovered each other. A full moon had bathed their bodies with opalescent light. The first time they joined, the unspent passion of their youth exploded in huge waves, drowning their senses repeatedly before returning them to and the soft night. The second time they came together, they delighted each other with the instinctive carnal knowledge nature had given them; and the third time was with love that allowed the man and woman to give freely, to please and in the end fulfill their deepest desires.

Even now, Landers could feel her warmth and sense her lips on his face as his mind relived the memory of them lying on the moss, with their passion stilled and the breeze from the ocean fanning their bodies, cooling them gently.

"You don't understand," the condemned man whispered. How could he explain to his father that they spent a lifetime with each other in a single night? "She took the blame for my leaving the post, telling her interrogators that she drugged me with the wine, so the Fort would be unguarded, open to attack." Tears ran down his face. "Father, we were discovered before she could get away."

"Landers, she was a spy for the Union!"

"Yes! No! She was just a woman who fell in love and then could not step back from it. The plan may have been like that at first. Instead, she chose to pay the price for loving me and stayed behind. She told me to go on, to live. And I believed I could!"

"Can't you see she was a witch? She came out of nowhere and picked you; she bewitched you!" He continued speaking solemnly, "Son, forget her. Make your peace with your Maker. Soon you will stand in front of Him, then what?"

"Father, all my life I did what I was told. I obeyed, I conformed, and I compromised. But whenever I prayed, there was only silence. No one ever answered. Yet, when I was with her, I understood. And when she told me, 'there is an answer,' I believed it." He smiled at his father. "She was not a witch, but she had the Gift and she loved me freely. She was earth, she was life."

Dawn, the continuum of life and rebirth, rose blood-red upon the land. Dew moistened the buds on the Magnolias and the mist gently dissipated, creating an almost perfect pastoral view that even the quietly swinging rope on the wooden gallows could not disturb.

Landers, shaven and properly dressed, walked with dignity toward the wooden platform. His hands were not shackled. He had given his word as a gentleman not to attempt an escape. A solitary drum roll accompanied him and added a haunting melody that silenced the small group of spectators hiding in the copse of aged chestnuts. The condemned man appeared eager as he ascended the steps. The rope was placed around his neck. The minister murmured appropriate words and then the noose tightened. Suddenly, the trap door opened and he whispered, "Mirrah!"

Faithfully she came, hands outstretched. The father stared at his son's peaceful face and was envious. There was a third kind of love. And the old man understood.

Brief comments on the short stories.

The Color of Rags came about when I looked down from the fifth floor rental apartment and saw a homeless person scavenging through the dumpster and picking up all of the cans and bottles.

Death Wears a Smile was written because of people assuming the right to judge other people, yet never recognizing, or failing to examine, their own life.

The Natural State of Being, was the most troublesome. When does responsibility for your actions enter into your life and does the state have the right to take a life?

The Price of a Plum Moon was inspired by reading "The Lottery," in conjunction with a difficult period in my marriage that prompted the question: do I have the courage to do what is right?

A Third Kind of Love was motivated when someone told me that when he prayed there was only silence. Yet, when he fell in love, he understood, which poses the question, do we hear once we love?

INSIDE THE BLACK BOX:
Possessed by the Dark

CHAPTER 1

THE ABOMINATION

Later he could not have said when he made the decision to kill Reba. Sometime after his ally had joined the Psychic Five–that group of intuitive New Agers perfecting their psychic skills in the flotation chamber. Doing things they shouldn't– like reading other people's minds and astrally projecting into other people's bedrooms–remote viewing, they called it. In the name of scientific experimentation.

Aah, he remembered now. His "Split" had made the decision to get rid of Reba. Inside the Black Box. Because Reba had the money. And Reba had put a halt to the most powerful experiments. Those inside the Black Box.

He wriggled through the dense watery passageway–the Way--his entrance to this strange but delightful new world that he could go into and out of almost at will through the "waterway." The faint shadings of light shook him a little. Was he still terrified of the light after being locked in his mother's closet for such a very long time? No. That was so very long ago. When he was a child. But wasn't that why he had this love-hate thing for all females? Still, he told himself, that was the "Split," not him. Now he emerged in front of Reba's city home where he paused making sure he had the right house.

Snowflakes dulled the Knoxville air. Although they did not chill him, he felt uneasy–as if something were wrong with *his plan. But what could go awry? Reba could not see him, not in his dimension–unless he wanted her to. Or had she a secret of her own?*

By the time his ephemeral form slipped into the frame house, he felt omnipotent once more. He floated directly into the bathroom, past the inhalator hanging on the wall, to the gas space heater. The gas in this old heater had no sulphur in it, no odor that an older person like Reba would smell–he hoped. In three swift movements he plugged the air vent, turned up the flame in the heater, and slammed the door shut. The seventy-year-old woman had a history of sinusitis and emphysema. Surely she could not detect the gas.

How many times had the old girl told him she would renovate this old house, install a central heating system? But he had known she was too stingy.

He chuckled and rubbed his hands together, barely able to stop himself from dancing with glee. His physical body had not danced–it was too crooked. He tore his thoughts away from "before" years, the years before he'd found the Black Box, determined to enjoy what was his, now.

And that included Reba.

He heard the whine of the hinges as the front door opened. The blood surged through his arteries, strong and throbbing, knowing it was her and the time was near.

But the voice that drifted in was that of the youngest member of the psychic group. Kris, the nature nut, called out, "Reba?"

He floated along the ceiling to a position above Kris.

Kris stood in the spacious living room, a pile of books in her arms, glancing about in confusion. She finger lifted her blonde dread-locks. She would have liked to have been born black, but lacking that coloration she affected their hairdos. The Afro hairdo made her round face babyish, the way he liked it.

Genitals tightening in anticipation, he wanted to flash down upon her. But no. That would destroy the perfect plan. He barely held back mirth as he watched her tromp through the house calling out to Reba.   When she paused before the bathroom, her gaze seeming to burrow into the closed door, he struggled to keep from pouncing on her.   The feeling that Kris might be psychic enough to sense him and reveal his presence heightened his excitement.

Kris glanced about, her brown eyes widening, as if she detected an eerie presence.   But instead of investigating, the young woman looked at the watch on her wrist briefly, muttered, "Damn, Reba, can I help it if you're not home?" deposited the books on a low book case in the hall and bounded out into the cold like a frightened hare.

Reba's old city house empty once more, the misty form lay down on Reba's canopied bed, smirking at how annoyed she would be if she knew he was invading her sanctuary.   But the bathroom epitomized her privateness.   He thought of her old-maid habit of locking the door behind her upon entering this retreat.

That act will be the death of you yet, my dear.   Shivers tingled his body at the thought of her shame when he first laughed at and then touched her wrinkled, naked skin. Guffaws wracked him until he felt weak but couldn't prevent the reaction.   This world and all it contained was his now that he'd found the "Split" and the "Way."

The click of a key in the front lock broke off his nervous laughter, and his heart beat faster as he shifted his station to the foyer where he could look down upon Reba–the one who could ruin everything–as she entered.   He wondered how such a dried-up old prune as she could have dredged up the trust to give keys to each member of the club.   It just showed how unstable she was, how incompetent to handle all that money.

Parkland, Florida (same time)

Dori Roberts strode through aisle after aisle of the bookstore looking for just the right Christmas gift for Aunt Reba. She'd know the book or the thing when she saw it, Aunt Reba always said Dori had a sixth sense about picking gifts that Reba would have bought for herself–but hadn't. Aah, here it is, thought Dori, as she halted before a unique display of embossed leather booklets. She picked up a brown one that had a gold tree of life emblazoned on its jacket and a brown-and-green forest complete with waterfall on its back. She flipped through the blank pages. It looked as though there were over 100 pages. Dori had overheard Aunt Reba telling Dori's eight-year-old daughter Rebecca at Thanksgiving that Reba needed to start recording the experiments she was doing with her metaphysical group–but hadn't gotten around to buying a notebook. This would be perfect for Aunt Reba. Dori paid the twenty-five dollars at checkout and left with the precious packet tucked under her arm. Tonight she'd show it to her daughter and ask if she wanted to put a dollar toward the gift and let it be from the two "ladies of the family."

Knoxville, Tennessee (same time)

Reba and Etta Mae stood for a moment on the tiny porch brushing snow from each other's coats with the only things free– their fingertips. Her arms sagging with packages, Reba pushed through the door first. Swinging her rump against the door to hold it open for her friend, Etta Mae, Reba felt the back of her scalp prickle in warning. As she laid the parcels of pre-wrapped Christmas gifts on the foyer floor, she ran trembling fingers through steel gray hair. Her gaze jumped around the living room from its Victorian sofa before the brick fireplace to its cocktail table with a horizontal crack in the pink Tennessee marble to its built-in bookcases lining the far wall. Warding off the subject she knew her octogenarian friend would soon broach, Reba said, "Etta Mae, could you believe the mothers in those stores– grabbing up computers for their grade school kiddies as fast as they could? My goodness, I hope Dori has the sense not to follow the crowd."

The shorter, older woman kept stride with Reba into the kitchen where Etta Mae reached into the cupboard for the herbal tea, snorting, "Dori must've inherited something from you,

Reba." Etta Mae grinned impishly as she filled two cups with water and placed them in the microwave while Reba put an old-fashioned teapot of water on the stove. "Besides, what do we know? Two years ago we were still brewing tea–without teabags-- two old witches over a cauldron."

Reba sat daintily on the flowered living room couch and drank some of the cinnamon-flavored brew. She had hoped the tea would calm her down but she felt more tense each passing moment. "I just don't hold with newfangled toys like automatic guns, and computers, and space ships."

"No, you'd rather 'float' than fly, wouldn't you, dear?"

Here it comes, thought Reba, too tired to spar with her stubborn old friend, but knowing she must find the energy to circumvent Etta Mae's line of inquiry. "Don't be sarcastic. My feet hurt too much to quibble with you today." Deliberately, Reba stretched her legs out and rotated her ankles in the air to relieve the aching. "Don't know how you do it. Walk the aisles all day and still chipper as a . . ."

"Say it, Reba. Won't hurt my feelings nary an ounce. A chipmunk. It's all in the genes. Don't you read the papers anymore? Soon those researchers will forget about sheep and such and beat down my door to clone me."

Following always directly overhead so that Reba would not catch a glimpse of him, he watched the way Reba's patterned eyes circled the room surreptitiously so her elderly friend would not become afraid. Good. Reba could feel his presence but couldn't see him in his current form. Today's was the ultimate test, and it was nearly complete. Now he would try to make this stocky woman do what he wanted by sending her mental messages–telepathy. When he was certain he could control this psychic woman, he would know he could control anyone.

His piercing gaze was glued to Reba who had set her cup down on the table and was stretching her flabby arms above her head–shaking them while her gaze traced the ceiling in rhythm with her arm movements. He heard the "thud" of

Etta Mae kicking off her heels and then she was leaning back in the living room recliner.

He hoped Reba was less powerful than he. The next few moments would tell.

The ominous feeling stronger than before, Reba dug out thumbnail-sized holes from her napkin while half-listening to her best friend.

Etta Mae continued with, "Lah, you'd think Christmas was tomorrow instead of two weeks from now the way you shopped today. But then if you're mailing gifts to Parkland, Florida, you should have started shopping earlier, shouldn't you?"

Opening her mouth to answer, Reba realized that Etta Mae had already gone into her usual monologue. Dear friend, if I didn't love you . . . Reba looked down at the hill of tissue but couldn't stop shredding it. One would think the atmosphere in the living room would be a little lighter, she thought, with a window on each wall. Instead gloom was building. The gray dreariness of the Knoxville winter was getting to her, that was all. It couldn't be . . .

Reba jumped up and went into the kitchen. She scanned the ceiling while she swallowed an aspirin. She saw nothing anywhere to prove her suspicions. She shrugged away her anxiety. Back in the living room she poured Etta Mae another cup of hot water over a fresh chamomile tea bag. Then she smoothed down her own red-and-white flowered polyester dress, balanced her teacup on her knees, and breathed deeply a few times to relax. But she could not. What was wrong?

"So don't tell me, let me guess." Etta Mae's high-pitched voice trailed on and on. "You loved the Cokes and cakes spilled on you at Thanksgiving by your grand niece and grand nephew so much you're going back for more goo on Christmas?" Etta Mae cocked her head and smiled sweetly at Reba over her teacup.

"Humph!" was all the satisfaction Reba would give her. She thought, heavens-to-Betsy, if you only knew. Reba wanted to confide in her older friend, but Etta could do nothing to help. And knowing would put her life in danger. Reba's eyes examined the living room again. Her stomach muscles tightened, as they always did before a disaster.

Etta Mae's blue eyes were bright and unwavering as she fastened them on Reba like an eagle targeting its prey before striking. When she spoke, however, her hesitant speech displayed concern. "Can't keep a secret from me, child. I've been second guessing you for more than forty years."

Fear entered the man at this. Could Etta Mae prevent him from fulfilling his task? He hated the thought of killing her. The vivacious eighty-year-old woman reminded him of the outgoing nine-year-old girl, his first love, his only love. Or was that the memory of his new ally? Sometimes he got confused. But that wasn't important. What was eminent was not letting Reba destroy his entrance into his time and place.

Etta Mae said, "I've already stocked the freezer with a ten-pound turkey for our Christmas dinner."

Reba ignored her old friend's subtle blackmail and again tried unsuccessfully to contain her crawling-the-wall feeling. She was happy when into her mind swirled a vivid picture of her eight-year-old niece last Christmas Eve–before all the black box experiments had begun.

"Rebecca," Reba had said, "in these mountains are special places. Magical almost. Once two other girls and I scrambled through drifts of foot-deep leaves, tee-heeing as the debris crackled underfoot when, Lordy, I stumbled over a hollow tree trunk. After I got up and brushed off my dress, the cutest little bear cub tumbled from the trunk's opposite end and tottered over to me. We patted the tiny thing and it rolled around in the dried leaves with us as if it thought we were its sisters.

"But all of a sudden the mother stuck her head through some mulberry branches."

Rebecca's eyes widened. "Were you scared, Auntie Reba?"

Reba raised an eyebrow. "The mother bear lunged toward us, roared, and clapped her paws at her cub. The frightened cub obeyed instantly, scrabbling up a tall pine. My friends ran but I couldn't move. Something froze me to the spot. I remember thinking, I wouldn't hurt you; why would you hurt me? The mother wheeled, stood tall like a person, and stared intently into my eyes. Then she grunted, fell to all four paws, and waddled past me.

"That was when I began to know the power of the Deep, of Domnu." Reba and Rebecca exchanged knowing glances. Reba added, "Not that mere knowledge *about* the Deep does much good. We must master its secrets."

Rebecca drew squares on the carpet with her bare foot. "You never told me the name before, Auntie. Will that keep the scare away?"

"A little. I've been there once–by accident–when I uncover how, we'll share. With your ability you should learn much faster than I have as you grow older. And, remember, honey, I'll always be here to protect you."

The young girl had climbed into her great aunt's lap and hugged her tightly.

The squeak from Etta Mae positioning the recliner interrupted Reba's reverie. Reba hated having lied to her young namesake about the last part. And now the test was at hand. Too soon, too soon. She felt unseen eyes watching her. His eyes.

"You could at least answer me, child." Etta Mae's voice was testy.

For more years than Reba cared to acknowledge, Etta Mae had directed those younger than she as "child." But the growing edginess upon entering her Knoxville city house made Reba even testier. She snapped back. "Etta Mae Briarley, just because you've got ten years on me doesn't entitle you to an interrogation."

Etta Mae smiled sweetly and murmured, "Humph."

Reba laughed out loud at this and wished she hadn't when Etta Mae leaned forward. "Oh lah! Why don't you come back to the Psychic Five meetings? And don't tell me you've been ill– you sounded fine on the phone. And you look fine. You've upset our balance; Jon doesn't have a decent partner for his exper–"

Reba felt the teacup slide through her fingers and heard it crash onto the table. She blurted, "Stay away from that black box!"

"So that's it." Etta Mae's eyes glowed. "What's gone wrong?"

He listened ferociously. Why didn't that old damn fool meddler Etta Mae go home? And what if Reba were stronger than he? He had to draw Reba into that bathroom. Remembering Reba's reliance on her inhalator, he drew a mental image of Reba's lungs folding inward.

Abruptly Reba felt her breath come quicker as her lungs constricted. She hadn't realized how panicky Etta Mae's probing could make her. She took longer, deeper gulps of air but couldn't fill her lungs. "Nothing has gone wrong," she answered with a wheeze. "I just . . . Frightens me when I stream into that oceanic world. And I *am* ill. You trust your own truths."

Etta Mae's mouth dropped open and her brow wrinkled. "What are you jabbering about? There's no ocean nearby. How could simple ESP projections disturb you so much?"

Reba squirmed. So Etta Mae wasn't experiencing the same phenomenon in the old mansion room as Reba, herself, was. Maybe none of the other Psychic Five were. Maybe it was just her. Could the Domnu be strengthening in her? But why? And why the fondling of her genitals? No, she wouldn't believe the Domnu was behind this. This presence was sinister, evil. The pressure on Reba's lungs increased until she felt as though she were pumping air through an iron honeycomb. She tried to keep fear from showing on her face.

"Doctor says the emphysema is worse–as if I need to pay him seventy-five dollars to tell me that. Don't want . . . face old age . . . Want see Dori and her kids. Sorry . . . Worried you. Use my mountain place until . . . make other arrangements."

Reba did not want to tell Etta Mae any more. Too embarrassing and too dangerous. Frustration over not knowing what she should do again made her irritation show. "Your curiosity . . . plagues me, Etta, really."

"I declare, Reba. Being ill doesn't account for your writing us out of your will."

"What? Who told you that?"

When Reba saw that the older woman wasn't going to answer, she said with labored breath, "Haven't cut anybody . . . yet."

Etta Mae looked down her nose at Reba, a disbelieving set to her features. Unexpectedly she changed tack. Sniffing the air, she said, "Lah, that ninny's been here again. She must shower in Chanel #5. But then I reckon she has to, to get the smell of those animals off her. Why any young lady would want to work in a zoo is more than I can understand."

Reba's chest felt so crushed that she could not concentrate on what Etta was saying. She struggled to her feet. "The inhalator, Etta. Please . . . don't leave." She motioned to the teapot on the tray and called over her shoulder as she bolted from the room, "Have another . . . cup."

Inside the bathroom Reba tried to get her breath. She went through her routine of locking the door behind her and testing it to make certain the lock held. She wished that she could lock It out of her memory that easily.

She grimaced into the mirror at an aging woman whose striated green eyes had dulled into a fearsome gray. She felt dirty again remembering the way those hands had infiltrated every crevice of her body while she lay helpless–in sleep-like stupor. Filth! Abomination!

After she placed her eyeglasses on the counter, she hunched over the sink. Even though she wanted the inhalator badly, she made herself wait a little longer for its relief. Control your body, she thought as she took deep breaths, control your breathing. Odd, instead of feeling clear-headed, as she usually did, she felt sleepy.

She rubbed the soap briskly between her hands under the warm water. Smearing suds over her face, she followed with two hands full of water to flood away her makeup. She snatched up the hand towel and managed to half-dry her face before lurching for the inhalator.

While rasping into the device with her efforts already easing, she felt a more urgent foreboding than the earlier ones grip her. Chill bumps rose on her arms. That *thing* was here.

Good Heavens, no! she thought. She sobbed in terror for the first time in her long life.

She must face It. Must confront It. Must acknowledge Its existence. She faced the door where she saw the vague form of a man.

What was It? A projection? A spirit?

He leaned against the pickled oak paneling, a mocking grin on incorporeal features, genitals exposed and erect.

It had come to her in daylight! Oh, Lord, help her. Reba's eyes closed involuntarily. She glimpsed a mental projection of Its Split–its Twin--lying in the cursed black box. What was the connection between them? "Go away–go away– why are you doing this?" Her voice sounded hysterical but she was beyond caring.

He–It–moved toward her. She swayed and held her fists to her eyes as she used to do as a child. She felt so sleepy. "Haven't you done enough? What do you want?"

She forced her eyes open but barrels of dark pressed in upon her. She traced his gaze to the gas space heater.

With a gasp she fell back against the cabinet of the sink.

He wanted . . . her life.

So easy to sleep. No, you mustn't, Reba. The next thought threatened to split her heart. It would kill Dori and Dori's little girl, Rebecca.

"No, you can't!" Reba lurched for him but plunged through the form onto the opposite wall.

She hugged the wall to keep from collapsing, calling, "Rebecca."

The image of her loved grand niece brought a feeling of love that swelled from inside Reba, expanding her lungs, giving her hope.

When her lungs thundered to breathe air but drew in gas instead, she crumpled into a heap on the wooden floor. She focused in upon her cherished grand-niece. Then, as the initial warmth of the child's contact fell away, hatred toward this thing from the darkness gave Reba strength to scream out to Etta Mae. "Eeee." Reba heard a scraping noise outside the bathroom door–from its lock--and lifted her head to see the insane grin on Its face. *Tell Dori about the force you and I call Domnu.* Reba "sent" this thought to Rebecca while the world crashed about her.

On Friday morning, nearly a week later, Reba's niece, Dori Roberts, stumbled into the kitchen a full hour before time to rouse the children for school. She yawned as she tried to remember the nightmare that had awakened her this time. A sea-serpent called Domnu? Good God, how ridiculous.

While habitually cleansing her hands at the sink before putting on coffee, she sent a surveying glance out the small window into the backyard.

The rising South Florida sun back-lit a spider web that hung like a jeweled net between the kumquat tree and the grapefruit tree. The web maker, a skinny black spider, hastily spun the finishing lines to his masterpiece in anticipation of dawn's tasty creatures.

Without warning, Dori's gaze was caught fast as something else blocked the spider from her view. A swirling, misty haze became dense. And from this ectoplasm the swaying body of Aunt Reba took shape. Dori gripped the counter with both hands, her tongue drying to the roof of her mouth.

Reba looked wasted–ill, at least forty pounds thinner than when Dori'd seen her three weeks earlier. A long black box, a coffin Dori surmised, appeared at the foot of the standing misty figure of the elderly woman. Green-patterned eyes lifted to Dori's. The horror in them caused the young woman to instinctively reach out to Reba. But Reba's thin arms flew up in a warning gesture.

Numb with shock, Dori stared while the foggy shape twisted toward the coffin object. When the ectoplasmic Reba spread-eagled itself over the box, a smothering sensation–claustrophobia–assaulted the Dori at the sink, and she shuddered. She couldn't stand closed spaces. And she had the premonition that if she came out of the coffin, she would be changed, metamorphosed. She blinked in confusion and the figures separated into cirrus clouds that scattered on the breeze.

Only schizophrenics hallucinated, didn't they? Like Reba's grandmother who'd occupied a room of the country mansion, unseen, for so many years–or so said Reba? Her hands trembling, Dori measured coffee into the automatic coffee maker. Her mind was a jumble of emotions as she sat at the dining room table staring out the bay window into the atrium. First the dream and now this vision. With the arguments over her increasing independence she and Will had been having recently, one more problem was too much for her to handle. What the heck was happening to her?

She looked up as Will slid onto a chair beside her and rubbed his freshly shaven cheek against her face, attempting to make up for their latest battle of wills. More like a skirmish since she was so dependent on his approval.

"Honey, what's wrong with you lately? Want me to call Doc Peterson? You've been moping around like a zombie–since Aunt Reba left."

Dori stiffened. She wanted to unload both the dreams and the apparitions on him. But she dared not. He'd think she had fallen off her rocker, for sure. "I don't need medicine, Will!" she snapped, and immediately regretted her outburst. But dammit, sometimes his concern brought out the worst in her–especially if she hadn't drunk her first cup of coffee before he started in. She knew she wouldn't feel so guilty over her testy replies if he'd raise his voice to her once in a while. His willpower was beyond belief. But wasn't that one of the reasons she'd married him?

While she sipped her coffee, Dori appraised her husband anew. His square-cut features reminded her of a Koala bear. Brown was prominent in his eyes and the wavy hair spilling down over his broad forehead. Even the slight intrusion of silver into the brown did not detract from the overall warmth he projected. A warmth she was beginning to sense was a cover up, a device to always get his way.

She wondered momentarily if she were wrong about thinking he'd ridicule her if she told him about Reba. No, she decided swiftly, remembering him loudly denouncing others on the same subject. Instead she said, "Sorry, sweetheart. I haven't been sleeping like my usual self lately."

His hand smothered an early morning yawn. "Thought maybe you were feeling guilty."

"Why? Because my seventy-year-old aunt had an anxiety attack and wanted me to ask her to stay on for a few months? Why should I feel guilty for not welcoming her with open arms? I mean, what did she ever do that she should deserve such royal treatment? Just give me tuition for four years of nursing school at a major university, that's all."

Will's hand closed over Dori's but she looked away so he would not see the tears in her eyes. Lately, whenever she tried her hardest to be sweet and do what he wanted, her voice took on a bitter tone that she hated.

"Sure she gave you money. But she didn't take you into her home when your parents were killed, did she? She, with two old houses, one in the country, one in the city, couldn't find room for *you*. Hell, no. She let older sister Lena do that, ill as the old gal was.

"And when Lena died, Reba shelled out that tuition out of guilt, baby. And for control. As her only living relative, she wanted you in a position to do what she wanted. So don't talk guilt to me. Besides," he said with that little-boy grin that had captivated her from the first time she'd met him, "we couldn't have stood another week of her incessant meddling–much less a month or two. She's a kook, Dori. And speaking of crazy, what's the new group she's involved with?"

"The word is eccentric, William, not crazy. Every family has someone like Reba hidden away. And I think it's great that her mind is open enough to delve into new ventures at her age."

Dori had to bite her tongue to keep from mentioning Will's crazy sister. But now that she was dead, he acted as though she'd never been born.

Will yawned exaggeratedly. "As open as Swiss cheese. She's a pushover for any new kind of psychology. You name it, she's tried it. Psycho-cybernetics-ism, TM-ism, EST-ism, Dada-ism, Erroneous-ism, Witch-ism, anything but William-ism. She's as closed as a padlock when it comes to me."

With a laugh Dori realized that Will had Reba down pat. "Yep, I'm afraid we prevented William-ism the day we married and I left nurse's training. She'll never forgive you for supporting me so well." She laughed again and Will joined in.

Later, after eight-year-old Rebecca Louise and five-year-old Billy had been escorted to their respective bus stops, Will and Dori sipped away at another pot of coffee while sorting through the morning's correspondence.

Will's architectural business had boomed the past year. So much so that they usually spent the first two hours of the morning answering mail. Will did the primary organizing, taking out those envelopes that appeared pressing and stacking the remainder onto Dori's "slush" pile. These she opened and sifted into two heaps–one for personal letters, the other for architectural transactions. Though it was only December 15th, the family/friend accumulation overflowed with Christmas cards.

Not so early, Dori reminded herself, when you consider you've already done most of your Christmas shopping. Making mental notes to keep looking for the imitation fur coat that Bethie–pardon me, Rebecca Louise she now wanted to be called--had asked for and to print out Christmas labels this afternoon, Dori slid the letter opener under another envelope flap. "I didn't realize you resented Aunt Reba so much. You're always so pleasant to her–even when she zings you."

"You mean like with the secretarial dig?"

"Uh huh, but it's not so much what she says as the dry way she rubs it in. So offhandedly you don't know you've been cut until the blood pours out."

Chuckling, Will mimicked Aunt Reba's caustic tone. "How much do you pay a secretary, William? No, don't tell me. You're much too smart to hire one for ten dollars an hour when you married a nurse who'll type correspondence for room and board."

After Dori quit laughing, she added, "Seriously, Will, I could not be sweet to a relative of yours who make remarks like that."

Will slid an invoice into an envelope and sealed it. "You're forgetting Jamie."

"Not really. That's one sweet kid. A bit of a joker at times, I admit, but sweet nevertheless." She remembered how ultra sensitive Jamie had been when he'd first come to live with them, and she credited Jamie's quick rise in self-confidence to his uncle's ceaseless, gentle teasing.

Will scratched his head. "Too much of a wise guy, if you ask me. You'd think college would sober him some. But getting back to Reba–since I knew she was wrong, her words didn't faze me. We both know I didn't force you to quit nurse's training after three years. *You* were the smart one. You saw how asinine it was to put in another year to become a registered nurse when you were already a practical nurse–and your hubby could supply all your needs, right?"

The abrupt trilling of the telephone saved Dori from replying. She held the receiver close to her ear to hear the quavering voice ask, "Dori Roberts?"

"Yes?"

"You're Rebecca Lang's niece?"

"Yes," Dori repeated, feeling suddenly cold. "Who is this?"

"Etta Mae Briarley, an old friend of Reba's. Maybe you've heard her speak of me?"

Dori pressed the receiver even closer to her ear as if that would make the tiny, far-away treble clearer. She thought back to some of Reba's visits. Of course. An old, old friend. Much older than Aunt Reba if Dori's memory was correct.

"Many times, Mrs. Briarley. I'm so glad you phoned; I've been worried about Aunt Reba. I've called several times this past week, but she doesn't answer her telephone."

"That would be about right–indeed. But call me Etta Mae, child. I've known you for nigh onto twenty-nine years– through Reba, naturally."

Guilt struck Dori as she realized she'd been in Reba's thoughts more than her aunt had let on if this stranger knew Dori's age.

"And I know you're an Aquarian," the voice chirped.

Dori recalled Will's comment about her aunt being kooky. "Uh, do you belong to Aunt Reba's psychic group?"

"I'm sorry, child. Mustn't mind me. A bit too intuitive for my own good. I'm just an old lady who can't forget old tricks–and startling people is one of my favorites."

Will called from the other room, "What does she want?"

Pressing the privacy button, Dori said loudly, "I'm not sure. She hasn't said yet."

As if she'd heard–which was impossible–the old lady explained. Dori understood only snatches–it sounded so unreal.

"Reba's in a coma. Couldn't recollect your married name. Reba never told me. But her lawyer called and it came to me where to look. Police say Reba tried to kill herself!"

"A coma? She what?" Dori whispered.

"Child, you will come right up, won't you? She has no one else in the world–just you and me." The reedy voice broke up as emotion tightened the words making them almost gibberish. "Can't get her to d-d-do anything. She just stares at the wall."

"Come up?" Dori repeated dully. She would have to ask Will to watch the children. Remorse squeezed her ribs into an undersized girdle of pain.   Dear God, her aunt needed her. "Yes," Dori whispered.   "Yes."

When she hung up the receiver Will was standing beside her, an odd look narrowing his eyes.   He asked slowly, "What were you saying yes to?"

Dori knew then she had to tell him everything, and she searched frantically around in her mind for a way to convince him that this was something she had to do.   Before she'd gotten two sentences out she saw the disbelief mount on his face.

LOVE'S EBBING TIDE

Digging her elbows into the sand, Loni propped her chin between her palms. She studied her fiancé's son, Eddy, as he hunched over the Styrofoam bucket of sea water. Inside, clinging to a chunk of coral, was the tube worm he'd just caught.

The ice cube that was the pit of her stomach melted, chilling her and forewarning another failure. Why couldn't Eddy accept her upcoming marriage to his father?

She had suggested the snorkeling trip in a last-ditch effort to win the boy over. Now she had given herself one day to reach this cool and distant young stranger who refused to admit her into his family.

Eddy brought the tube worm for her to admire. The animal slowly stretched out its head, a dozen or so red-and-white banded petals that resembled the passion vine flower. Its tentacles quivered in a test for the tide that swept plankton into its filaments. How was it that such a delicate-appearing creature survived the two ebbing and two flooding tides everyday? The answer was beyond Loni. But somehow its kind had adapted to the intertidal zones, for millions of years timing their rhythms to tides chained to movements of earth, moon, and sun. She wished that she could adapt to Eddy's moods that easily.

She looked from the sea worm to Eddy. His red hair flying in the ocean breeze, he stroked the plant-like worm. Instantly, its fringed crown withdrew into its tube in a motion faster than the eye could follow. Maybe it was his delight in observing the protective instincts of nature; at any rate, his usual reserve toward Loni relaxed into a spontaneous whoop of amazement. A grin broadened the band of freckles that bridged his pug nose, creating a twelve-year-old version of his father Dan.

Her heart went out to the boy. Then, just when he was beginning to open up, she waded in too fast, too deep–again.

Smiling at him, she said, "You know, Eddy, that plumed worm would landscape my marine tank. I could get some of that gunk from the pet store and feed it with an eyedropper–until you take over in two weeks, that is."

Her indirect reference to the imminent marriage dissolved his grin, narrowing his expression of joy into a scowl. Jumping to his feet, he grabbed his snorkel and mask and retreated to the inlet, muttering over his shoulder, "Nah . . . I'll throw it back in before we leave."

Loni nibbled her bottom lip. The harder she tried to become friends with the kid, the more distant he became. When she had expressed her worries to Dan last night, he had laughed, stroked her cheek, and said softly, "He'll come around, Lon, give him time."

But she knew differently. If Eddy had not warmed up to her by the time they left Jupiter Beach Park, she would give Dan back his ring. Still vivid in her mind were the cruel methods by which she and her two sisters had made their step-father feel like an outsider. She shivered, remembering also the years of bickering because their mother had believed her daughters' lies. Loni guessed she and her sisters had needed that feeling of control over their lives. Was this thing with Eddy about . . . power?

She lowered her head onto the beach towel while she scanned the shell road that paralleled the inlet shore. There had been no cars or other signs of human life since she and Eddy had arrived over an hour ago. Becoming uneasy, Loni shifted around until she could see the water. Her gaze swept its surface for Eddy.

The water areas were held in the grip of a crooked giant T, its vertical line comprising the inlet, its horizontal line containing the eastern channel that dropped off abruptly into the Atlantic Ocean. A fishing boat chugged through the channel on its way to the open sea, furrowing the lime-colored water, churning out wavelets that slapped against the rocks and spat white fog into the air.

A flash of light reflecting from Eddy's holstered knife caught Loni's eye, and she relaxed a bit while watching him play. He sprang up out of the water, dove down and under, then surfaced again, spouting water out his snorkel like a baby whale. She longed to join him, but she knew that for now she would be intruding.

She sent a sweeping glance past Eddy to the narrow bridge of creosoted posts arching over the neck of the bay. This planked bridge was a transitional point marking the joining of the lines of the T, the melding of shallow bay waters into deep channel waters. She thought of the forces of nature that controlled the deceptive waters. Four times daily the Intracoastal and ocean battled. Both claimed two victories: the low ebbing tides were the prizes of the sea while the high flooding tides were trophies for the Intracoastal.

Her gaze trailed the river where it flowed under the bridge, her focus pausing upon the hulking boulders making up the seawall that held the channel waters captive. But rocks alone could not withstand the warring; every now and then the rock-lined channel released a stone in homage to the inexorable tug-of-war.

Loni sighed. She felt as if she and Eddy were tug-of-warring. She had ended two previous engagements. But Dan had seemed different. His gentle teasing and pleasure with life made marriage to him seem secure and happy, with none of the emotional ups and downs of her current lifestyle. Yet she was drawing back from him. Was it because of Eddy? Or was she scared to take a chance, to let herself be caught up in a new experience?

And if so, what was wrong with clinging to what she knew? The answer came in a flash. She was bored and unfulfilled with single life. She wanted to marry Dan, wanted it more than she had ever wanted anything in her life. And the knowledge that she would not go through with it, would back out again, filled her with self-contempt. Oh shit, what was the use of stewing over the inevitable–at thirty-two her nature was fixed for life.

She lay back on the towel and draped another one over her face to shield her from the sun. She dozed. Eventually she became lost in a dream. She was a long, twisted mass of seaweed that Dan and Eddy were fighting over. Eddy wanted to return her to the ocean, but each time he headed for the water, the seaweed shrouding his shoulders, Dan would yank on it and topple Eddy into the sand.

When she awoke, Loni felt as though she'd been buried alive. Her eyes burned, her body felt heavy, and her breathing was labored. She stripped the terry cloth from her face and sat up. Her mind was no longer sifting alternatives. Instead, she was eerily quiescent as though while she had slept a decision had been made for her. Remembering the starfish Dan wanted for his collection, Loni waded into the bay with a bucket. Her feet and legs were heavy as marble and once again ice coated her stomach. It was as if a primitive section of her mind was cautioning her against joining Eddy, but she discounted any real danger.

Fighting off the sluggish reaction of her body, she waded into the stream. But even though the immersion cooled her skin, she did not feel refreshed. She moved into deeper water where Eddy was snorkeling, an ominous sense of foreboding circling her mind in tighter and tighter bands the farther out she went.

Eddy surfaced in a spray of foam, and Loni called to him. "Hey, fella, I'd of thought you'd be in to rest before now."

Yanking the mouthpiece out, he said teasingly as though he'd forgotten she was his father's intended, "I got out for a while, but you weren't such hot company–covered up like a mummy and snoring away."

As Loni handed him the bucket, explaining about turning over rocks to uncover starfish, she wondered why she felt no relief at his mellowed mood. Her misgivings seemed to emanate from her dream that hinted at unexplored parts of her life far from the iron control she maintained.

Annoyed at herself for yielding to intuition instead of to reality, she dove down about six feet and opened her eyes, blinking against the burning salt. Immersed in the flux of fresh seawater that had poured into the inlet while she slept, she saw the mangrove roots, rocks, and fish as clearly as if the water were a magnifying glass. The finger snapping crackle of thousands of tiny shrimp clicking together the two joints of their one claw echoed in her ears like the ghosts of background music from old horror films.

A slight motion to her right caught her attention. Turning toward it, she saw the lemon-yellow, white, and black colors of a disk-shaped fish. The four-eyed butterfly fish, so named because of two black replicas of eyes near its tail, swam toward her, circled lazily, then returned to guard duty outside a tiny cave.

Loni wondered if it was true that these fish mated for life. Would Dan be that devoted? When she had first become interested in the man, he had been arguing with their psychology professor in a half-serious, half-bantering tone.

Loni had glanced up at him and become transfixed by the soft-voiced, red-haired man. Was it the aura of good humor in those warm brown eyes? Or the curving welcome in his lips? She only knew she felt drawn by a sense of belonging, a symbiotic feeling that she did not understand. On their third date she had learned about the complication called Eddy.

Her lungs gave out and she kicked to the surface. The water seemed much more turbulent. Loni looked first north then south of the inlet searching for the red tip of Eddy's snorkel. Locating it, she watched the current snatch the foam bucket from the boy's grasp and propel it downstream toward the Intracoastal. Eddy raced in pursuit, but it bobbed away, just out of reach. Loni's eyes lifted to the towering whitecaps, raging against the eastern sky like Titans.

Finally realizing he was a pawn of the ocean, Eddy screamed, "Loni! Help me!"

The terror in his childish voice unleashed a primordial instinct in Loni. She paddled desperately in his direction.

Eddy had been carried under the bridge and around the bend into the open throat of the inlet. No longer concerned with the disappearing bucket, he grabbed the first outcropping and clung to it.

Loni called, "Can you make it back, Eddy?"

"I think so."

Too late she realized her mistake. Idiot. Oh, God. "Don't! I'll come get you!"

But Eddy had already loosed his grip. Although he dug in frantically, his light body was no match for the strength of the tide. He was drawn closer and closer to the roaring mouth of the Atlantic.

Loni knew then that the boy was a goner–even she was helpless against the channel current. She had been aware of the danger of the ebbing tide and should have foreseen its intensity instead of mulling over her problems. *Oh, God–let me be strong, just this once, and I'll do whatever you want me to,* she prayed.

Her hand struck a submerged rock. Glancing down she saw a sea worm, its body squeezed into a crack, its bicolored plumage extended. How had it survived this turbulence so long? Even though its young was pelagic and drifted with the plankton that fed it, the adult was assaulted by billions of gallons of water, by a tide whose daily friction is slowing down the earth's rotation.

Oh, my God, she thought, why am I wondering about an insignificant worm when the only child I've ever loved is drowning?

Out in the neck of the Intracoastal, Eddy sank beneath the surf. Loni held her breath until he emerged. His voice shrill, he screamed, "Loni, help me! Help me!"

She groaned when he went under again, bobbing up seconds later. How much longer could he last? How could they get out of this?

The solution came to her with an image of the plumed worm rolling on the waves. She screamed the answer, "Ride the current, Eddy. Don't fight it! It'll eventually take you close to shore."

Eddy did not take her advice. Instead, he flailed at the water in a frenzied attempt to retreat from the whitecaps. Their roar seemed to rise in response to his helplessness, angering Loni.

"Damn it, Eddy, ride the current! I can't reach you!"

Loni sliced through the strait with longer, faster strokes. When she was within several yards of the boy, she lunged for him. But the channel's lust to mate with the sea was more savage than her puny efforts. It carried her farther and farther beyond Eddy.

Eddy began to respond. As if he were a raft, he pointed his arms in front of him and toward the south side of the waterway. He was obeying her, was being carried out into the ocean!

Oh, sweet Jesus, had she told him wrong? Loni saw the frothing monsters waiting for them. The closer she and Eddy came, the taller the waves seemed to have grown. Now they loomed higher than a rooftop. How could Eddy ride them?

Then she remembered the boulder-strewn seawall. If she could scramble onto an outcropping before being sucked into the maelstrom at the channel cutoff, maybe she could pull Eddy out.

Moments later her knees grazed the rocks, slowing her forward momentum and scraping the skin from her legs. She grasped the closest outcropping and winced as the slimy edges gashed her hands. She could not hang on, felt her flesh tear with the effort. In desperation, she leaped for the rocks, blanking out the agony of her lacerated hands and feet.

Thrown onto her knees, she clutched at anything for support. Both legs were skinned from ankles to knees, but still she held tight, sobbing with the effort. Then, unmindful of sharks, of barracudas, of anything but pulling Eddy from the surf, she wedged her legs between two boulders and yelled to Eddy to take her hand.

His body limp and partially submerged in the current, Eddy rushed past. Loni grabbed for the hand he held out to her. Her fingers slid down between his; they interlocked and the tug nearly jerked her in. With her last bit of energy, she dragged him out onto a flat rock. She stroked his thin back in a circular motion until his shuddering subsided.

By the time they reached their beach towels, Loni's legs burned as though she were covered in fire ants. Glancing down she noticed blood oozing from the cuts.

Eddy slipped his knife from its holster, snatched up his beach towel, and flashed Loni a questioning glance. She nodded. After he bound her legs with strips of terry cloth, the two of them rested for a few moments. Without speaking, they stared out over the plunging lime water.

When Loni got up and began gathering the remainder of their snorkeling equipment, Eddy said, his eyes still on the ocean, "You'll never be my mother, you know." His face was set and his words, though soft, held a note of finality. "I already have a mother."

The sudden ache in Loni's chest was greater than the spreading pain in her legs. She sighed and nodded. "You're right, Eddy. I guess I knew it all along."

When she had loaded the masks and snorkels in the car, she turned around and bumped into him standing beside the car, the bucket of seawater in his hands.

Glancing down at the crimson petals of the tube worm in the pail, he said in his soft child's voice, "Are you sure it won't be too much trouble to feed it? Just until after the wedding, of course."

Feeling a burning behind her eyes, Loni slipped on her sunglasses. "Sure," she said. "If it can live in the ocean, it can learn to adapt to my tank–with a little extra care."

(Like Shades we slip through Life neither seen nor heard.   Only upon Exiting do we make our Mark.   Liana Laurens, 2020)

SHADE STALKER

Wiping the sweat from my brow, I turn around in the steaming hydrogen 2020 Rabbit to see how long the line has gotten.

"Jesus!"   For at least a mile ahead of me and a mile behind, cars are lined up, waiting for either fuel or a DC battery exchange.   With diesel juice at ten dollars a gallon, this is insanity. "What a piss-drinking week this has been!"

I glance over at the automatic riveting gun and other construction tools on the seat beside me wondering briefly whether to fling them in the back to make room for Fred, decide with a lightning jab of mine to hell with it.

I wonder if the Old Man meant the words still ringing in my head: " 'One more time, Shit-head! Punch in late one more time and you can haul ass out of here!' "

If I had the balls, wasn't worried so much about helping Terry make a living for our family, I'd stuff those words back down that skinny throat.

It isn't just the boss, though; the whole damned system is against me, I think as I jerk the car into gear and gain a few inches. I can buy hydrogen only twice a week, and wouldn't you know it, these two days just happen to fall on Monday and Thursday, my driving days?   Luck of the damned steeplejacks. And on those days I'm supposed to pick up Fred in exchange for riding with the creep on his two driving days. But lucky-ass Fred has no problem getting to work on time. His fuel-ups alternate with his rider days.

Hell, twenty-eight years into the new century and the whole world has soured. Inhalators on every big city corner. Only way a person can get across a carbon-choked intersection is to snort a lung full of oxygen before sprinting over. Myself, though, I only leave the safety of an air conditioned and purified car or house for a sky-jock's sling on the skeleton of a rising skyscraper.

Somebody honks from far back of the line and I give her the finger. Oh, for those lost days back in the late 90's when a jock felt like King of the Heap shooting bolts into the side of a superstructure, chest thrumming with each smooth beat of fresh air, eyes wide-angling to hold the swoop of town below.

No more. No more. Now holes in the ozone and swarms of exhaling creatures below bring searing madness to straining lungs.

I glance at my atomic watch: 9:35. I fume, drumming my knuckles on the steering wheel, remembering Fred hanging up on me a few minutes earlier when I called to let the little worm know I'd be late again. Well, the hell with Fred, I think, chewing the inside of my cheek. For that matter, the hell with all of them.

You'd think, with air so gloppy you needed a shovel to stumble through it, some genius somewhere would invent a car that doesn't swill H 2/0 like a thirsty dinosaur–for Christ's sake. And the DC battery is nearly as bad, needing a charge from FPL every time you turn around. To get the energy, of course, the power company burns oil–talk about your vicious circles.

Liquefied coal is worse. Even with bacterium gobbling up sulfur pyrites like emaciated armadillos loosed upon an anthill, organic sulphur still gloms up the works.

I cough, a phlegmy rattle deep in my chest, that doubles me over in a paroxysm of pain before I can breathe again.

Not like me to bitch and moan, I think, disgusted with a disposition as sour as nuclear winter. What's happened to me lately? Then I remember that Terry asked the same question just yesterday, less politely. When I was too tired to make love, those warm brown eyes hardened into shining lumps of coal. " 'The hell's wrong with you, Lee? You only happy thirty stories up, staring at the tree topping off another condo or skyscraper? Dear God, just what this world needs, fifty million more blackout curtains.' "

I didn't answer. What could I say–fuck you, too?

A tiny hole opens up ahead. But I've had it with inching forward, wasting fuel starting and stopping. With my luck, the Rabbit will run out before getting to the pumps and I'll have to push the damned thing in. No, I'll wait for a larger space.

Not even ten o'clock and already the sun is a jaundiced South Florida eye peering through the thick haze caused by the burning of high sulphur oil.

A girl of nine or ten, sporting a yellow-flowered filter nose-piece, smiles hesitantly as she approached my car with a paper cup of lemonade, cooled with an artificial ice-cube.

The good old American Way. Making money from other people's misery. But deep down I wish just one of my three kids had her initiative.

Not until I give the girl a five and tell her to keep the change do I noted the damned AC/purifier has died on me. Shit. Idled too long. Utter helplessness in the face of scummy surroundings and even scummier louses inhabiting it crush me. Throwing the liquid down my throat, I crumple the cup and flick it out the window, for once elated to add my crap to the effluent.

I squeeze my eyes shut against the sweat stinging them, rocking from side-to-side to resist the building pressure. A horn blasts me into instant awareness that the Rabbit is creeping forward. I kick the brake in a delayed reaction to the jolt I feel as my bumper thuds with that of the fiery red sports car ahead.

Damned foot slipped, shit. And wouldn't you know I'd have to hit a 2028 Maserati? Couldn't of been an old car, no way, had to have just slid off the assembly line. I jump out and scamper over to apologize. Leaning my head down into the open window, I say, "Hell, man, just a tap. No damage."

The door swings open catching me in the gut, doubling me over. In a haze of pain I watch the biggest sucker my eyes have ever fallen upon unfold himself from the little red job and stalk over to its trunk to pick at the zit on its shining rear end.

Straightening up, I slit my eyes and study the man. Young . . . glittering with modish neole clothes. Popper peddler, no doubt. Who else but a sex-runner has the capital to finance a Maserati these days?

He kicks the front tire of my VW, screaming, "What a bitching . . ." After he stomps over to his open car door where I stand, the giant pauses to sink his palm into my left shoulder, a gesture as fleeting as swatting an insect. The impact sends me staggering back to my VW.

He briefly surveys my one-piece steeple-jock's fatigues, and shouts, "Shouldn't allow baboons like you out at the same time as us?" After he rakes me with one last burning gaze, he stuffs his very long limbs back into the cramped red interior, still sputtering. "Put your toe up your ass where it belongs and off the goddamned gas pedal, Neanderthal . . ."

There is more but I retreat to the inner sanctum of the VW Rabbit and roll up the window. I am shaking, for God's sake. I have to take a leak so bad I swear I feel sand in my . . . what the hell did Doc Wilson call that thing when he rammed the catheter up it? Oh, yeah. Urethra. I beat on the steering wheel with my fists over the injustices dumped on we mortals daily.

More and more lately I've been feeling like a cog in some crabby giant's machine. It wouldn't surprise me if this monster sets out daily busy work for us all–to keep us from mischief. After all, the more buildings I rivet, the more squalling brats are born to fill them. And the more vaccines that researchers develop, the more diseases pop up to send them scurrying back to their petri plates.

A line from a poem by my favorite author reels through my mind–and for the first time I think I understand it. "Like Shades we slip through Life, neither heard nor seen. Only upon Exiting do we make our mark."

Shit! Who will "mark" my passing–Terry? The three terrors? Another fit o coughing shakes me. In the midst of it my head itches and I scrape broken fingernails against the shedding scalp, momentarily giving myself over to the sensation.

The line of cars crawls forward but I hold my section back, allowing the Maserati to edge ahead. The further away the other car moves, the better I feel, as though there was a spring stretched between us that snapped.

Wearily I slump back and close my eyes, wondering why I didn't slug Mr. Maserati. Images of Terry leap-frog into view. Five foot six on redhead temper. Terry'd go toe-to-toe with that slag heap in an instant.

I sigh. Lately the only time I feel as though I'm alive is when I'm topping and tall building and squinting down at the skittering flecks beneath my feet. Thinking that this is the sort of day that make a person feel like coming down off a tall one the fast way, my eyes close against the disturbing outside world while I comfort myself with images of panoramic view.

Not until the slant of incoming sunlight warps into shadow do my eyes pop open and I see the restored antique Caddy. My mind refuses to believe it. I blink to make the image go away, but when I peek again the huge car is still there, wedged in sideways between my VW and the Maserati ahead.

It is a swanky number from the sixties with gleaming layers of paint and svelte baby blue upholstery. The guy probably paid several hundred thou for it, I think.

Has it been here all along? Hell, no, I conclude feeling my face flush from warm to hot. My right hand gropes along the tattered seat feeling for the familiar object. Closing my fingers around it, I slide it toward me in a reflex motion of chemical impulses jetting across an abyss. The rage of released frustration heating my spirit makes me heady.

Grabbing it up like a catcher's mitt, thumb on one side, fingers on the other, I hug the automatic gun to my side.

Then I am out of the VW and tearing around past the Caddy to the Maserati. I yank the front door open against the protesting grip of the giant whose eyes grow into saucers as he claws the seat, trying to burrow into it. As I glare into his gelatinous back, my thumb falters. His throat bulges with the effort to speak.   Only gargling noises dribble out, "Ghuuu ghuuu!"

The next instant, in a blur of speed and strength I didn't know I possessed, I am straddling the legs of the quivering popper peddler. My thumb unleashes the surge of electrical energy.

The Ultima bolt gun rat-a-tat-tats, bucking slightly in my grasp, the whining hum of its gadgetry tattooing an invisible shield over my soul as the tool roars to my aid. Again and again I jab the weapon into life, giggling with the pleasure of my actions.

The quivering hunk under me sobs in rhythm with the gun. Finished at last I look up to see the old man from the Caddy leaning against the Maserati, his blue gaze pinned to the precise rows of spikes I've riveted into the plush dashboard. The class of studded metal letters against the red cloth are a satisfying incongruity screaming out my thoughts louder than spoken words.

The old man continues to stare in horror at my handiwork blasted an inch deep and four inches high into the once velvety cloth of the Maserati dash: "SHIT-HEAD! LIANA WS HERE!"

As I climb out of the Maserati and stretch, the giant lifts his head briefly to take in my artwork then blubbers and buries his face in the seat cushion.

I saunter back to the VW singing my name-sake's poem over and over, "Like Shades we slip through Life neither seen nor heard. Only upon Exiting do we Make our Mark."

I wrote "Love's Ebbing Tide" after reading about a boy swept from the Jupiter Inlet out into the ocean where he drowned.

("Love's Ebbing Tide" was first published in *Woman's World*.)

INSIDE THE BLACK BOX: *Possessed by the Dark*

In *Possessed by the Dark*, a psychiatrist driven by a tormented past experiments with the supernatural in a flotation chamber called the Black Box to cure sexual aberrations. But zealousness propels him into realms that split his psyche. *Possessed by the Dark* is ambition run wild, bi-location, and obsession.

In the style of the characters in the novels of Dan Moffet, Stephen King, and Dean Koontz, Dori Roberts leads a peaceful existence as a nurse with a loving husband and two cute children in the cypress-laden atmosphere of her Parkland, Florida, home. When her Aunt Reba mysteriously falls into a deep coma, though, Dori is catapulted into a psychic arena that imperils both her life and her sanity. She must clash with the terrors of the unknown to save the lives of the people she loves.

Ginger Curry lives in South Florida with her computer, her books and the natural habitat that surrounds her. A member of The Metaphysical Church of the Palm Beaches, she leads book discussions at a local bookstore. If you would like to contact the author–or buy the book–her e-mail is skywoman@stis.net

IN CONFIDENCE
Novel Excerpt

Leann's feet throbbed. She walked across the parking lot with a box of files cradled in her arms, wearing shoes that pinched her toes. The soles of her shoes slapped the asphalt with each step she took. She wished she was barefoot. The closer Leann got to the building, she could hear voices drift from the walkway. Blinded by the glare of the sun's reflection off of the white stucco façade, she couldn't see faces. The voices intermingled with the filtered noises of early morning. Leann's skin tingled and her arm hair bristled.

"Dr. Regent, am I glad to see you." A uniformed man came toward her. He was a big man with a belly that extended over his belt. He sounded out of breath.

Leann blinked and concentrated on his face, but she couldn't remember his name. Her arms floated upward, as he took the box she carried from her grasp.

"He's just sitting up there," he said as he wedged the carton under one arm.

"Oh, Ralph." She tested her memory. "Thanks." She remembered now, he was, Ralph, the security guard.

Ralph pointed at the roof and the red border that encircled the building just above the fourth floor. Leann looked over the top of his head. Beyond the silver sheen of his hair and the building's red stripe she saw the reason for the stillness. This wouldn't be a morning for admiring her new office plaque,

Leann Regent, Ph.D., Clinical Psychologist. She would begin her work from the sidewalk.

    Leann quickened her pace to keep up with Ralph. Her toes were numb now, the pain was gone. The group of people who waited along the side of the building, held their heads thrust back, and each set of eyes focused on the figure at the edge of the roof. Ralph said something about police, but Leann didn't catch it. Bystanders turned their attention toward Leann and Ralph. Now she could see their worried facial expressions with brows arched in concern. Their words bounced off of the stucco wall like echoes in culvert pipe. When she and Ralph reached the walkway, they were met with the crowd's unified concerns..

    "Please talk to him." A twenty-something, redheaded woman looked their way. Her arm extended upward.

    "Can you do something to get him down?" A balding man asked. He mopped his brow with the back of his hand, but didn't take his eyes from the scene on the roof.

    A young boy wearing sandals and faded jeans said, "He says he's waiting for you." He looked directly at Leann through plastic sunglasses that were too small for his head.

    Leann looked up and over their heads. She could see two legs dangling over the roof's edge and a face looking down toward the crowd. She knew the face, Brandon, her first scheduled appointment of the day.

    "Dr. Regent!" Brandon shouted and waved.

    Leann leaned her head back and cupped her hands around her mouth to call back. Then she changed her mind.

    "How long has he been up there?" Leann turned to Ralph.

    "I'm not sure. I heard him first. He was saying something, like chanting the alphabet or a rap song. Then I looked up and there he was." Ralph shifted the carton of files to his other arm. His middle bulk appeared to get in the way.

    Leann felt her stomach muscles contract in rhythm with a flutter in her throat. She knew her negotiating power would be better if she were on the roof. Perspiration beaded along her hairline and the palms of her hands went damp. Thoughts of being a kid swinging too high on the playground swing triggered her discomfort and left Leann with a fear of heights.

"Ralph, can you get me up there?" She asked. She winced to hear her words. Pushing her shoulders back, Leann resisted the temptation to wrap her arms around her middle in self-protection

"Sure, come on."

Leann cupped her hands over her mouth and this time she called out toward the roof. "I'm coming up, Brandon."

In her past experience with Brandon he didn't express suicidal thoughts. At least for the moment, his posture, perched on the roof's edge with his legs hanging over the side, didn't suggest he was bent on self-destruction. But she couldn't dismiss the possibility. Brandon expressed himself in dramatic ways. He was creative at devising a show of risky behaviors. Generally, his behaviors succeeded in gaining the attention he wanted. Brandon was referred to her by a local psychiatrist for treatment of obsessive-compulsive behaviors. His need for continual reassurance took on an obsessive nature of its own. However, he was a dedicated patient. Dedication in Brandon's case was defined by his over dependence on therapy, not a willingness to make changes.

The elevator doors opened at the fourth floor. Ralph put the box down in the corner on the elevator floor. Then he and Leann walked toward the narrow stairwell that led to the security door to the roof. A siren blared out sounding like it was in the building.

"It's the police," Ralph said shaking his head.

Leann tugged at his elbow. "Wait until the siren stops," she said letting out the breath she held in to keep her stomach from jumping. Leann looked toward the window at the end of the hall and saw a police car and another car parking along the access road by the river.

"This isn't good," Ralph said pursing his lips and shaking his head. "Too much commotion gets my boss nervous."

The sirens stopped, then the elevator began to move. Leann and Ralph watched the numbers light up above the door.

The doors parted and out stepped a man surrounded by a blur of brown and tan uniforms. Dressed in navy blue slacks, a plaid shirt and a mismatched suit jacket, he walked toward Leann and Ralph, reaching inside his jacket revealing a holstered pistol. He and his escort stopped just short of Leann, almost stepping on her.

"Detective Clayton Hammon, Ft. Lauderdale Police." He announced his title as he flashed his badge. "We need to secure the area and talk the man down."

"I'm his therapist." Leann crossed her arms over her chest and moved slightly into his path. "I'm going out to talk to him."

Hammon hesitated, then said, "Can't let you do that." He raised his sunglasses. The detective's eyes focused on hers, like a father confronting his teenaged daughter for coming home late.

"You do know, those sirens don't help the situation." Leann felt her jaw tighten and teeth clench. The urge to protect her client set her in motion. She turned toward the roof door, knowing the detective's eyes were on her. Ralph didn't move.

"Detective, *I'll* talk him down," she said over her shoulder. Leann's words echoed in her head, as she passed Ralph. She heard her voice, its low raspy tones. She was told that her voice was seductive. It didn't fit in this situation or any other. Once the door opened her words and thoughts were lost to the grating sound of the metal door scraping across the gravel surface of the roof. Ignoring the voices she heard behind her, Leann stepped onto the roof. She didn't hesitate. As she walked toward Brandon, the gravel shifted under her feet making a crunching sound. Her breathing quickened, more from the exhilaration of defiance, than her fear of heights. She slowed her pace. An involuntary gasp of air escaped from her throat when she caught the sight of the tops of the palm trees.

Leann stopped. The sudden silence felt as sharp as metal on metal. She wiped her sweaty palms down the sides of her jacket. The roof was already hot from the morning sun and she felt the heat rise up her pant legs. *Relax, relax.* She focused on Brandon's face. Stomach bile surfaced in her mouth. She swallowed it away.

Brandon waved. His legs no longer hung over the edge. Now he sat parallel to the roof's edge with his arms wrapped around his knees, forcing him to balance on his tailbone.

"I broke the chain," he said, "I broke the chain." He smiled and gave a thumbs up.

"Brandon, that's great." Leann paused, relaxed her jaw and smiled. She needed to keep saying his name to ground him in reality. A heaviness left her shoulders, replaced by a tingling in her arms and fingers. She felt lightheaded. The palm fronds at the tops of trees slapped together imitating the sound of light rain.

"Brandon, let's talk in my office." She pushed the words from her head through her mouth, squeezed her hands into fists, then relaxed them.

Brandon teetered on his backside, curling himself into a tighter ball. His feet rose from the ledge, as he looked over the side of the building. He wore his hat backwards, the bill of the cap at the back of his neck. His pants were frayed at the bottoms and there weren't any laces in his shoes.

"What are those sirens about?" He snapped his head around to look at Leann. His chin dropped. "It's me isn't it?"

She held her breath, but air forced its way from Leann's throat making in involuntary sound like a groan.

"I caused trouble, again." Brandon's complexion was gray. The outline of his mouth whitened. "Right?"

Leann stayed focused on his face avoiding the view of the of the swaying palm fronds. *Calm, got to be calm.* "Brandon, the best thing to do is go down to my office." She lowered her voice hoping to sooth Brandon's anxiety.

"Are the cops here?" He looked over the edge of the building again.

Leann was about ten feet from Brandon. She wanted to grab him. His slight build gave him a childlike appearance. He waved his arm in the direction of the road between the building and the river like he was about to fly off of the roof.

"Brandon." Leann pulled warm air into her lungs hoping to stifle her urge to yell.

Brandon turned, but not in response to her. The door opened and the metal scraped along the gravel. Leann didn't dare turn around. She didn't want to take her eyes off of Brandon.

"It's okay," she said, "let's go downstairs."

Brandon focused on something over Leann's shoulder. She moved into his line of vision, hoping to block his view of whoever stood behind her. Her move sideways gave her the sensation that the building moved under her. She stretched her arm out toward Brandon and offered her hand.

"Who's that?" Brandon asked.

"Brandon, take my hand and I'll introduce you." Leann hoped there wasn't a uniformed cop behind her.

Brandon stood up on the ledge, brushed his pants and then rubbed his palms together. Leann felt the corners of her mouth twitch from her forced smile. He moved toward her. She could hear him whispering, counting each step he took. When he reached Leann's side, he took her hand. She felt his damp hand in hers, but wasn't sure that the dampness wasn't her own. Together they turned to face the door. It was the detective who held the door open.

Like a child Brandon continued to hold Leann's hand as they walked to the rhythm of his counting. For once Leann was thankful for his obsessive counting, one of his repetitive behaviors. Knowing it calmed him, she made no comment, as they walked through the doorway. The detective held the door for them. He nodded and smiled, but his glasses covered the expression in his eyes.

Brandon's eyes widened when he saw the uniformed officers. Both men stood at the end of the hall, one was leaning against the wall with his arms folded and the other officer appeared to be cleaning his nails with a pocketknife. Neither of them looked at Leann or Brandon.

"Are they here for me?" Brandon asked. He gripped her hand even tighter.

Leann watched Brandon's eyes fill with tears. She squeezed his hand, but ignored his question. The elevator doors opened and here sat the box of files. They stepped in and the door shut behind them. Leann pushed the button with a worn number three, that was barely visible. Brandon's head dropped forward and his chin rested on his chest, as he muttered words of apology into his shirt.

"Brandon, would you please carry that box for me?" He needed a purposeful act to do to keep him calm. Brandon let go of her hand, straightened his shoulders and picked up the file box.

Brandon put the box on Leann's desk and settled onto the couch. His eyes darted around the room taking in the new office. He looked over his shoulder at the door, then rocked in place. Leann sat opposite Brandon in her familiar chair and waited. She stroked the arms of the one piece of the past she brought with her. Leann gave Brandon time to get used to the new surroundings.

"Nice place," he said. His body rocking slowed.

"Tell me what happened, Brandon, " Leann said.

Brandon moved toward the seat's edge with his hands clasped and lodged between his knees. His eyes focused on Leann's. "Last night, I tried to get to bed, but locking the doors, turning off the TV, unplugging the toaster, microwave, blender . . . all my stuff, took an hour from start to finish. I couldn't stop, I kept checking, so I never finished. I was getting mad, you know, and tired, too. I tried all the stuff you tell me to do, breathing deep and all, but nothing helped, so I tried to think of, what'd you call it? "*Opposite behavior?*"

"Opposing behavior." Leann noted Brandon's body rocking. She didn't recall seeing him do that before. Well, he was never on the roof of her office building before either. His focus on her face was a good sign.

"Right, opposing behavior. Well, I locked myself out of my apartment on purpose. I don't remember what I left on, what I turned off." Brandon added, "I turned the stereo on." Talking to himself, he said, "I hope I didn't turn on the coffee pot . . . my neighbors are probably mad."

"Would you like to call the building manager and have him check the apartment." Leann hoped to bring Brandon to the reality of his actions. She handed him the cordless phone. "Do you know the number?"

"Yeah, it's easy. It's on the sign by the parking lot. I know it," he replied in a high pitched voice. He seemed pleased that he knew the number. He fumbled with the phone then dialed.

When he got an answer, Brandon repeated "sorry" over and over. With each apology his voice grew faint and his words unintelligible. He held the phone to his ear for a short time, then placed it on the floor next to his foot. He stared at it for some time.

"The super's pissed at me, the neighbors called him at 4 AM." Brandon picked up the receiver and disconnected the call. "He said, the music, TV and all were blaring." He shook his head and rested his chin on his chest again. "I'm in trouble. I'll have to do something, special like." He looked distracted. "Maybe, a cookout." His face brightened. He got up and walked around the room. His feet shuffling through the carpet.

Leann studied the expression on his face, inattentive, but hopeful, lost in his own world. Brandon claimed that he is allergic to the sun, and that's why his complexion is the egg white. He's in his late twenties, but his slight build makes him look like an adolescent. His work history suffered because of his OCD. The need to repeat unnecessary rituals at work got in the way of productivity. He reported that he hadn't stayed at any job for more than a couple of months.

"A note of apology to the other tenants would be a good idea." Leann watched Brandon as he meandered back to the couch and sat down. "How did you get on the roof?"

Brandon looked up, but stared out of the window. "I did the opposing behaviors and left my apartment. That way I would stop checking stuff. It was hard to stay away. I was walking around, couldn't settle down, so I figured if I got here, I'd be far enough away. And I wouldn't miss my appointment." Brandon rubbed his palms together and looked toward the ceiling. The muscles in his neck twitched. "I got here and came in the building behind that security guy. He didn't see me. I hid around the corner from the elevators. When his back was turned, I took the stairs up to the top floor and saw the door to the roof. I didn't think when I went out." Brandon paused and put his hands under his thighs and shifted his weight. He rocked back into the couch cushion. "The door locked. Stupid idea, huh?"

"Did you want to harm yourself?" Leann asked. She was more confident that he didn't have suicidal thoughts. His level of concern for others was a good sign.

Brandon's eyes widened. "Oh no, I never want to do that. I don't think of that anymore. I know I do stuff that doesn't make sense, but I don't want to . . ." Brandon's hands released from the grip of his legs and flapped in the air.

"If you ever have the idea to hurt yourself, you call me right away." Leann watched Brandon. His hands found each other. He rubbed his palms together again. One of his OCD gestures. "Brandon, we have to agree on a better plan for the next time." Leann looked at his face. He avoided her gaze. His mouth drooped into a pout. "Are you with me?" She asked.

Brandon nodded and looked directly at Leann. Good, she thought. The diligent patient, he signed a contract for a plan he designed to interrupt his obsessive compulsive behaviors. He thought of a friend, who he didn't name, who would help him leave his apartment in a safe way. They practiced the apology he planned to give his neighbors. Brandon left the office in good spirits with his plan and an appointment for the next week.

"I won't go higher than this floor next week. I feel better now," Brandon said rubbing his hands on his pant legs. He stepped into the elevator.

"Don't forget to see the doctor about a refill on your medication. It may help, Brandon." Leann was relieved. She leaned her back against the door jamb watching the "L" light up over the elevator door. This wasn't the morning she expected.

Leann stared out the window at the boat traffic on the New River as she ran her fingers along the edge of the business card the detective left under her door. He must have shoved it under when Brandon was here. She read the script, *Detective Clayton Hammon.* There was nothing on the back of the card. She wondered if she should respond in some way. Surprisingly, the detective didn't say anything when she and Brandon passed him on the roof. Her thoughts were interrupted by the horn sounding the opening of the bridge.

A knock at the door brought her to her feet with an imagined urgency that wasn't there. She opened the door. A medium built, dark haired, blue-eyed man, dressed in what they now call "business casual" stood almost face to face with Leann. Her 5' 10" stature put them almost eye to eye. With a cursory survey she surmised that he was in his forties and probably the outdoors type. A broad smile eased across his suntanned face.

He tapped the name plate on the door, as he said, "Hi, ah, Dr. Regent?"

Leann acknowledged his question with a quick nod. "Can I help you?"

Waving his arm in the direction down the hall he said, "I'm one of your floor mates, Ron Spencer. Everyone calls me "Spence." His smile surrounded his every word. He ejected his right hand from his pants pocket and extended it to Leann. "Welcome." As they shook hands, Leann noticed the naked ring finger on his left hand. She was taken back by her own unintentional observation. Leann felt caught in an emotional squeeze. She missed Joel.

Leann widened her stance and spread her toes, she felt off balance. The discarded new shoes embraced each other under her desk. She was barefoot.

"Well, thank you for your welcome." Leann found it difficult to move her eyes from Spence's. "I appreciate it," she said as she blinked her eyes to refocus on his chin. Spence smiled again, or maybe he was still smiling. Regardless, she found his looks captivating.

"I wanted to let you know, we, the tenants, like to look after each another. We have a small association of sorts. You know, for our protection and our clients too. So, we request a schedule of the tenants' business hours for the building security. Just a listing of your office hours, days you'll be here. I keep it on file." Spence paused and jiggled the change in his pocket.

Interesting habit. Leann thought.

"Of course, Ralph, you met him, our security guard, likes to know our routine hours." Spence looked as though he had just finished a persuasive talk in front of a public speaking class.

"Sure, that's not a problem," Leann said. She didn't want to ask any questions that might lead him into another breathless explanation. She stood in the doorway trying to maintain a professional stance in her bare feet.

Spence's smile relaxed as the corners of his mouth dropped. "Well, that was quite a greeting this morning, with that guy on the roof. Does that kind of thing happen often?"

Leann felt her spine arch. "No, I can't say that it does."

When she was looking for office space, She found resistance from a few landlords. They asked whether her clients included criminals. The question wasn't too much out of place, since the courthouse and county jail sat right across the river. The owners of this building didn't ask questions. But, she didn't recall being told about an "association." She wondered if there was another fee.

"Oh, no problem there. Well, we're glad to hear that." A forced laugh escaped, then the smile reappeared on Spence's face.

Leann wondered how he assumed the position of "we." Maybe he was elected. She thought *maybe he used his smile to get votes.*

"I'll be glad to drop off a schedule," she said as the corners of her mouth rose to a smile.

"Great, I'm at the end of the hall, Spencer Engineering. That's me." He shifted his weight and freed his hand from the change in his pants pocket.

Leann didn't say anything. The moment was just a little too long for comfort. A blast of heat stroked the skin on her face and she knew a flush of red was on her cheeks. That was another striking feature she had been told about. She couldn't figure how a blush on her face contrasted with her russet colored hair was attractive.

"I didn't mean to question you about your patients, but, well, as the rep for the association, sorry." Now his face colored, his tan gave way to a burgundy hue.

Leann felt her defensiveness slide away. The awkward moment ended when the elevator doors parted and a man entered the hallway.

Spence turned toward the man. "Oh, Mr. Kane, I'll be right with you." Spence looked toward Leann. "Welcome again."

She nodded and stared at his broad shoulders and his long stride as he approached his client, shook his hand and steered the man toward his office. Leann let out her breath. She hadn't realized she was holding it.

Leann stared at the streaks of sunlight on the window. Michele talked rapidly about feeling overwhelmed. This young woman was experiencing clinical levels of anxiety. But the source of her anxiety remained a mystery. Leann's instincts told her that Michele was well aware of the source, but was not presenting her situation to Leann realistically. Not an uncommon behavior in the early stages of therapy.

"Dr. Regent, do you think I should tell my boyfriend about what happened?" Michele was crying. Her large brown eyes blinked as Leann handed her tissues.

"I know that he'll be angry, especially since he's away." Michele added as she took the tissue. She dabbed it along her mascara laden eyelashes. A pretty girl, but too thin. High fashion demanded low calories and no carbs. Her looks assured her success as a local model and semi-celebrity. South Florida is known for its Hollywood mentality and glitz.

"Michele, you have time to decide what to do, or to decide to do nothing. I want you to do the relaxation exercises and log the moments in each day when your anxiety is the highest," Leann said. She scribbled *address eating habits* on her notepad and looked at her watch.

Michele agreed to her weekly homework. She demonstrated the breathing exercises she learned in yoga. Here was a young woman who placed all her hopes and future on her looks. But she has the good sense to learn business skills. Michele worked for a small communications firm by day and modeled by night. Leann was concerned about the "modeling" concept and what that meant. Michele justified her evening work as required exposure. She explained to Leann, that the actual photo modeling took place on the weekends. Michele's perceived celebrity status came from an occasional job modeling for local businesses on TV commercials.

Michele took her appointment card, dropping it in her purse, she pulled out glasses and a scarf and placed her oversized sunglasses over her brown eyes, now smeared with mascara. She wrapped her blond hair in the teal colored scarf, turban style. It actually didn't look bad on her. Concealed from the public in her disguise, Michele left. Leann thought Michele's anxiety about being seen might have more to do with the parts of her story she didn't feel free to share. At least not yet.

It was past 4 PM and time to get home. Leann's feline boat mate, Molly, was waiting. The cat escaped the northeast with Leann. She rented a sailboat, a 41 foot Morgan, for their living quarters. Absentee boat owners rented their boats like apartments. Leann was one of the liveaboards in the Venice of the Americas, a part of Fort Lauderdale's charm. The boating community consisted of canals that meandered beside the fingers of land running perpendicular to Las Olas Boulevard. Living on the *Sandollar* was economical. Leann hadn't met the owner. He lived in Washington state and was happy to have someone aboard his boat to look after it. Leann fell in love with the lifestyle. She wished Joel was there to share it with her. Leann's feelings of loss came in waves of nausea. She kept thinking she was forgetting something important. It was a void, empty feeling, like her insides were gutted. They made plans for the future, a warmer climate for sailing and enjoying the outdoors. After he died Leann needed a change. There were too many layers of emotions now and remembering Joel's death was an endless nightmare for her.

Leann pulled into her appointed parking space at the condo marina. She opened the car door and was immediately distracted by a commotion across the street. Godfrey, the manager of the property where the *Sandollar* was docked, appeared to be a participant in a heated discussion. Another man was demanding that Godfrey's dog stay on a leash. Leann was out of the car and able to see that the man yelling at Godfrey held a pooper-scooper in one hand and a brown bag in the other.

Godfrey came across the street at a quick pace clutching his Shih Tzu, Mitzy. "That man will be the death of me, raising my blood pressure. Now my baby's shaking all over." Stroking the dog, he nearly collided with Leann.

"Oh, please forgive me Dr. Regent, I didn't see you." He adjusted the collar of his shirt with his free hand and relaxed his tense facial muscles. With a smile he asked, "How was your day?"

"Good." Leann smiled at the sight of Godfrey. "It doesn't sound like yours was the best." At times he was so formal. Godfrey's posture was angular. A man in his late fifties, tall and lanky, Godfrey's gait appeared to defy gravity. With his left elbow pushed back and his right shoulder slightly raised, he looked like a paperclip that was yanked out of shape. His colorful shirt decorated with palms and seashells made him an accessory to the tropical garden he created in the courtyard. During the first week that Leann lived at the marina, he learned of her occupation. Godfrey asked what types of problems she treated. She politely gave him an overview, feeling that he wasn't actually interested. She was right. He took the opportunity to confide that he was gay and had been in a long-term relationship until a year ago, when his partner, Kevin, died. She figured he told her what he wanted her to know, and that was that.

Godfrey continued walking toward his office with Mitzy cradled in his arms. The sound of his large, plastic flip-flops smacking his heels accentuated Godfrey's soothing comments to the dog.

"You have mail, doctor." He grabbed a pile of mail from his office doorstep and presented it to Leann with a sideward movement of his chin and extension of his neck in her direction. That was a mannerism Leann saw him do before. She wondered if it was a tic.

"Thank you. I hope the rest of the evening goes better for you." Leann shoved the mail in between her appointment book and the files she held in her arm.

Godfrey stroked Mitzy and nodded. The dog sat in the crook of his arm looking like a furry growth on his forearm.

It was high tide. That meant more maneuvering than usual to get aboard the boat. Leann climbed the finger pier ladder, tossed the mail, appointment book and files on the cockpit seat. She heard Molly's affectionate meow. Once she was down below Leann changed into her favorite jersey shorts and one of Joel's old T-shirts. She busied herself making something to eat and talking to Molly, then she followed Molly into the screened cockpit carrying a bowl of chili, crackers and a glass of wine. Molly did figure eights between Leann's legs then settled on the cockpit cushion as close to Leann as possible. Molly purred her thanks while Leann rubbed her ears and under her chin.

Leann's thoughts wandered in patterns like unattached sound bites of her cerebral synapses. Abruptly her attention turned to raised voices, this time along the dock. She craned my neck around to see the bulkhead in front of the adjacent boats. The shades of early dusk left Leann unable to see clearly, but there was the sound of someone jumping from the houseboat a couple of boat slips down from the *Sandollar*. The sunset cast an orange and gold hue on the docks and water. The houseboat swayed and tugged against the lines that secured it to the pilings, as the person's weight shifted from the boat deck to the pier. The sound of a light splash in the water followed, then it was quiet.

Leann sat back and relaxed. The voices were gone. *Probably someone in a hurry.* Molly took advantage of her position and used Leann's lap as a cushion. She settled down with a steady purr. Leann slid down and eased farther into the cockpit cushions. The air was still, the quiet took over and so did sleep.

Leann awakened to the chilly breeze in the cockpit. With the exception of the dock security lights, it was dark. No moonlight. She pulled herself from a dream of childhood. It wasn't the first time for this dream. She recalled waking up as a child . . . *those feelings. The kind that sent jolts of butterflies through her stomach. Lying in her grandmother's poster bed, swallowed by the feather comforter and surrounded by the warmth of sunshine making its way through the window. She looked at the clock. Too early for voices, adult talk.*

Leann tried to block the voices. She kept her eyes shut tightly and set the stage for her fantasy to take her away. She pictured the clock behind her eyelids. Its dome over the little girl with blonde pigtails, swinging back and forth to the rhythm of the ticking. She imagined the girl on the swing, stopped and leaning against the glass dome. No, move, pump your feet, keep swinging. She was the little girl on the swing. Leann slowly slipped into herself. She could feel the breeze against her skin and hear the rustle of her petticoat as the swing went back and forth, back and forth. She was protected under the dome.

Voices again, she covered her ears and head with the pillow. Her legs were wrapped in the sheets, tangled so tightly, she couldn't move. Then she knew, she shouldn't move, better to pretend sleep.

"I don't want to hear it." She heard her mother say. Was mommy crying?

Her Grandfather's loud voice was clear. "All night they were together." His voice faded away.

The house was quiet again. She moved the pillow from over her head, but kept her eyes closed. She heard her mother in the room. Mommy was crying. Leann wanted to cry too. But knew she must be still . . .

Leann jerked awake for the second time. This time a fine sandpaper tongue moved across her chin and whiskers brushed her cheek. Molly.

Voices floated in her head, her mother and grandfather, both dead now. The same fuzzy dream at her grandparents' house. She was nine, maybe ten years old. Now forty-seven, and widowed, she still searched for an answer to these fragmented memories.

Feeling chilled all over, Leann coaxed Molly to the cabin below, put the screen over the companionway opening and pushed the security button. She smiled. Even though he insisted the marina was safe, Godfrey installed a motion sensor alarm. It would sound if someone boarded the boat. Leann promised him she would use it at night. For all his formality, Godfrey let his nurturing and protective side show. The aft cabin nightlight glowed showing the way. With Molly in her arms she crawled into bed and Molly nestled in the covers along side of Leann.

The agreement Leann had with the owner of the *Sandollar* included simple maintenance and occasionally running the equipment on the boat. That meant running the generator and water maker. These nautical tasks became a part of the household routine. Leann's reward was a ride in the dinghy to keep the small 5 hp Evinrude in good working order.

Godfrey helped her lower the outboard from the stern railing of the *Sandollar* to the dinghy. She secured the outboard and attached the gas line from the portable fuel tank. She thought about the times she and Joel explored the island anchorages in their small wooden dory. The motor started right away. With sunglasses, straw hat, T-shirt and shorts on, Leann looked and felt younger than her years. There were only hints of gray mixed among the auburn strands of her hair. People told her that her green eyes and russet hair were one of her striking features. She never knew whether to take these "striking" descriptions as a compliment. She pulled away from the stern of the sailboat and waved to Godfrey.

"Have a nice ride," he said with his arm waving high above his head.

"Thanks," she called out over the noise of the engine. She gave a quick look toward the cockpit and saw Molly lounging on the cushions staring through the screen with her nose raised working the breeze.

Godfrey's figure become smaller and smaller. He stood on the bulkhead with Mitzy, in his arms. His flamboyant gestures and colorful shirts was one way he proclaimed his pride in his alternative lifestyle. Leann liked Godfrey. His honesty and interest in others reflected the comfort he obviously found with himself.

The dinghy moved smoothly through the water. At the waterline Leann read the names of the boats and their home ports. Neighbors waved as she passed. She headed the dinghy through the canal that ran parallel to Las Olas Boulevard. With high tide she had to duck under the bridges that led to the Isles from Las Olas. Leann came into the mouth of the New River where the main channel was filled with pleasure craft, the same boats she admired from her office window. Large motor yachts and tour boats hid the bulkhead along the river. Leann maneuvered the dinghy up the river hugging the portsides of the yachts to stay clear of the channel traffic. She heard her name called.

"Dr. Regent!" Ron Spencer waved at her from the walkway in front of their office building.

"Hi, there." She eased the dinghy toward an opening between a small sailboat and a huge yacht, then hesitated. Maybe she would just wave and motor passed. On second thought, she opted to be friendly. Spence took the line that Leann tossed.

"You'll have to get in, I can't tie up with this wake, the inflatable won't last a minute, rubbing against the concrete," Leann said. "Come take a ride." Her words sounded as though they were coming from someone else, not her.

"Hey, great." Holding up his briefcase and a roll of what looked like building plans, he said, "I'll just put these in my car, be right back."

To keep the dinghy away from the concrete Leann held onto a line that extended from the bow of a large yacht and a cleat on the dock. She watched Spencer jog to his car. When he came back he wore a baseball cap with Spencer Engineering across the front. He lowered himself into the dinghy. Leann pulled at the back of her hat fingering her neck to capture lose hairs. She felt exposed. *Foolish.* A lump formed in her throat, then fell deeper into her chest and stomach. Her physical attraction to this man was unexpected. Simultaneously, Leann felt pangs of guilt for the second time. While Spence released the line from the bulkhead cleat, Leann found herself watching his leg muscles move up and down.

Spence said something to her as he sat on the bow seat. Leann put her hand to her ear and shook her head. She couldn't hear him. Spence nodded. She steered the boat up the river, passed the restaurants and shops and gazebo along the Riverwalk. Reggae music filtered through the air. The steel drums and the halting beat faded as they motored farther up the river toward an area known as Sailboat Bend. Leann throttled back on the engine. It was quieter.

"Most of Lauderdale's historical sites are right on this river." Spence said. He took off his hat and raked his fingers through his hair.

"I've only been here three months and haven't learned much about the area, " Leann replied. She pushed loose strands of hair from her face and tucked them under her hat.

"I'll give you a little history lesson." Spence gave a tour guide version of the founding of Ft. Lauderdale, specifically the history of the Cooleys and Stranahans, the early settlers along the New River. Leann found herself focusing on the mellow tones of His voice and the ease she felt in his presence. She wanted to know more about him. They motored up the river a short way along the bend in the river and then turned back toward the commercial riverfront.

"Why not tie up the boat and we'll take a walk along the Riverwalk?" Spence leaned toward Leann.

He had her interest. After a fleeting feeling of panic, she found her voice. "I'm afraid I'll have to take a rain check." With a raised voice she made her excuses saying that she needed to get back before dusk. Leann wanted a chance to sort her thoughts. Besides she knew nothing about Spence except that his office was down the hall.

Spence smiled, but his eyes suggested disappointment. "How 'bout collecting on that rain check at the end of next week, say Friday? I'll be out of town for a couple of days, but back late Thursday afternoon." They had passed the commercial section of the Riverwalk.

"Sure, that would be fine." Leann let out a breath of relief. She maneuvered the dinghy toward the bulkhead. Her throat pushed the raspy tones into her voice. Sometimes her voice cracked like an adolescent boy's. This was one of those times.

Spence nodded as he reached over the side of the dinghy for the cleat and secured a line to steady the boat while he stepped onto the walkway. "I'll call you at the office Friday afternoon."

Leann caught the line he tossed into the boat. "Okay." Leann waved as she moved the dinghy toward the Las Olas canal.

The shades of late afternoon were visible on the water as Leann made her way back to the *Sandollar* in time for dusk. The tide had receded, so she was able to motor under the bridges without ducking her head. She approached the stern of the *Sandollar,* cut the motor and secured the dinghy lines. Preoccupied with her thoughts, she climbed the stern ladder. *Silence.* Molly wasn't at her usual post greeting Leann with a demanding meow.

Leann felt perspiration form across her forehead. She opened the cockpit enclosure and called for Molly. An opening where the jib sheets thread through the cockpit screening was unsnapped. An opening that looked stretched just big enough for Molly to squeeze through. Leann checked the cabins below, but no Molly. She walked across the deck toward the dock. "Molly, Molly."

"Have you lost a cat?" Godfrey called from his patio.

His voice startled Leann. "Yes, I think she slipped out through a jib line hole in the screening."

"I'll help you look," Godfrey replied. He put a yapping Mitzy in the condo.

They each went in separate directions. Leann took the southerly docks of the neighboring property. There were a few liveaboards on this side. She felt like she was trespassing. Dusk faded into a smear of pastels and gray. She called out for Molly and could hear Godfrey at the far end of docks doing the same. Leann heard a scraping sound and stopped in her tracks to listen. The boats swayed gently with the outgoing tide. The sound came from the houseboat, *Villa*. The same houseboat she noticed earlier in the week.

"Molly," she said with a sigh of relief. There Molly was perched on the top of the houseboat's sundeck. But the sounds that attracted Leann continued. The noise intensified as she moved closer to the slip of a houseboat.

Leann knocked on the hull of the boat. No one responded. She knocked again. Boarding the boat without permission was a violation of seaman etiquette, but Leann had no choice. She realized Molly wasn't going anywhere. Molly got herself up the ladder to the sundeck, but wasn't able to figure out how to get down. The distance to the top step may have appeared overwhelming to the cat. Leann looked at her furry friend.

"Got yourself in a fix, didn't you?"

Leann stepped on the houseboat and reached for the ladder to rescue Molly, when she heard noises come from the cabin of the boat. She noticed a faint light shining through the swaying curtains. The air conditioning unit sat precariously in a cut out on the side of the cabin wall. There were beads of moisture dripping from its corner, but it wasn't running. Leann wanted to grab Molly and go, but something wasn't right. Knowing Molly was secure on the roof, she walked toward the door of the cabin.

"Molly, sit tight," she called over her shoulder. Leann remembered seeing a man on the sundeck several times, but didn't know his name.

Nearing the door, Leann caught her breath. A wave of nausea took over. She gagged and swallowed then gently tapped on the door causing it to swing open. Out came the obvious reason for Molly's visit, a small gray kitten with dark spotted fur. Leann wasn't prepared for what hit her next, an odor, nothing she had ever smelled before. It was a sweet and putrid smell. The air was both warm and cool at the same time. It pierced her nostrils and her skin tingled with heat. Her eyes watered so she couldn't see. As the door swung open farther her hand involuntarily rose to cover her mouth and nose. Bile filled her mouth. She gagged. She blinked away the tears to clear her vision. Then she saw it. Her body went rigid and she couldn't move her eyes from the sight of a human figure slumped against the cabin wall. The faint lighting cast what looked like shadows around the body. Leann focused her eyes on the shadows and realized they were irregular patterns of blood, slivers of skin and body parts soaked into the carpet.

The kitten rubbed its stiff fur against her leg. She jumped back. Her throat closed and she felt like she couldn't breath. But a guttural sound moved from the rolling muscles of her stomach to the tense muscles of her neck. A shrill scream forced its way out of her mouth.

Under the nom de plume, Diane Duritt, introduces her protagonist, Leann Regent, Ph.D. in a first novel, *IN CONFIDENCE*. Currently in revision, this Fort Lauderdale based novel follows Dr. Regent, Clinical Psychologist, as she faces the fallout of a murder that threatens to jeopardize her clients and her life. To contact the author - DianeDuritt@aol.com

FLING TRAINING

Patricia Carpenter wasn't laughing now. Not like a few hours ago, when she was at the stadium. She loved being at the ballpark. It was there that she could root and cheer with abandon and as she became entranced in the game, her breathing rhythm harmonized with the pitches and the swings on the field below. Only she knew the brief spell would be shattered by the time she found her car in the parking lot after each game. No wonder she loved a tie in the ninth.

Now she was home. She chided herself for thinking she could pull off such a coup and anxiety began to creep into her. She stood, leaning against the sink in her spacious kitchen, surveying some of what had come her way over the years--the blue-black granite countertops, the sleek marble floor and the huge cabinets, the chrome patina doors framing the etched-glass inserts. Her eyes were drawn to the double picture frame on the counter of the butler's pantry, displaying the two high school graduation photos of her daughters, smiling, their caps perched lopsided atop their heads, the tassels hanging over their eyes. She missed them a lot; the house was still and seemed even bigger, now that they were away at school. When they were little, the older used to look just like Mark, the younger like herself. You could always tell they were sisters, but the older they got, the more each looked like the other. Even the four of them looked alike after a while- all sharing that classic oval-shaped face, and distinct brows, each perfectly arched, the highest point directly above the outer edge of the iris. They all had dark hair too, except Mark's was already more salt than pepper. You could tell they belonged to each other, that they were family.

What would she make for supper? Mark would be home late as usual. "Honey, I'm home," he would say and come to her in whatever part of the house she would be. He was trim and tall and would have to bend a little to give her a peck on the lips, a peck that wouldn't last long enough for her to blink. Tonight when he came home, she knew she would have to find a way to close her eyes.

Since she had arrived later than she planned, she went straight to the fence near the dugouts to see if she could get autographs. This was the first time she went to a spring training game; she wanted to see the Mets play the Orioles. She heard the players were supposed to be friendlier than at regular season games. She really wanted Al Leiter to sign the ticket stub she saved from the May 11, 1996 Marlins game. That was Al's no hitter against the Rockies and she remembered the thrill of holding her breath each time the ball left Al's hand until the umpire called the strike. By the seventh inning, the crowd was engulfed in anticipation, and the eerie silence waiting for the pitch and the explosive roar as the umpire made the call filled Patricia with a nervous vitality. By the ninth, she could hardly bare the tension. A shame not to share the exhilaration with someone, especially Mark, at least a friend. So she imagined she was the center of the group, alternately intruding on the chit-chat of the fans sitting in front of her, behind her, on the left and on the right. But in reality, it was only she and Al, as if he even cared. Al had since been traded to the Mets. So much for loyalty.

She was too late. He must have gone back into the dugout. Her dark hair fell on her shoulders as she removed her Orioles' cap and flung it over the fence to a tall, husky fellow. "Will you sign my cap?"

"For you, anything." He winked and scribbled illegibly right in the center of the cap.

"Do you know who he is?" she asked the kid next to her.

"Elrod. A coach."

"Oh, no!" she said. "He took the best spot. I knew I should've gotten to Cal Ripken first." She laughed. A *bird in the hand is better than two in the bush*. Only at a ballpark could a teacher bask in the joy of cliche.

She fluffed her hair with her fingers, relieved it had grown back even thicker than before, and put the cap back on. She climbed up the concrete steps, found her row and set her pillow on the hard seat before she sat down. She smiled at the old man sitting next to her.

"You from Baltimore, like me?" he asked.

"New York." she said.

"Oh, a Met fan."

"Marlins- all the way, but the Mets will do today."

She could tell by the crowd that spring training was different from the regular season games: the old-timers- carefree trailer park retirees, gray or balding snowbirds hobbling their way up to their seats, the young northern grandkids, on recess, hustling to get autographs along the fence, the cute spring-breakers changing the venue of their hunt from the beach to the ballpark. Fort Lauderdale Stadium was so much smaller than the Marlins' Pro Player and Patricia enjoyed the fragrance of fresh-fruit smoothies wafting in the breeze, a pleasant change from the stench of beer at Pro Player.

Always a stickler for appearances, the forty-six year old seized the opportunity to sing the anthem out loud, for at the stadium, even her voice was lost in the crowd, and it didn't matter to anyone that she couldn't carry a tune.

"Peanuts, be-e-er, sod-a-a." The cackles of the vendors, with their particular chants, floated through the stands as they hustled and sweated while swinging their bulky cartons. Her eye caught one of them whom she presumed to be younger than she, but still a bit too old for the job. His slightly gray, curly hair was hanging out of an Orioles' baseball cap, and his rugged, boyish face betrayed his age. Unlike the others, this hawker seemed to really enjoy being where he was despite the heavy load he was lugging. He joked about the game with the old men, and smiled and winked at the women in the stands, the pretty women, the young women. He winked at Patricia, too, when she called out for a bottle of water and sent two crumpled singles down the row. "'Spe--shh-ly cooo--ld," he sang out in accentuated syllables, "for the lady in lavender at the end of the row," and sent the Deer Park on its way. Patricia let the sounds of his alliterated melody linger as she and some others who were involved in the relay of goods and cash started to laugh. In a flash he was gone, yelling and selling his wares somewhere on the other side of the stands. But not before she noticed his cute butt and slender physique. She felt a little chill, probably from holding the ice-cold container.

The Orioles were down by three runs in the eighth inning when Roberto Alomar got up to pinch-hit for the first time. She joined in the loud booing of the crowd.

"I hope he'll never live it down," she remarked to the old man sitting next to her.

The power and precision of Alomar's swing split the bat in two, and the right fielder botched the catch as the ball sailed toward the fence. Alomar drove in two runs.

The old man laughed. "See what happens when you boo! My team's gonna win now." And it did.

She didn't know why, but she looked for the vendor as she was leaving the stadium, and there he was tapping her shoulder from behind as the throng made its way down the exit ramp.

"Enjoy the game?" the vendor said.

"It was great. Who'd you root for?" she said.

"Had no time--it was a real thirsty crowd. I could sure use a drink myself. Join me? There's a lounge in the Travelodge on the corner of Commercial."

Glancing at the half-full water bottle she was holding, she hesitated for a moment. She felt drawn to him. His happy-go-lucky demeanor made her feel ten years younger. She smiled at him. "Just for a little while," she said.

"You confused me," he said as they met up at the hotel's parking lot, walked to the lounge and sat down.

"How so?"

When the waitress came by, Patricia ordered a Perrier with lime. The vendor asked for a bourbon.

"First, I saw you yell when Leiter took the mound. I thought you're from New York. Then I saw you cheer for Cal Ripken and Eric Davis. So, okay, you're a Baltimore fan. But then Alomar came out. What gives?"

She was on the brink of asking him why he was watching her so carefully, but caught herself, afraid of complicating things. After describing the no-hitter, she told him she was fairly new to the game, that she had always hated sports, but when Florida got the Marlins, she went to a game and got hooked. "I admire Cal's work ethic and Eric's courage in his fight against cancer." Kindred spirits they were, she and Eric. Different genders, different races. They both fought colon cancer, and both made it back to the ballpark.

"And Alomar?" he asked.

"Bad attitude, spitting at the ump like that."

"Attitude, work ethic," he said. You sound like a teacher."

She was impressed with his insight. "I am, but I'm on leave until the fall. This is my last stab at freedom. What's your story?" She recoiled at the huge question the moment it left her mouth. She really didn't want to know too much, and trying to narrow it down, quickly added in a wry and playful tone, "If you were a *full-time* vendor, you would have invested in a black felt bowler or a nutty elephant balloon hat, like your *colleagues*."

"I've been in construction since high school. Left Boston a couple of years now. It's a good life down here. Tuesday's my day off. I love baseball, and hawking gives me a chance to make a few extra bucks." He conversed easily and she started to relax. He still sent money for his kids back home, even though his wife left him a long time ago. Patricia got the feeling baseball wasn't all that he loved. He was thirty-eight. He was just the kind of man Patricia would never have looked at twice.

She told him she had tickets for all the Tuesday games in March. "I want to get familiar with the players and teams. Season's almost here." She mocked herself as she knew she would never fully understand all the nuances and endless statistics of the game, no matter how hard she tried. She had just learned they don't play extra innings in pre-season. "There's so much to learn," she complained. "You'd think a pitch is a pitch, but no, there's a splitter and a...." She hesitated.

"And a slider," he said.

"Sinker," she said.

Before they knew it, they were engaged in a contest of wits, seeing who would be last to come up with a pitch.

"Change-up," he added, gloating. "Well?"

"How about curveball, smarty?"

"Fastball."

"Cut Fastball," she retorted.

"Hey.... That's pretty good. Knuckleball?"

"Knuckleball!" she screamed. "No way! I never heard of that one before," and when she remembered she was in a quiet lounge and not the stadium, she shrugged back into her chair and cupped her hands over her mouth, feigning embarrassment. They laughed heartily, like two grade school kids conspiring- she distracting the teacher and he putting a thumbtack on the teacher's seat, and both giddy because they got away with it.

She glanced at his watch, and noticed his jagged fingernails. "Boy, it's late," she said as she pushed the lime around with the stirrer. "At least rush hour's over."

"How come you're by yourself?"

"For baseball, are you kidding? No one has time." She laughed, wishing someone did.

"That's a sad color," he said of the matte greige as he stroked each of her meticulously polished nails that were wrapped around her glass.

His hands looked so strong, yet they felt so gentle. She hoped he couldn't hear her pulse thumping, or see her veins quivering. His touch felt good. What was she doing here, she thought. She retracted her hands from the glass and got up to leave. "I really have to go. Thanks for the drink."

"See you next week," he said and smiled.

Patricia left him sitting at the table drinking his bourbon. She'd never flirted before, much less had a drink with another man. She enjoyed the lighthearted moment. Amazing how she lost so much and still wanted everything. If only she weren't so serious. She wished she could be detached; it just wasn't her. Life was supposed to be precious, especially now, and it seemed ironic that at her age, she was confused and ungrounded.

The Red Sox were in town the following Tuesday. Patricia was impatient as she set up her pillows. She heard the familiar Boston voice, turned and caught sight of the vendor, and settled comfortably into her seat.

"Er-ic- Er-ic," she chanted, poking the air with her fists. As her ally came up to the plate, she slipped into her own private world. No one ever told her how to deal with the uncertainty of survival. Or how foolish it was to think she could put her life in abeyance while she waited the five years it took to be declared cured. Or how she could acknowledge her defect and vulnerability and still consider herself appealing. No one told her how to forget about her disease while routinely checking for swollen nodes. Maybe the support group was right- live for today. Don't waste a moment.

The Boston vendor passed by her row and asked for her Orioles' cap. He caught it with one hand and tossed her a bag of peanuts with the other and disappeared.

She munched on the peanuts, sharing them with the same old gentleman she met the week before. No willpower, she thought, as she finished the bag, salvaging as many of the flavonoid-rich redskins she could. She looked at the big pile of shells at her feet and was happy she didn't have an aisle seat, for then everyone passing by would see she was not only a pig but a slob as well.

The Orioles were down by three runs, and when a rookie Boston pitcher wearing red and white knee-high argyles took the mound in the bottom of the sixth, a fan shouted to the chubby guy at bat, "Knock the *Socks* off him." Not to be outdone, she shouted, "It's not over till the fat batter swings!" Everyone around her laughed.

With his team still in the lead, the vendor smiled when he came by Patricia's section during the seventh inning stretch. "No more he-re. Time to go-o-o home!" he shouted, tipping his empty case toward her. She took his cue, and they met up at the ramp. He wanted to give her a lift on his motorcycle. She had never ridden on one before, and got a little excited about the prospect. But after a few seconds, she thought better of it. She wanted to have her own transportation.

They met up in the parking lot of the Travelodge and headed for the lounge. He ordered bourbon on the rocks, she needed hers straight up. They didn't speak much, but he grasped her left hand and lightly traced her veins from her wrist to her knuckles. "I like this color a lot better," he said of the glossy lilac polish on her nails. He looked at her and smiled. No particular rush. They lingered over their drinks.

She was captivated, too late to flee, mesmerized by his attentiveness. He must have sensed her trepidation, her shyness. She had been faithful to Mark for twenty-three years and she felt ridiculous. She didn't belong here, in a hotel. What could she possibly have in common with this construction guy? Baseball? Yet she wanted freedom from the sting of her husband's indifference. Gratification and intimacy, once integrated in a comfortable synergy upon which they had built a life, had become starkly separate and that made her feel old. She longed for a raison d'être that would validate her remission.

Patricia appreciated the delay. She knew what he wanted, what was expected. She wanted something new and carefree, too. She suffered plenty; she deserved a break. But she was awkward, and probably more nervous about casual sex than her collegiate daughters. She wanted to be worldly and sophisticated, and in front of this virile, patient hunk, she felt like a fool. At least she could take advantage of the meditation and visualization skills she learned during her illness to help her hop remorselessly between this new wild world and her real one.

"Shall we?" he asked.

"Did you bring protection?" she said. Her cheeks got hot. She was more of a stranger to herself than the vendor was. Sex with Mark was always protected and they never needed condoms. At least she was starting to float a little from the liquor. He nodded and they walked to the elevator.

She felt a surge of mischief and daring when they entered the room. Patricia fumbled trying to unclasp her necklace. He got behind her and unlocked it for her. She started to calm down as he rubbed her neck. He edged up closer, pulling her toward him. He wrapped one arm across her breasts and the other around her waist, his palm slanted slightly downward, so it rested on her hip. She leaned back into him, drew in a deep breath and closed her eyes, incapacitated with fear and pleasure simultaneously.

He turned her toward him, holding her close, and slid his hands along the lean small of her back. He lifted her tee shirt slowly, and his lips made their way across her breasts, teasing her, making her wait for more. He pulled her onto the bed and they embraced, rocking back and forth. He kept his arms around her and she felt protected. He did not rush her, and his soft strokes on her face and back felt pleasing and comfortable. He caressed her in all the safe, non-threatening places- her upper arms, her calves, her outer thighs. He kissed her flat, girlish abdomen and let his index finger glide over the red, six-inch long incision. Though hardly a touch, barely a tickle, Patricia flinched.

"Everybody has a story," he said.

She knew he would listen to it, but he didn't compel her to tell it, and she kept it to herself.

He kissed her navel and said, "One small blemish on the body, one giant impression on the soul." Then he kissed her on the mouth, hard, and her self-consciousness dissipated amidst the constant sensations of his touch and the mild wooziness of the liquor. The longer he held her, the more relaxed she became, until she was lost in a passionate, guiltless frenzy.

She was comfortable afterward, cuddled up in the sheet, and must have dozed off briefly. Quiet sounds of gentle stirring in the room awakened her, and when she opened her eyes, she saw him standing next to the bed, stark naked but for her Orioles' cap on his head. She bit her lips in a grueling effort to squelch her giddiness. He sat down on the edge of the bed and handed her the cap.

"Here, I almost forgot. I brought it down to the clubhouse for you."

She looked over the names and smirked in jest with one eye closed.

"Well, I couldn't tell Alomar not to sign, could I?" he said, and they burst out laughing.

"Hi, honey. I'm home," Mark called out as he came into the house. Patricia felt weak.

"Hungry?" she asked him. "Want some supper?"

"My clients brought me a burger and fries. How about a sandwich, just?"

"You're incorrigible, always eating junk food."

"Lay off, hon. I'm tired," he told her, as if she hadn't known he would be tired, as if he hadn't said it a thousand times before.

He sat down at the kitchen table. She placed a tuna sandwich in front of him.

"Enjoy the game? I heard the Orioles had a big rally in the eighth."

The once wistful and distant ballpark infringed on the sanctity of the past, and Patricia saw the stadium right there in front of her, plunked down like a giant 3D monopoly board taking up the entire tabletop, the infield littered with broken, crunched up peanut shells spread out like a tarp during a rain delay, and her husband sitting high up and far away in the bleachers, eating a tuna sandwich.

She turned around, pretending to scour a stain in the sink. "I missed the whole thing. I went to the ladies' room and by the time I got back...." She wasn't used to lying. She pushed the SOS pad a long time.

"Too bad," he said. "You never had sports-sense."

"Heaven forbid you should come with me and explain it."

He continued to eat silently, and put his plate in the spotless sink when he finished. "Thanks for the sandwich," he said and left for the bedroom. "Good night," he called out. No kiss. No peck. She knew he would fall asleep almost as soon as his head hit the pillow, yet she stayed in the family room to watch the news and then flicked between Jay Leno and Nightline.

The next game was sold out. The Mets and Orioles both were hoping to end their losing streaks. The sun was bright. There wasn't a cloud in the blue sky, but it was unseasonably chilly. She was dressed more for a winter football game as she huddled in her seat, sipping coffee, hoping the wind would die down.

"This El Nino is crazy," she said to the man with the season ticket sitting next to her. "Who ever drinks hot coffee at a baseball game?"

"The world's topsy-turvy, seems like. So your guy is pitching today," he said, referring to Al Leiter. "Some people have all the luck. I've been going to games for sixty years and never saw a no-hitter. And how many games did you go to, ten maybe, before you got one."

"Yes. I'm a pretty lucky woman." She searched her fanny pack for the ticket stub from the no-hitter and showed it to him.

"Hot dogs he-re. It's lunchtime!" the Boston vendor sang out as he came by her row. He asked for the ticket stub and gave her a bag of peanuts. The instant their hands touched in the exchange, a jolt pierced through her, inaudible screams shouted from her gut, "I-ce cold beer- three dol-lars! Au-to-graphs--a lay a piece! "

Patricia was cold and couldn't concentrate on the game. She gave the peanuts to the man sitting next to her and left. She spent half her life with Mark. They had some hard times, but still he was there for her. He put ice chips on her parched lips. Damn the support group- "don't take your remission for granted; put yourself first," the members touted. Live for the moment; destroy a lifetime. She should have known better.

The cool winter weather gave way to the typical humidity by the last Tuesday in March, the final game of spring training. Patricia got dressed and studied her reflection in the mirror longer than usual. When she clasped her necklace, she ran her fingers over the slippery facets of the heart-shaped amethyst. She remembered the day Mark gave it to her, to celebrate her one-year anniversary check-up. The doctor gave them a thumbs up, and afterwards, in the car, Mark handed her a box and said, "I don't want you to be afraid of doctors and check-ups. Think of good things and be strong." That was a good day, a great day. It had been a long time since Mark had been that tender, and on that day, he made her remember just how in sync they used to be.

She finished getting dressed and left the house. By the time she climbed to the top of the stairs, she was puffing, all out of breath. She stood at the door to his office, unbeknownst to him, observing him, his fingers flying over the calculator keys, five ballerinas leaping to allegretto tempo. She always loved watching his hands in action, his fingers moved so fast, his nails perfectly trimmed.

"And you tell me you're skinny because I don't cook. It's these stairs that keep you in shape!" Her presence startled Mark as he looked up in response to her voice.

"Hi. This is a surprise." They walked toward each other and embraced for a moment. "So what brings you to this part of town?"

"We never have time to talk. I thought maybe we could do lunch. My treat," she laughed.

"You should have called first. I've got wall to wall clients today." He was distracted. Patricia could tell by the way his eyes scanned the files and texts strewn around the office. He walked back to his desk and sat down.

"Look, Mark. We can't go on like this. We need to be close." She sat down across from him.

"You know I've been working on some big cases. A client's on the way over now. Give me a break."

"You've always had big cases, and we always had a marriage." She leaned over toward him. "I want you close to me. I want you to want me."

"I want. I want. Listen to yourself. What about me, Patricia, me? You're not the only one with troubles. You don't know what it's been like for me. Doctors, medical decisions, bills, employees, mortgages, tuition, clients. I've got to solve everybody's problems. And you're no fun anymore. You're a nut with health food. You won't die if you eat French fries once in a while." He started to tap the calculator keys, and suddenly, as if the tapping annoyed him, pushed the calculator away and got up.

"I'm just trying to keep us both healthy."

"You strangle me. I don't even want to come home. 'Don't get crumbs! Don't drag in dirt! Leave the cake for company!' Don't you care if your *friends* get high cholesterol?"

"Stop it." Patricia felt like a piece of tin foil, getting more crumpled with each slur Mark hurled at her, until it was ready to be tossed in the trash. But she wasn't surprised about Mark's reaction. Whenever she exposed her feelings, Mark would take it as a personal assault and attack her in self-defense.

"I can't even make love to you the way I want," he said.

"I'm nothing to you but prostate relief!" She fought back tears.

Mark's face turned red. He walked toward the window and looked out at the courtyard below.

"What do you mean, you don't make love to me the way you want?"

She could barely hear him when he spoke. "You feel so sorry for yourself. Sometimes, I think you'll break. You do nothing important. Just waste time at ballgames."

"That's not fair. I'm going back to work. And golf is so exciting?" she mocked.

He turned around to look at her. "At least on the golf course I'm free. I see the trees and the fairways, and I'm happy to be alive. You hide in the ballpark. You rave about Eric Davis. Well, he got back into the game. You're so afraid of losing, you don't know how to keep what you have."

She glared at him. "What did you want from me? Should I have bowed down and thanked the doctor for telling me I might die? Should I have been grateful for the opportunity to have chemo because such an enriching experience was going to make me a better human being? I'm sorry. I'm sorry I needed so much time, that I was a burden. Nobody handed me a script telling me how to be a perfect patient, an expert survivor- no fear, no pity."

"I'm worn out, Patricia. Finished. Enough."

"I'm your wife, for God's sake. Don't you have any compassion? The people who say cancer is the best thing that happened to them, that it's a gift from God. Well, that's crap. I was terrified." Her voice trailed off. She moved closer to him, but he backed away. "Come on, Mark. I came to tell you that I'm on my way. I don't want to be a scared victim and I want you with me. I thought you'd be happy."

"Look. I know it hasn't been easy for you, and I tried to support you. But if I had the guts, I would sell the house, the practice and move to a trailer in the desert."

"As long as there's a golf course nearby!"

"Absolutely. The sand traps there would be better than the yoke around my neck here." He threw his arms out in front of him. "My clients will be here in a minute. I need to get my files." Not, 'we'll talk about it later,' or 'we'll figure out a way.' Just, "I need to get my files."

"Speaking of yokes!" she said, as she yanked the amethyst from her neck and threw it at him. Her eyes were watery from his rejection and the burn on her neck. "I was a fool. I let you buy me off too often."

He grabbed at the gemstone in mid-air, catching it just before it was about to hit his chest. "Good aim. At least baseball's good for something."

"More than you'll ever know!" She scooped up her bag from the desk, turned her back and left.

Patricia struggled down the stairs, her stomach aching with the queasiness that comes when learning someone close has died. After all, Mark had been her best friend for such a long time. She walked toward her car, grappled for the keys, turned on the ignition, and stayed in her seat for a long time, composing herself. She knew Mark wouldn't come after her.

She sucked in a deep breath of humid air, and when the wrenching eased up a little, she gripped the wheel and pulled away from the curb. She didn't know exactly where she was going, but by the time she made a right turn at the corner, her grip loosened and the car seemed to move of its own volition.

The farther she traveled from Mark's office, the more elevated she felt, as if she were ascending in a hot-air balloon. Airborne, she was free--her clothes flapping against her skin in the wind, her long hair flicking across her cheeks, damp strands sticking on her lips. Her entire being luxuriated in the thrill of gliding above the city in a swaying wicker basket.

Patricia meandered across the sky until she saw the big, bright blue letters of the Travelodge sign peeking through the clouds below. The wind slowed down just gradually enough so that balloon hovered above the center of the stadium. Leaning over the side of the basket, Patricia observed everything- the Yankees were playing and the stands were packed. She sniffed in the tart scent of pineapple smoothies rising in the air. She narrowed her line of vision to where she thought her Boston vendor would be, and there he was, lugging his case near her row. She heard his familiar voice shouting, "Ice cold be-er! Pea-nuts he-re!" He kept turning toward her empty seat, again and again, and by the seventh inning stretch, he finally gave up.

"Hey, kid." He grabbed the arm of a boy, maybe ten or eleven, running toward the ramp. "Know what this is?"

The boy looked quizzically at the teal and white stub held up in front of him.

"It's a ticket from Al Leiter's '96 no-hitter, and see this," pointing proudly to the writing, "that's his autograph. You want it?"

"Oh!" Patricia gasped and she brought the palm of her hand up to her mouth. Tears filled her eyes.

"For real?" the boy said.

"Sure, kid. I don't need it anymore. Here."

"Wow! Gee thanks, Mister, Wow!" He squealed in delight and in a flash was lost in the crowd.

The vendor returned to his section, his near-empty case strapped around his neck. Patricia heard his usual shout and saw him wink, catching the eye of a thirty-something blonde sitting in the middle of a row. He smiled and tossed her a bag of peanuts. Patricia smiled, too. Then in tandem with the tropical breezes blowing in from the east, she released the blast valve and jolting the giant balloon with one last shot of propane, sailed away in a gust.

RHYME AND PUNISHMENT

Life is a mere series of moments- of expectations and disappointments, joys and sorrows, victories and vulnerabilities, hardiness and ill-health. But making life more palatable is the knowledge that there is a sense of nobility and constancy allowing us to believe things will turn out, not necessarily as we would wish, but rather as they must, for we are what we are. Then something snaps and the unpredictable happens, the unthinkable thought, the unspeakable spoken, the undoable done. We are left in a lurch, devastated, shocked: desperate to find sanity where there is none, driven to rationalize the irrational.

I pulled the newspaper from its damp plastic sack Friday morning and confronted such a moment. There the headline lay, sprawled on the first page of the local section in bold, black letters. I was aghast, my pulse raced, and little drips of hot coffee spilled from the cup that was shaking in my hand. Is this the same Bernard? How could it be?

I had thought the monthly poetry meetings were just that, but the moment I saw Bernard's photograph on the right side of the page, I realized how much more than poetry our group meant to me.

Do not ask me why I go to poetry meetings; that is not important, except to say that since I was a child I dreamt about publishing poems and stories, gripping readers' hearts, signing autographs during exciting book tours, traveling around the world--relishing in the glare of celebrity.

It was here at these monthly sessions that on occasion, I would have the opportunity to bask in a fleeting moment of satisfaction and accomplishment. Reciting a poem, I could see tears well up in a random eye here and there, especially Bernie's. He loved my work, but was never too shy to tell me how to make it better. "Bring it to a more artistic level," he would prod.

I had been slaving over a poem for several weeks and for fear of making a fool of myself in front of the group, I rehearsed reciting it, using a pedestal in the family room as a make-do podium, and spoke into the microphone of a pocket tape recorder. I had to be certain my tone and inflection were perfect. After all, this was my big chance. *"Why Can't I Make Music?"* was my autobiographical confession proclaiming my musical shortcomings: my voice was flat, I couldn't carry a tune and years of piano lessons yielded only the ability to play with an abundance of expressiveness. Nimble, technical acumen and talent remained abhorrently lacking.

When it was my turn to recite, I passed around fourteen copies, enough for each participant to have one, and walked to the center of the room. "This poem is really important to me," I said, the sheet of paper shaking in my hand. "It reflects the feelings in my heart and soul."

"You shouldn't give us commentary about your poem," Katherine, a middle-aged member of the group castigated me. "We need to get that from your poem itself. And if we don't, than you didn't write a good one."

I shrank back from the podium, and my already fragile esteem seemed to shrink as well. I wanted to flee the room but my pride overtook my humiliation.

"Don't mind her," Bernie said as he glanced at me. "Apparently Katherine hasn't forgotten the many suggestions we gave her the last time." He slapped his palm on the table with authority, as though he had a gavel in his hand. "Go ahead," he said, leading the workshop.

I sucked in the deepest breath I could, thankful for Bernie's comfort, and after reading a line or two, I melted into my own thoughts, oblivious to the crowd listening to me.

"I'll start," Bernie said after I finished. "You can't use an old World War II jingle. Your poem deserves better," he said. "The language must speak of you. You just can't get away with *tune* and *croon* in the year 2000. It doesn't sound authentic."

What does he know? I thought, my spirit crushed, once again left to wonder why I even attend these critique sessions. Sometimes Bernie seemed pompous, the possessor of an artificial prowess of literary skill, as if he were a former literature professor and not the retired electrical engineer he was. But I must admit, it sounded like he just might have been on to something. I thought of a way to change the jingle.

> *There is a song somewhere in my soul*
> *But I cannot squeeze out its sound.*
> *Notes scurry to and fro between my ears*
> *The pitch is off, the key nowhere to be found.*

Then I had to put up with this newcomer who should have written her own poem on the topic. "You should say fear, because you are afraid of your ineptitude." I explained that first of all, I, the poet, was not the subject of the poem; that I, the writer, was resigned to the talents the Omniscient One did or did not bestow upon me, and furthermore, that fear was not the emotion I wanted to conjure up. I intended to convey the sadness of that vacant spot where talent should have been. "It's a mistake," she insisted.

> *There is a verse of energy*
> *bursting from my lungs*
> *But it gets checked inside my cheeks*
> *while lyrics garble on my tongue.*
> *The melody mute, locked within my tear*
> *My song unable to be sung.*

Bernie's wife Hilda came to the rescue and cut off the obnoxious, obstinate wench. I could always count on Hilda. Her voice was as soft as the poetry she read, and her motivation as innocent as it was honest. She scanned to the final stanza and suggested a different couplet to strengthen an image I longed to portray. I had not even thought of the possibility, and I saw its potential immediately. The way she fashioned the concept also misconstrued my specific meaning, but she was not so stubborn, and I knew I could make it work for me.

I mused on her recommendation, not even waiting until I got home, but while on the way. I struggled to memorize these new phrases as I drove, and was happy to get caught at red lights so I could jot them down. At one intersection, I noticed Bernie and Hilda stopped in the right lane, and gave them a high-five. They smiled at me, this perfectly-suited, diminutive couple, sitting low in the old maroon Chevy, two gray heads barely peeking over the dashboard. I worked through the night to finish the revision and I awaited anxiously to read it at the next meeting.

> *The beat I crave eludes my heart*
> *Bereft I am, useless to create*
> *Yet I soar immersed in songs and symphonies*
> *Feats of others easy to appreciate.*
> *And therein lies my gift, a loud, resounding*
> *passion-*
> *Let others make the music while I fly on*
> *chords they fashion.*

"A caterpillar into a butterfly right before our eyes," Hilda gasped. Others nodded their heads in agreement. "You shouldn't feel bad about not being able to play," an old-timer encouraged from across the room. "You do with words what others do with a piano." He didn't get it either, but I was, to tell the truth, flattered and buoyed by their approval. I quipped to mild, soft-spoken Hilda, "Do I have to share my byline with you- after all, it was your rhyme that I fashioned to fit?" Her laugh was modest and there was a sparkle of genuine satisfaction in her eyes.

That was the last time I saw Bernie and Hilda, at the meeting two months ago. I will never again hear her soft voice read those intimate, passionate love poems she composed- poems devoted to Bernie, and poems written long ago of motherhood, when she was young and unsure.

I got hold of myself as I tightened my grip around the warm coffee mug. I had to read the headline once more. HUSBAND CHARGED IN WIFE'S DEATH. Poor, suffering Hilda. Gone. Dead. Poor Bernie. Inconceivable. Even his mug shot didn't do him justice. I read the article, slowly, trying to absorb the facts. He was arrested and charged with second degree murder after he confessed to stabbing her ten times in the chest. SUSPECT WEPT AS PARAMEDICS REMOVED BLOODIED BODY FROM CONDO, "I COULDN'T STAND TO SEE HER SUFFER." The words of his weeping echoed in my mind, grating at me like the scratching of a record spinning on a turntable after the song was finished: "I couldn't stand to see her suffer." So he stabbed her! Ten times! In the chest! The article claimed Hilda had been terminally ill. That was odd-she didn't seem sick. Diminutive and subservient, but not sick, suffering no more than anyone else who chooses to be cheerful rather than grumpy.

I was devastated not to have perceived even a hint of her infirmity, his insanity, their anguish. I was enraged at myself. I never offered them anything during our workshops- no ideas, no help. I never thought to give back. I will miss them. Bernie will no longer attend our meetings, and even if he could, I would never be able to look at him in the same way. The rhymes Bernie and Hilda selflessly offered—the very ones I selfishly took— have become a burden all my own. I crumpled up our poem and tossed it in the wastepaper basket.

SUICIDER

Abulafia Cohen picked up his denim floppy hat and walked with a limp, courtesy of the Yom Kippur War, to the front door. Arnold was his given name, but when he was old enough, he changed it for something more exotic than the one his American parents gave him and something more indigenous to the heritage of which he was part.

"*Shalom, motek*," he called to his wife who was cleaning up breakfast dishes in the kitchen. He still called her "sweetie," after 28 years, and after such a time, he knew when to take leave of her quickly so he could avoid the criticisms, the questions, the nudging.

"*T'zahir*," be careful, he heard her shout from the kitchen.

"I don't have my itinerary yet but I have my cell," he said as he shut the door, balancing the walking stick on his muscular arm as he jiggled the keys in the lock. It was almost an out-and-out lie, for today he had an urge to go to Musrara, and he knew, more or less, that was where he would go.

When she heard him close the door, Galit Cohen went into the salon where she crashed onto the sofa like a crystal chandelier whose wire was cut. The money problems, the health and rehabilitation struggles, even the other women, nothing broke their marriage apart. But this flirting with danger to prove a point made her crazy. "*I don't have my itinerary, yet.*" She heard his voice in her head and pounded her fists on her thighs.

She would worry if something happened in the city, not knowing if he were there or somewhere else. At least, she conceded, the bastard knew enough to take the cell phone.

"I'm not going to let them change me." Abulafia would insist.

"You're obsessed with this. Resilience. It doesn't mean a thing when they pick you up in a million pieces from the sidewalk."

"They will not break my spirit. Who do those savages think they are?"

"You never rode buses before. Only when you had to. They changed you all right. They made you a nut. A new version of Jerusalem Syndrome. JTS. Jerusalem Terror Syndrome," she screamed and paused a moment to catch her breath. "You should take the bus to Hadassah…for treatment!" She'd carry on until she was spent, limp, to no avail.

She couldn't take him anymore. She cradled her face in her hands and rocked back and forth like a grief-stricken mother. She felt the wetness from her tears on her fingers, and dried them on her skirt. *This is it,* she resolved. *When he comes back, I'll put my foot down. No more needless bus trips to tempt fate. Not one more. Not one.*

It was a perfect spring day. Abulafia sucked in the clean air, savoring the delicate fragrance of almond tree blossoms that swirled in the warm breeze. The sky was pure blue and he could see the Judean hills far off into the horizon. With every step he took away from the house toward the bus stop, he felt lighter and freer from Galit's tirades and attacks. *Things were worse these past two weeks. Every time there's a push for peace, nothing changes but more pieces of Jews strewn on the streets. Look at what happened after Aqaba, on the #14. And Powell is coming again. That's good for another two massacres. If only the Arabs would disappear, if the Americans would go away, if we could just be left alone before there's nothing left of us.* By the time he got to the bus stop in front of the main post office on Rehov Yafo, the scent of blossoms dissipated, replaced by the contradictory smells of falafel balls sizzling in hot oil in the sidewalk kiosks mixed with the blackish exhaust fumes polluting the air. He waited for the #57 to Musrara.

He remembered the neighborhood well from the crisis days just before the Six Days' War. Then it was a poor slum of mostly religious immigrants from Morocco, Tunisia and Algeria. The men of the country had been called up for army service and sons - nine, ten years old as well as teenagers - took over their fathers' jobs, manning shops, delivering goods on bicycles, even some driving buses.

Fifteen year-old Abulafia did his share by walking his father's mail route, delivering letters to the dilapidated apartment buildings of Musrara, which at that time lay along the border of No-Man's-Land. He remembered it like yesterday: the long barbed wire fence to keep out Jordanian infiltrators, and the high stone walls built to protect people walking in the streets, pocked-marked throughout their length with rifle bullets. Beyond the fences and the walls, was the majestic expanse of rolling hills and mountains, white with barrenness, stone huts of Arabs painted in pastel blues, yellows and greens.

Back then, from the edge of a hill, he could see the narrow road winding through the slopes to the original Hadassah Hospital and Hebrew University on Mt. Scopus. The convoys on the old road bringing water and provisions to the isolated hospital in 1947 and '48 were constantly attacked and decimated by the Jordanian army. A grave defeat for the Palmach, the territory was lost altogether, and the jewels of civilization and science lay fallow in a demilitarized zone since 1948.

He recalled a moment the day before the war started in '67, when he was entering an apartment building on Rehov Hessed with a mailbag on his shoulder. He passed a group of elementary school children who were just dismissed. They were mingling with the group of American university students on a break from filling and piling sandbags in front of the school windows. It was a terrible hamsein day, dry and scorching. The air was laden with desert grit making it difficult to breathe. A twenty-something American woman wearing a purple straw hat sat right in the middle of the sidewalk, drinking water, gathering some children around her.

"Want to learn a song?" she asked. Curious and excited, a boy said, "BEE-tles, BEE-tles." They all sat in the middle of the sidewalk singing one phrase after the other of "I Want to Hold Your Hand" in broken accents.

All of a sudden, shots rang out. A Jordanian man was standing on a rooftop in No-Man's-Land, shooting a rifle into the crowd of frightened kids. Abulafia, on one side, and the American on the other, led the children into the school building and comforted them until it was quiet. A policeman showed up and said, "Go home now. The Arab's gone; it's safe."

The kids scattered, all but one little girl who was crying. The American woman stooped and put her arms around her. "Come with me. Don't be afraid. I will walk you home." She plopped her big purple hat on the little girl's head, which brought a gentle giggle from the child, and took her hand. As they started to walk down the street, she called out to Abulafia, "Thanks for your help. Be careful."

That's the way it was in those days, and pretty much these days, too. Looking out for each other, strangers. He loved to see how the surroundings changed since the '67 war. The hospital and university were once again in Israel's hands, modernized and flourishing. The walls and fences were torn down right after the war, and those barren, sparsely populated hilltops were thriving with beautiful apartment buildings, five stories high carved right out of the gold-hued stone hills. The architecture was imaginative, the entrances built right into the mountains on the third floor so you didn't have to walk up or down more than two stories. Stone terraces lined the sides of the buildings, and from the distance, they looked like stuffed pockets jutting out in front. Potted plants hanging from the ceilings of those terraces appeared like giant green periods and exclamation points in distance. The streets were filled with traffic and kids and life and life and life.

Everything was different in the modern suburb. Except when he looked toward the east side across the valley, there was a new stone wall, maybe just a year old, a high stone wall to protect the people in the streets and apartments from the machine guns and homemade missiles of the newest intifada. Things were so different but little had changed. Only the weapons were more modern and lethal, and the pock marks deeper and more damaging.

Why the urge to come here? For Abulafia, this spot was the crossroad where past, present and future collided, none being perfect, all fraught with blood and loss. One man's wound another's victory. History's tennis ball slammed back and forth over a barbed wire net achieving nothing but every player's exhaustion and frustration. From this intersection called Musrara, he could see stability, and even if it wasn't good or easy or bursting with the potential for joy, it was stable. If nothing else, he could count on stability.

Husam Nasif dreaded saying goodbye to his parents, and he dreaded coming home. Everyday it was the same. They would warn him not to get into trouble on his way out, and upon his return they would question what he did, where he went, what he ate, and if he got into trouble. His grandparents, too, had warnings to issue, advice to give, and he couldn't stand any of it. He almost hated his grandfather, his cowardice, his stupidity, and he didn't even feel guilty about it.

Husam was surprisingly clean-cut considering he lived in a refugee camp on the outskirts of Ein Sahar, a quaint village nestled in a valley midway between Jerusalem and Bethlehem. For all of his seventeen years he shared a two-room apartment with his parents, grandparents, seven siblings, and was maddened by the squalor and the smell. He was tall by Middle East standards—almost six feet, and slender. His hair was thick and black, and he wore it slicked back. Two lush, distinct eyebrows crowned his sad, haunting hazel eyes. He wore his shirts tucked inside his slim, tight jeans, and the wide buckle on his leather belt was always polished. The sole flaw he had was a small but deep scar on his chin, the result of a stone-throwing, Molotov cocktail melee with the Israeli army. But it made him seem more rugged and even more appealing. The girls swooned over him, flirting and offering him sweets as he passed them on the streets. He knew they would have offered more, but he wasn't interested. Only sometimes would he smile half-heartedly at them, when he was in the mood to hear their giggles and banter.

"You look tired," his mother said that morning, raising her hand to brush across his face as if to make sure he was all right, even *there*.

He shooed her away with a swat of his arm, not wanting to feel her touch on his face. She smothered him so; she might as well have raised a pillow and pressed it against his face.

"I was up late studying." He bit his lip, realizing he might have raised a red flag, and he quickly added, "History. I'm playing soccer after school. I'll be late."

Her face paled. "The one who did the #14, he did the soccer, too. You can go to university next year. Please, don't stay with those boys. They'll spoil it for you."

"Leave me alone. You always worry."

His old grandfather, his father's father, who was drinking coffee at the small table in the corner, still in his pajamas, scoffed at Husam's coldness. "Don't be so harsh with your mother. She thinks only for your health and goodness."

"You. It's all your fault, you and all those other cowards who brought this catastrophe on us. Why didn't you stay and fight. You're all still afraid to fight."

The grandfather retreated. How could he demand respect from Husam when he was ashamed of himself? How was he to know then that everything he was told would turn out the opposite? "Leave. Don't get in the way. We'll get rid of them, drown them in the sea and you come back in a few days." That's what the soldiers said, and he did what he was told. He didn't stay. No one expected such battles. He could understand the disgust Husam had for him. He began sipping the cold coffee, staring at the newspaper in front of him.

Husam turned back to his mother, lowering his voice, trying to reassure her. "Don't worry so much. I don't play on Jihad Team Soccer." He didn't like lying to her, but he resented that his family didn't encourage him, and wouldn't be proud of him the way his friend Fawzi was honored by his family. They celebrated with wedding feasts and blessings, befitting the bridegroom ascending to Paradise. They were proud of Fawzi, who was courageous and brought honor to the family. They didn't lament; they rejoiced.

Husam tried to trap the bad thoughts and push them out of his head. Time was short and he needed to reach the proper frame of mind. He had studied the Koran all night. He was ready and embraced his mother without saying goodbye, as was prescribed, but he couldn't tell her not to cry if something happened to him, for that would draw too much protest. "I love you with all my heart," he said, and kissed her three times on her cheeks. Then he walked over to his grandfather, and squeezed his hands on the old man's tired shoulders as he leaned over to kiss him. Without another word, he left. Without looking back, he closed the door behind him.

The bus driver scrutinized the people getting on his #57. He had, of course, searched for hidden explosives under the seats before he left the depot, and as usual, he checked everyone stepping up to the coin box, looking for anything, a speck of suspicion, praying his intuition wouldn't fail him.

"*Boker tov,*"- - good morning, Abulafia said dropping his token in the box. "A beautiful day, yes? Not a cloud in the sky. A good day for a nice ride."

"Nice ride," the driver muttered under his breath, annoyed with Abulafia's distracting burst of friendliness. "Who cares for weather?" he said, his forehead creased as he bobbed his head this way and that to get a look at the people shoving their way on the bus. It was getting harder for him to discern the bombers. They had a new angle, dressing like Jews—soldiers or black coats—so they could blend in and blow-up. At least it was still summer. His task was more difficult in the winter— everyone bundled in coats and jackets, anyone could hide an explosive belt under so much clothing.

The driver's mood shifted from irritation to anger. The Arabs were taking everything over from the Jews. First, it was the term Diaspora. For thousands of years, Jews were expelled from here, there and everywhere. Now the Arabs claim a *Diaspora* of their own. Then the "Law of Return," the guarantee for any Jew to be permitted access and citizenship in Israel which had been denied to them in so many other countries of the world throughout the centuries. Now Arabs profess the right to return, even though most of them were never even here. And Jerusalem, the city Jews built and yearned for thousands of years, hardly mentioned in the Koran, all of a sudden, Jerusalem is holy to them. When they had control, they urinated on The Wall and paved roads with broken headstones from ransacked Jewish cemeteries. What a joke. And now, dressing up like soldiers or Hasidim. This used to be a good job he thought, union pay, good pension. Today, it's life or death, a heavy load, too much responsibility. Who could count on reaching retirement? It would be enough to reach the depot at the end of the run.

Abulafia took note of the passengers, nodding here and there, as he made his way to the middle of the bus where he preferred to sit. It was before the rush hour and the bus was crowded, but not mobbed. No one was even standing. There was a single vacant seat near one of the center poles, and he sat down, leaning his walking stick against the seatback in front of him. The bus worked its way through the traffic tie-ups on the main road, passengers entering and exiting at every stop. Outside it was noisy- horns honking, police blowing whistles directing hordes of rushing pedestrians. By the time the bus reached the King George stop, people were already standing in the aisle.

At the next stop, in front of the Mahane Yehuda marketplace, a young man in a green uniform got on, nodding inconspicuously to the driver as he stepped up the three stairs. Soldiers didn't have to pay fare and he walked past the token box. It was important to reach the middle of the bus; that would be most effective, and he wound his way there carefully, twisting and turning, avoiding contact with the other passengers. He had already grasped a pole with his left hand, prepared for the coming jolt as the bus pulled away from the curb. He looked around and saw Abulafia's gaze fixed on him. The young man smiled tentatively at him. He stood still and seemed nervous. A nice looking boy, Abulafia thought, but for the scar on his chin. Abulafia smiled back—deliberate, determined, defiant.

Galit Cohen waited for the cell to ring.

MONSTER ALLEY

Lyman trudged east up a dark, deserted side street, slowly becoming aware that night had long descended, of brightly lit Broadway two blocks ahead, that he must be in Manhattan now. But mostly Lyman was becoming aware of how tired he felt from being on the lam all day. He had no idea of how many miles he'd walked since fleeing the Bronx this morning.

Finally emerging from his dilemma, he suddenly felt a great need for people—for chatter, lights, music—all the signs of life. And most of all a new life of his own. Which meant a new scam. And he'd better find one quick.

Who'd of thought a whole neighborhood could get so worked up over the theft of a few wheelchairs? Hell, didn't he always point Huey to the cripples and have him give them first crack at buying their crummy chairs back—at half price yet?

Where the hell did people get off saying he had no conscience?

But now, with the law onto him, he couldn't even sneak back to his pad for his duds. He was stuck, out in the night, with nothing but the threads on his back: his knockoff of a blue satin Yankee's jacket, t-shirt, chinos, sneakers; not even socks or skivvies.

He'd ducked out at seven this morning for his coffee and immediately heard that Huey'd gotten nabbed, again. Idly he wondered how the little crack freak would wiggle out of it this time. Then, shuffling back to his pad with his coffee and cinnamon, he'd spotted the two 'suits' in the 'unmarked' in front of his brownstone and knew exactly how the little crack freak was wiggling out of it this time. By ratting out the *Notorious Wheelchair Thief* was how.

Damn! His livelihood blown, he did an about face and had been walking ever since—bumping into people, lampposts; blaring horns and windy gusts swishing by—trying to get his mind around his devastating reversal of fortune.

Now, head down, shoulders hunched in his jacket against the night chill, Lyman plodded on up the dark street toward the Great White Way, not a sound to be heard but his footfalls. The only signs of life the spill of reds and greens across the sidewalk from the few bars still open; across the street a peon sweeping out a late night bistro with jack-o-lanterns in its diamond-paned window. Suddenly Lyman realized he was hungry, and that he might get a lot hungrier yet.

Jesus, to be down to forty bucks in New York, a city that eats money. Thank God for his ring, watch, and the solid gold bracelet heavy in his chinos' pocket. These he could hock for a quick duce. But how far would even two hundred go in this money-grubbing berg?

Besides, this jewelry, which he never left home without, wasn't for food. It was his case ace. His quick conversion to cash for just such emergencies as this, all he had left in the world now to get him up and running again with a new scam.

But where to find a good new scam in the dead of night? Lyman threw up his hands to the empty street. Was he doomed to eat out of dumpsters and sleep in cardboard boxes till he could at least find a mark? But, again, where to find a nice fat mark in the dead of night? Who ever said there's a sucker born every minute?

Lyman kicked a crumpled tin can through the cone of lamp light coming up, sent it clattering out into the gutter, when a tall, pasty-faced figure in a high-collared cape leaped out of the alley before him, claws raised, booming, "I vont to dreenk your blood."

Lyman's heart leaped to his tonsils and he threw up his dukes to fight.

"Oops," the figure piped in a freshman voice. "Sorry, sir. Didn't mean to scare you quite so bad." The lanky figure lowered his claws to a tray slung around his neck.

"A pitchman," Lyman blurted, "you're a pitchman? Jesus."

"Au contraire," the figure piped bowing low with a sweep of his cape, "Not a pitchman, sir. Pray, an actor if you will."

"An actor. An actor?" With his heart fluttering back down into his chest again, Lyman could finally size the dude up and Lyman had a keen eye for the brown spot on a piece of fruit.

Theatrical dinner dress sagging off tall, bony frame; rubber Dracula mask and monster claws right out of Woolworth's. Throw in the high-pitched voice and Lyman realized he'd been stopped by a 6-foot-4-inch kid who couldn't weigh over a hundred-and-fifty pounds soaking wet—one of them stringbean types that probably shoots up quick and fills out later.

Lyman wasn't worried. Though eight inches shorter than the fool—and probably twenty years older—he was a savvy, hundred and eighty pound gang-banger. He'd match his forty years of street smarts against this silly stringbean's any day. In fact, one more hinky move out of the dip and he'd kick a hole in him. Oops, listen up, he's . . .

". . . what did you expect, sir, coming through Monster Alley at this time of night?"

"Monster Alley?" Lyman screwed up his face to show his confusion.

"What, you haven't heard of Monster Alley?"

Lyman winced to the pitch. "Fraid not, pally. Bronx boy, born and bred." He planted his meaty hands on stocky hips. One more hinky move.

"Ah, well, 'Ask and ye shall receive.'"

Oh, no, not a Holy Roller.

"You're in Manhattan's theater district, sir. On the street with the most legitimate theaters. We call it Monster Alley now because it's presently offering a revival of all the old, classic horror hits." The stringbean swept his cape to the darkened theaters up and down the block, "See?"

And, indeed, now that Lyman looked at the marquees he could see Mary Shelley's *Frankenstein,* Bram Stoker's *Dracula,* the original *Wolf Man,* Tickets now on sale for *The Mummy.* Maybe he should look better where he's walking.

"Monster Alley, sir, is where we actors step out in our costumes to get live reactions from the passers by."

Lyman slipped his cuff to peek at his watch. "At 2:00 a.m.?"

The stringbean sighed his soul to the inky sky, weary of explaining yet again. "I know, I know, sir. We tried scaring people in the daytime but they just laughed at us. Uh, say, wanna see something neat?" he piped, raising the lid of his tray to the chalk-white chin of his mask.

Lyman blinked at the blunt, stubbled face peering back at him in the lid's underside mirror. Another thing he left without this morning, his shave. He ran a hand through his unkempt hair.

"Uh, *we?*" he said up to the mask.

"Me, Frankenstein, the Wolf Man, the Mummy. They're all hiding up the block. We're not the shows' stars, mind you. Just their understudies, seeking, ahem,"–hairy claw to black tie— "our 'Big Breaks.'"

"Big breaks? In the middle of the night?"

"Ah," one cautionary claw popped up, "you never know who might come along in the theatre district, sir. Wanna see my Groucho? I got Groucho down to a T." The caped stringbean spun into a crouched profile of the comedian, clawed mitt to mouth tapping ashes off an imaginary cigar. "Say the magic word and make the duck come down," he mimicked in Groucho's voice. "Uh!" Straightening again with a paw to the small of his back, "So, what do you think, sir?"

"I think if that's Groucho, one of you'se is pretty lousy. But, hey, pally, 'Seek and ye shall find.'" Lyman knew how to give a Roller as good as he got.

"Touche', sir. But you won't have to seek to find my cohorts. They'll jump out at you as you pass their alleys."

"More actors subbing as vendors?" Lyman cocked his head up to the lanky stringbean in his sagging dinner dress, "Why?"

"Our kingdoms for a ham on rye, sir. You'd be surprised at how little we understudies make."

"And as vendors?"

"Ho, all the difference in the world, sir."

Hmmm, Lyman thought, street hawks dressed like monsters. Could there be anything here for him? Could this holy roller be Heaven-sent—literally? For the first time since his livelihood had been snatched out from under him this morning, Lyman felt a twinge of hope. Of course, having a good product helped, too.

"So," he drawled hiking up his beltless pants and tucking in his T-shirt, "what're youse kids pushin?"

"Pushing? Oh, you mean selling? Franky's selling golf balls, sir. Titleists at half price. Wolfie's selling rubbers. A gross or one, he'll give you a good price."

"Rubbers, at two in the morning? Who buys?"

"Golly, sir, see these bars still opened, up and down the block? Ever hear the saying, 'The girls all look prettier at closing time?' You'd be surprised how many rubbers Wolfie sells at this hour to drunks still hoping for a meaningful one-night stand."

Lyman had to grin at the kooky kind of logic. And what more should he expect anyway from dips who lurk for marks in the dead of night?

"Mummy, up the block," the stringbean piped, flipping a clawed thumb over his shoulder, "is selling encyclopedias. If you think condoms are hard to sell to drunks at two a.m., try unloading twenty-pound books on them at this hour."

Rubbers, encyclopedias, golf balls; Lyman shook his head at the incongruity of it all. He couldn't push enough of that crap to buy Cheez-its if he dressed like King Kong. He'd hoped for something that suckers would lunge for like cripples lunged

for their chairs back. But, alas, nothing here for him, unless. . .
Lyman peeked into the mirrored tray on the stringbean's chest—a
display case for sunglasses, if he knew anything about vending.

"And what're you pushing, pally?" he asked, rummaging
a finger around in the jumble of metal under his nose.

"Gasp!" Furry paw to sagging collar, "I thought you'd
never ask, sir. For you this," he said clawing out an old alarm
clock with a red button on its top where the bell should be.

"A clock?" Lyman chuffed a laugh. "Shove it," he said
brushing the stringbean aside to hoof it on up the block. "Jesus,"
he muttered, "a clock."

"Please, sir." One long, caped arm shot out to stay
Lyman. "Don't be too quick to understand it. This is no ordinary
clock. This clock's on steroids." The stringbean stood hunched
over Lyman like a praying mantis with the gizmo up before his
mask in both hands.

Who's he supposed to be now, Lyman wondered, that
Merlin guy with his crystal ball. "Yeah," he said, "Well, you c'n
take your steroids an' shove them, too!"

"But, sir, if you turn this clock backwards you'll go back
in time. If you turn it forward, you'll go forward in time."

Backward and forward in...? Lyman rolled his eyes to
the antennaed rooftops. Not just a holy roller but a Loony Toon
to boot.

Either the kid had him figured for somebody who just fell
off a turnip truck, or he'd let himself be stopped by a dip who
couldn't find his ass with both hands. Either way, he was an
even bigger dip for wasting minute one with the dude, from his
rubber widow's peek to his pruny claws the kid was a joke.

Lyman squinted up at the glint from within the mask's
eyeholes. "And people actually buy this crap?" he gruffed.

"Why. . . yes, sir," backing a step; furry paw to pencil
neck, affronted. "Hand to God, sir. It's the quickest way to a
new life."

Ha, if only. Lyman felt amused in a con-man to con-man
sort of way. But the onions on this kid, expecting to sell him on
such a pitch as time-travel! Insulting. After the blow he took to

his finances this morning, he didn't need another to his intellect. He was beginning to feel just mean enough to screw with the kid, slap his tray up, crap flying everywhere, teach him a vendor's version of *fifty-two pick up* that he'd never forget. In fact...what better did he have to do with his time? "Oh, yeah?" he said warming to the idea. "Quanto, Tonto?"

"Oh, ye of little faith. Pray, try it before you buy it, sir." The stringbean leaned back, holding the gizmo out to Lyman in his monster mitts.

Ho-ho, this was going to be good. He snatched the chunky gizmo out the hairy claws and hefted it. Hmm, surprisingly heavy. Solid, too. Two qualities that marks linked with value. And 'Try before you buy'—hell, no better hook than that.

Ridiculous as the kid looked in his sagging Dracula costume, maybe he shouldn't be too quick to understand him. Maybe there was something to learn here. Something he could maybe pull on somebody tonight even . . . if it wasn't too late.

Lyman leaned around the caped clown for a gander at the Great White Way still inviting in the distance: traffic flowing; hordes still crossing at the green and not in between. Yeah, maybe tonight even. And if this scam's already old down here maybe he could still pull it off in the Bronx. Bronxites were forever behind the curve when it came to the scams springing up in Manhattan.

"How do I use it?" Lyman said eying the gizmo's five dials, one within the other, labeled Year, Month, Day, Hour and Minute.

"Simple, sir. You turn the dials back in time to correct your mistakes or forward in time to see your future. Press the red button when you're ready."

"Yeah, yeah. Just tell me how ya make money with it."

"Money? Hmmm." Rubber claws stroking chalky chin.

Actors, this one would break his leash for a slab of ham, Lyman thought. Well, let's see him act his way out of this. Ha. Time travel indeed.

"Okay, sir," the stringbean piped, "Say, for instance, you're concerned for your financial future." Boy, did that hit home. "Just turn the clock ahead to see which of today's stocks has gone up the most by the time you're sixty-five and ready to retire. Then go out tomorrow and buy it."

Lyman rolled his eyes at the premise, but, going along with the gag till disproven, he spun the gizmo's dials, one by one, setting them exactly to his sixty-fifth birthday twenty-five years ahead. Then, feeling a bit silly, he pressed the jobbies' little red button.

Instantly a hot 'rush' surged through his body. He felt a singing in his bones. His knees buckled and his left hand shot out for the lamppost, the sidewalk beneath him fading in and out before his eyes. Hoo-eeee! He shook his head. Gradually, blurs in the sidewalk came into focus as cracks, then his sneakers were standing in a circle of light. Odd, there was somebody else standing in the light with him. Then the present flooded back and he remembered he was under a lamppost, at two in the morning, readying to teach a lesson to a dip dressed like Dracula. Wow, what a rush. Better'n Acapulco gold, Frankenweed even!

He pressed off the lamppost to wobble on watery legs and ran a strange-feeling hand through strange-feeling hair. He shook out his fingers like a pianist at a keyboard, then, not knowing what else to do with them, he jammed them into his chinos' pockets, hunched his shoulders against a gust of wind whipping up the block and looked around.

Imagination, or what, but had the night grown darker? He craned up at the strip of sky between the rooftops. No moon. But had there been...? Gone behind...? But, no, there were no clouds. And around him now the apartments, stores and theaters all looked different, too. More shabby maybe. Then he glanced across the street at the little bistro and his heart clutched.

The jack-o-lantern decorated window of only moments ago now stood dark, a big red FOR RENT sign plastered across its little diamond windows. How?

Lyman snapped around to a rustle under the marquee behind him. Torn playbill of an actress fluttering in the gusty wind, a spray-painted moustache turning her smile into a mocking smirk. Was it there before, that playbill?

Damn, either he'd just had a heart attack or this kid had one hell of a Houdini going for him here.

Then Lyman remembered: Manhattan, Theater District, actors trying out props. He slumped, his bubble burst by the dust devil swirling up the gutter toward them, nature breaking in on the kid's intended spell. He almost wished it hadn't. Lyman raised an arm to his eyes to fend off the flying debris, a sheet of newspaper wrapping around his calf. He bent to free it.

"No—read it!"

Huh? Lyman craned up at the unexpected command; had he missed a spot on this piece of fruit? He rose, slowly; eyeing the tall stringbean staring down at him from over his shoulder, caped arms folded over starched shirtfront like Dracula playing Batman. Or was he Mussolini now with his chin hiked up like a chorus girl's tits? Hmmph, actors. Lyman opened the paper and held it up to the lamplight. The front page of The Wall Street Journal. And, dated twenty-five years ahead...right to his birthday! How? Featured was an article on Archer-Cardin, an advisory firm that took five percent from every one of the Fortune 500 companies.

"Top stock over last quarter century," the caption read. Lyman studied the accompanying chart showing that every dollar invested twenty-five years ago—which was today—would have returned ten thousand dollars on his sixty-fifth birthday.

How had the kid...? Lyman spun about, half expecting to see prop men stepping out of doorways, popping up out of garbage cans, rolling out from under cars with battery-powered fans and sheets of newspapers in their hands. But no. And even if. How could they know his age, his very birthday? And make the paper blow right to him?

Oh, he'd learn this trick. He'd learn it if he had to kick it out of the kid. But first do the math like a mark would, gauge the scam's 'sucker effect.

Ten of the two hundred bucks he could get for hocking his jewelry would return him one hundred grand; a hundred would bring him a million. And his whole two hundred would bring him . . . two million dollars!

Wow, would this pitch ever appeal to the larceny in men's hearts. A mark could be made to feel happy washing dishes for twenty-five years thinking he had that much loot coming. And Lyman could already think of an even better way to pitch the scam. Tell the mark to bet tomorrow's horses, fights, ball games. That way his profits would be immediate, ultimately bigger—and bookies didn't stiff you for taxes. No need to wait twenty-five years for your money this way, pally. And in twenty-four hours he'd be long gone.

Considering the size of New York, he could work this gig forever, never pitching the same neighborhood twice. But if this time-travel business was the hook, what was the catch? In a scam this technical, the profit would have to be big, way big, to be worth its while. Wait'll the dip finds out all I got on me is forty bucks. What you get for not qualifying your mark, sucker.

Lyman yawned and stretched the stiffness out of his bones. Fordham Road all the way down to Manhattan's theater district—whew, and he was only forty. God, he felt eighty. But this was no time to stop. Learn now, rest later. He turned the gizmo's dials back to the present and looked about him. Now we'll see how this trick works. He pressed the red button.

Nothing. Silence as dense as the night around him. He pressed the button again. Again nothing. Then again and again. Behind his shoulder that fluttering sound. He spun about to see the actress's smirking smile. "Silly boy; time travel, indeed," it seemed to mock.

And just when he thought he had life's problems licked. The kid really had him going. He cocked his head up to the chalky mask with its black lips and bloody red canines.

"Whaddya do, Dracky-poo, gimme the broken one? What's the point' a showin' a mark his future if he can't go back to buy into it? Here, keep your piece of crap." Lyman tossed the gizmo into the tray, when he suddenly glimpsed himself in its mirror. Whoa!

His hands flew up to his cheeks and his eyes bulged out like stalks. He stared, transfixed, at the wizened face with its elfin ears and hairy nostrils bulging out at him like a fun mirror, its shocked-wide eyes and wrinkled chin quivering in fear. From cracked lips came an anguished wail and Lyman recognized the voice as his own.

"Easy, easy, sir," the stringbean piped. "Don't panic. It works. 'Knock and ye shall enter,'" he said pressing the clock back into Lyman's hands, "Set it forward another…"

"The hell…"

"No, no. Just for another minute, sir. Please. Time it by your own watch. It works—see if it don't."

"It fuckin' better."

Lyman snatched up the gizmo, nudged its minute dial exactly one increment ahead and eyed his watch's second hand coming up on 2:09. He pressed the button, felt the sidewalk ripple beneath his feet and saw the hand sweep across 2:10. Whew, success. He looked up at the kid, embarrassment wrestling with relief, and got a caped shrug that said *I told you so.*

Lyman smiled back at the veined-nosed, picket-toothed grin in the mirror. No more for you, pally. Ever so carefully he turned all five of the gizmo's dials back to the present. Then, double-checking to see that he'd made no mistakes, he offered a shaky smile up to the kid and pressed the gizmo's button.

The wizened face in the mirror eyed him, expectant, seconds ticking. Then the wrinkled chin began to quiver again, the hesitant grin morphing into a sickly frown, and Lyman felt a worm of fear begin to gnaw in his gut.

He peered up at the dirty, old buildings looming over him, milky windows in their dark facades peering back down at him like blind men's eyes. Never had night felt so ominous.

Enough! He wanted out of this scam, to be away from this spooky kid. But not frogged like this. He winced at the decrepit face in the mirror and the cadaverous face winced back.

God! Don't panic. Panic only plays into a con man's hands. "Listen!" Lyman snarled, nothing summoning courage quicker than trying to recover from looking stupid. "You said *forward* for future and *back* for back—right?"

"Wrong. I said you could go forward or back. I never said you could do both, sir. Both would be greedy, avarice. Avarice is one of the seven deadly sins."

"Why, you holy rollin'...." But something told Lyman to cool it; he no longer felt strong enough to kick a hole in a wet paper bag. "Okay, okay," he wheezed, collecting himself, "how do I get outta this?"

"You could buy another clock, sir."

"Oh, so ransom's the game. Dupe the mark into thinking you stole his life with the first clock, then scare 'im into buying another to get it back—right? Cute. But I been in worser spots, pally." The scam's catch divulged, Lyman permitted himself a smug smile. "So," he said rocking up on his toes, "push a lot of these gizmos, do you?"

"Sir, there isn't a billionaire on the planet who doesn't own one. Are you sure I can't sell you one, too?"

Lyman almost thought he saw old Lugosi smile. "Okay, kid. What the hell, ya got me fair an' square. You can take that silly mask off now an' tell me what's your price."

"Oh, come now, Mr. Lyman," the stringbean said in a deep, mellifluous voice, while bowing his mask to reveal stubby horns and a black goatee, "I think you know the price."

HUNGRY, THEY JUST KEEP COMING ONE BY ONE
Beauty and grace once blessed this place. Angels guarded the
door. Now beauty's dead, the angels have fled and Grace is the
local whore.   –Unknown

THE AMAZON
An Excerpt from a Novel of Adventures in the Remote South
American Jungles

The eight, raft-like diving platforms proceeded up the
river in tandem at four knots, their bows pushing little wakes
fifteen feet apart. There were six men to a raft, forty-eight men
in all. In the overhang above them, spider monkeys screeched
and macaws squawked. Secured to each platform's stern were
two 250 hp Merc outboards; one churning at half speed, the other
tilted up out of the water, cutting drag.

Save for each rafts' helmsmen, the other five men lounged
on crates and barrels in flowery shirts, cutoffs, sockless in their
boots. They scratched their stubble, occasionally yanked their
baseball caps and planters' hats down against the bright sun.
With boom boxes playing, they drank, waved off insects, joked
and boxed the colorful balloons tethered to their rafts' air hoses,
compressors   and   generators...outward-bound   vacationers
exploring the Amazon's western tributaries.

From the youngest member--a big, blond, pony-tailed ox
of a youth aboard the lead platform--to the oldest--a stocky,
fortyish, gray-stubbled Mexican in a sombrero and green poncho
on the last platform--the forty-eight revelers made quite a sight:
here in the depths of the Western Amazon Basin, such a massive
intrusion or partying vacationers was never seen. For from here
to the Eastern foot of the Andes Mountains stretched nothing but
jungle undisturbed for millenniums.

Suddenly the ox-like youth heaved himself up out of a coil of rope and peered forward shading his eyes. "Opening ahead," he shouted pointing to a break in the jungle wall on the river's left bank. Down the line of rafts over the drone of outboards past, "Opening ahead!" Instantly the horseplay stopped, the revelers jumping up and shading their eyes to see. On drawing nearer to the opening, a loom appeared in their vision, then cooking fires surrounded by thatched huts--a village!--Indians swarming to the river's edge. On the platforms came, the revelers waving and raising their bottles to the stupified Indians.

When all eight rafts were abreast of the crowd, the stocky Mexican raised his bullhorn and called out over the procession's drone, "Left flank!" The eight dive platforms executed left turns as one, closed ranks and headed in for the shore; eight bows abreast, plowing an unbroken, little green wave before them.

The revelers shouted greetings to the Indians in Tupi and Guarrani, extended their bottles, blew party favors and yanked their balloons up and down. Several men tooted New Year's horns.

The Indians, some two hundred strong, in feathers, paint and skins crowded the shore, their children jumping up and down. The helmsmen nudged their platforms up to the river's bank before them, then opened their Mercs' throttles to hold them steady against the slight current.

The revelers twisted round to their crates and barrels over the churning drone and when they turned back, their bottles were gone and in their hands were MAC-10s, AK-47s and Uzises.

"Aim high," the Mexican bull-horned as the weapons bucked into action.

Screams pierced the morning air as the Indians leapt, spun, jerked and twitched under the withering fusillade. Through a rising mist of red, automatic fire diced the crowd's front ranks like a Veg-o-matic on high. Behind the back-flying bodies the rest of the tribe scattered like roaches for the jungle wall.

"Runners out!" the Mexican bull-horned over the chattering fusillade. The racket ceased and, with the blond ox leading, three men on each raft dropped their weapons, pulled their stun guns and sprang ashore, above them creature screams in the two-hundred-foot high trees; behind them their comrades cheering them on.

The runners leaped the dead bodies before them, fanning out swiftly, merging into the ranks of the fleeing Indians, ignoring adults, girls and the smallest children; shocking down only the tribe's middle aged boys then racing on to stun as many more as they could before the remains of the tribe disappeared into the jungle wall where they would not follow.

In minutes the raid was over, sprawled bodies carpeting the compound, furious thrashing in the jungle growing fainter. "Guards out!" The Mexican bull-horned.

Two more men from each raft leaped ashore, shotguns cocking, and fanned out in a semicircle facing the village's jungle wall, ready to discourage any counter attacks while the runners dragged the stunned boys back to their respective platforms where they laid them on their stomachs and tied their wrists to their ankles behind their backs.

"Vamos," the Mexican bull-horned. Then, when all were aboard, "Back," he bull-horned. The synchronized helmsmen threw their outboards into reverse, all eight rafts backing out into the river as one and, on the Mexican's command, backed around to face down river. In line again, they lowered their second Mercs into the water and pulled both throttles out to their stops.

The crews stumbled and lurched for holds as the rafts' bows rose up out of the water onto twin-hulls. Back down the river they skimmed now, eight diving platforms in line making 15 knots under dense jungle overhang.

"Count off," the Mexican bull-horned over the multi-engine roar.

"Two!" the pony-tailed ox, whose raft was now eight, shouted to a man on raft seven.

"Plus three makes five!" shouted that man to another on raft.

"Plus four makes nine!" shouted a man on six to the men on raft five, and so on till, "Plus two makes twenty-three!"

shouted a man on raft two to the thickset Mexican whose raft was now one.

The Mexican sat facing backward on a barrel, legs spread, bullhorn and left hand on one knee, his right hand on the other, his poncho billowing up green around him. He nodded over the river roar, acknowledging the count then crabbed around on his barrel, fished out a scrap of paper and a pencil, licked its tip and, adding the four aboard his platform, wrote a jittery 27 on it in his palm. Bueno, he thought, Senor Rhinoman will be pleased. He swiped off his bandana and shook out his long gray hair to the river's breeze.

Hungry They Keep Coming is the first chapter of a work in progress about a burned-out football star, King "Wahoo" Kelly, who finds new purpose in the Amazon jungles while searching for a giant anaconda. It is also the parallel tale of slavery and a female lawyer.

THE GAMES PEOPLE PLAY

Lucie knows Hank will be waiting for her when she arrives in Florida. He'll also know she's staying with his sister Jacky and arrange to be at her house. Lucy will, as a matter of course, play her role of aloof but charismatic businesswoman on vacation, out for a good time. Hank in turn, will function in his usual capacity as rejected but adoring swain. This year's adventure will provide extra entertainment as Hank has recently married Claire, his long-time, live in girlfriend.

Still, Lucie knows he'll show up. She doesn't want him, doesn't love him. In fact, most of the time she doesn't even like him. But for some reason he loves and wants her—always has—and that makes the game worth playing.

In Jacky's driveway, Hank's baby blue Cadillac convertible shimmers under the streetlight, the pearly white top a quarter-moon stretching over the stereotypical vehicle. Poor Hank. This illusion of wealth, big spender, playboy, so essential to his psyche, only typecasts him as insecure—using material objects to supplement his impotent existence. She shakes her head and grimaces as she walks beside her chattering friends toward the house where he awaits.

The party is already in progress. Jacky weaves through the crowd and embraces Lucie. "So! Welcome back to Florida!"

Jacky's estranged husband, Roland, beams down at Lucie then crushes her against his chest. "Love the feel of those great tits!" He glances at his wife's flat bosom and grins broadly as he releases Lucie. Hank waits next in line.

She sums up his condition as normal for eleven o'clock—only about half shitfaced. She notes that he has put on weight since the last time she saw him. His shirt stretches tightly across his stomach. He's a big man with small hands and feet. She glances down, checking the toes of his shoes, gratified to see the ends still curling up from buying a larger than necessary size. His wavy hair, longer than usual, isn't properly styled, giving him a sort of rumpled Ted Kennedy look.

He reaches for her hand, draws her to him and brushes her lips with his. "Good to see you," he says eyes alight with pleasure. Over his shoulder, Lucie scans the crowd then steps back. "Where's your wife?" she asks, one eyebrow raised, a smile spreading across her face. Hank throws back his head and laughs aloud. "I think she's at home." Lucie knows they've tossed the dice and spun the wheel. Let the games begin.

The evening progresses according to guidelines set long ago, in another life. They dance and chat, he fetches her drinks, following her from room to room. Lucie bestows part of her attention on him, but not too much, concentrating instead on another available man and acting interested in his offer to leave the party and go night clubbing. She can't decide if she's really attracted to the man, then decides he's just a diversion until Hank's next move.

Right on time, Hank seems to have picked up his cue. He approaches and tucks her arm through his in a proprietary manner. "We're all moving on to another party. You can ride with me." Lucie blinks and sidesteps—too much to drink she realizes, her reflexes are slow. She disengages her arm, smiles and says, "I don't think so."

"It's okay," Hank argues, pulling her back against him. "Jacky'll ride with us. You're safe!" The sly smirk she has always associated with deceit, slides across his face and lingers. But Jacky heads toward the door behind them and Lucie decides to let him play this round his way.

He slips too quickly into the driver's seat and starts the car. He hasn't opened the door for her. Whoa! He loses points for that. She slides into the car, holding the door open for Jacky who is crossing the front yard. Hank guns the engine and careens out onto the street. The jolt slams Lucie's door shut and she looks back to see Hank's sister standing under a streetlight looking bewildered.

Lucie twists back around and leans as far into the corner of the seat as possible. Hank's smile, no longer deceptive, shines triumphantly from his eyes as they meet hers. She's been outplayed but it's no time to show her hand. She'll start the necessary repartee to cover her losses.

"Kidnapping is a federal offense, you know." She relaxes into the plush seat and stretches her arm along the back in what she hopes is a pose of nonchalance. You can go directly to jail without collecting your two hundred dollars for this."

He picks up the challenge without a hitch. "Well, you took a—'Chance Card'. His hand drifts from the steering wheel to her knee. "And who would I send the ransom note to, may I ask? I'm still the person who wants you the most."

Lucie considers his comment as she lifts his hand from her knee. "Possibly, but hardly relevant, since if memory serves me, you just got married. By the way, won't your bride be wondering where you are?"

He nods. "I'm sure she will. However, I'm going to take you to see a really great show. You'll love it. Twin piano players. You always loved piano." Lucie knows he holds the high cards for now. He parks under a giant, neon keyboard and they go inside. Hank over tips the hostess and procures a table directly in front of the stage. Lucie settles in for an entertaining evening. Hank can always be depended on for diversion—of one sort or another. She won't be bored.

After the last show Lucie glances at her watch. Nearly three-thirty. Weaving her way through the smoke-filled club she zigzags to the restroom. Notes from the finale tinkle and skip through her mind as she combs her hair and stares at her wilted face in the mirror. "Lucie girl, you're shitfaced!" she exclaims to her sagging image. The good news is, Hank's bound to be drunker than she. He always is.

Leaving the restroom she tries to get her bearings. Lumps of people stick out through hazy clouds of dim lights and smoke. She can't remember which way to go to find her table. She panics. This game has turned into a maze and she can't find her way out. Then she remembers she only needs to find the stage, the brightest lights, and she spots Hank's hulking shape outlined in the murky distance.

Relief floods her body and for a moment she weakens. He appears so familiar, so solid, so—always there for her. She shakes her head clearing away cobwebs from old memories and knows this moment for what it is—a bizarre illusion. He is none of those things. Hank has never been the oasis of her emotional desert. She's just drunk and sentimental. The stakes are too high to begin thinking like this.

They leave the club and drive, who knows where, until Hank pulls up in front of a hotel. He takes her hand and says softly, "Come on. Let me have the rest of the night with you." She detects a red light going off in her addled head, a tilt sign flashing a warning yet she allows him to steer her through the revolving door up to the desk clerk. He signs the register with a flourish, Mr. and Mrs. Harrison Maxwell. "Has a familiar ring to it doesn't it?" he asks, leading her to the elevator.

In the glitzy room he undresses and slides between the satin sheets. "Come on," he urges, "I just want to hold you." Sitting on the side of the bed she considers her options—win, lose or draw. She'll sleep with him but there will be no sex. They both know that. During their ten years of marriage his chronic impotence has been an embarrassment to him and a source of frustration to her. She'll have to settle for a draw.

Removing her clothes, she slips into bed, her back to him. He stretches against her body in spoon position, his arm tense beneath her breasts. His breath is hot as he whispers into her ear, "I don't care what happens tomorrow. No one can ever take away tonight."

As Lucie drifts off to sleep, she reflects on their foolish, almost childish game. There's a good chance something similar will happen again next year. She just doesn't know why.

SAILOR BEWARE

The night before we leave on our two-week, Bahamas excursion, the phone rings.

"Hi, this is Danny down in the Keys. I hear you guys are flying a private plane back from the Bahamas and can bring my son back with you."

My brow furrows and I shoot an aggravated look at my husband. "No, Dan, I'm afraid not. I don't know where you heard that." I answer. "Jim, a friend of ours is a passenger on our companion boat and we promised he could fly back with us. It's a four-passenger plane. Of course, a pilot flies it over from Fort Lauderdale, so that's a full load coming back. Besides which, we have a lot of diving equipment."

The news of another child accompanying us on our Bahamas trip comes as a surprise. Our hosts, Sue and Roger Brake, friends for several years, have two children, ages eight and eleven. They will of course, be members of our entourage but there's been no inkling of another child joining the group for our three-week voyage on Roger's fifty-foot trimaran.

Danny seems somewhat disgruntled. "I sure hate to have Kevin fly that island shuttle alone. I wish Roger'd get his stories straight. Oh well, there's nothing I can do now. The boat left

Marathon two days ago." With Kevin's return arrangements up in the air, I agree to tell Roger that Danny called when we meet the boat in Miami tomorrow.

Rupert and I discuss the new ramifications. Between the two of us we have raised six children and are cognizant of what the sum of one fifty-foot boat, three children, assorted animals, plus three weeks equals—possible insanity. Then we consider the alternative. Sitting by our front door are boxes of borrowed videos and supplies purchased solely for this adventure: cases of beer, wine and soda, various sun lotions, blocks and soothing creams, fishing gear, mats for sunbathing on the deck, and many bags of unfamiliar canned goods which we would never consider eating at home.

Besides this we have contributed several hundred dollars to Sue's kitty that I assume will include the purchase of rice, pasta dry goods and paper articles already stowed aboard the vessel.

The Brake family's yearly itinerary is to cruise all summer on their trimaran, visiting many uninhabited islands. They inform us that food supplies are meager even on populated neighboring islands and the cost is prohibitive so they purchase non-perishable provisions at home and stow them on board.

Rupert and I are a stalwart pair and decide to go for it, children and all, and the following evening my son-in-law drives us to Miami. From the dock we spot the triple-hulled boat moored out in the harbor. We whistle and wave to our friends milling around on ITASHA's deck and the deck of a companion trawler commanded by Jack and Brigitte. The setting is perfection: boats bobbing gently in a protected harbor, sunset embellishing the sky, the seductive scent of salt-laden breezes teasing the senses. I inhale deeply and smile at Rupert. Surely a heavenly vacation awaits us.

Roger and Sue gallantly relinquish the master cabin and their king-size bed which occupies the main room of the boat, a combination bedroom, kitchen and living area. They opt to bunk with the children in the forward cabin where there is also a large bed. This arrangement suits us just fine. When we retire we open the hatch over our bed and are rewarded with an evening sky studded with stars. The compressor hums, the pulsing air conditioner freshens our bedchamber and the icemaker clunks frozen consignments of cubes into the proper receptacle. This is roughing it smoothly.

We wake early. We do, after all, sleep in the kitchen and children rise with the sun. As I search for paper plates to serve breakfast, outside the door I hear the ship's radio broadcasting today's weather, six to eight foot waves.

"We can't sail today," Roger announces," it's too choppy. The family will get seasick." This is the first I have heard about his family not being good sailors. I find it odd since the family has lived aboard the ITASHA all their lives and every summer when the school term ends, Roger and Sue up anchor and cruise the islands until fall.

There have been hints from Sue that she is less than pleased with this arrangement—both living quarters and summer vacation activities, but apparently Roger is king of his castle. I have called him a male chauvinist in the past and am sincerely convinced that Sue believes her fate would be that of a bag lady if Roger hadn't married her.

They are a tall, slim, handsome couple. A boat mechanic, Roger's nails are never free of imbedded grease. He bears a striking resemblance to an imaginary pirate with thick, black hair, sun-browned face and gleaming eyes. The only thing lacking is an eye patch.

Despite her forty-five years and two marriages, Sue seems naïve. Her vacillating personality makes her a bit difficult to figure out. However, living for twelve years aboard a boat attests to her good nature. Her outstanding feature, shoulder-length, blonde sun-streaked hair, frames a face abundant with smile wrinkles. Katherine, the daughter, is a clone.

We spend the day reading, sunbathing and swimming beside the boat. The boys, Kevin and Joe, buzz around the bay in the dinghy. Later in the day Roger and Sue ferry the kids to shore for ice cream. That night Jack and Brigette and Jim ferry over from their boat and we play Trivial Pursuit.

It's a pleasant, lazy day in Miami's harbor but we're getting anxious to sail away to exotic lands. Besides which, the absence of paper goods has become apparent as we are using regular plates for meals and are washing dishes. I'm not particularly happy about this turn of events. I question Sue about the omission of paper plates and her answer is vague.

"Well, Roger says paper makes too much garbage to dispose of and besides, he likes to get back to nature when we sail. He really doesn't approve of paper plates."

I suggest that Roger do the dishes every night. The arrangement is for one couple to cook and the other couple to clean up every evening on alternate days. The rest of the time it's everyone for himself. So far this works.

The next day dawns clear and sunny. Today Rupert and I rush to the marine radio for the forecast. Again Roger turns thumbs down on crossing the open water because of choppy sea. He radios Jack of his decision and our group disbands to execute their individual missions. Rupert and I grouse to each other quietly.

"Are we going to sit in this harbor for three weeks?" I ask. "What if the weather doesn't break?" He suggests we take the dinghy to shore. We tour the mall, buy funny-looking boating hats we don't need and eat lunch. On our way back to the dinghy I stop at a grocery store and buy Oreos. The kids have already devoured three weeks of my cookie ration—three weeks worth.

The new ones I will hide under a seat with the rest of our provisions. I also purchase paper plates, cups and napkins—not so many as to be insulting but enough to make a point.

The third day we wake to chaos as Roger finally reels in the anchor. Everyone scurries around 'battening down the hatches,' readying for our first day at sea. I'm psyched. My husband and I are both good sailors and love the ocean. Followed closely by Jack, the two boats motor out of the harbor at last.

Inside the cabin I observe Sue dispensing seasick pills. Shortly thereafter they all disappear into the aft cabin where they spend the day sleeping. Roger steers the boat to open water and sets the controls to autopilot. The sails will be raised only once on this voyage as Roger finds the task of raising and lowering sails too strenuous. The three of us lie back, basking in the shimmering rays of nirvana and inhaling the brisk ocean breezes.

Later that day Roger anchors in the bay of an uninhabited island. Sue, Brigette and I swim to shore with the children and investigate. The beach defies comparison—deserted, sand clean and white and dotted with large conch shells. The men don scuba masks and prepare to dive for our supper. Lobster, being out of season, they will spear whatever edible fish is unlucky enough to swim past. Although Roger's method of cooking seems rather primitive, we dine on fresh some-kind-of fish, rice and canned vegetables.

The kids pick at their food and another family secret comes to light. Sue's children are not overly fond of fish. We discuss supplies and first realize that we have only limited refrigeration. To make ice cubes or keep food cold the generator must always run. So far the generator has only run at night to facilitate watching movies on the VCR and to run the AC. Within a few days we will be eating canned meat or dining exclusively on whatever fish the men catch. The children don't look happy. I am less than thrilled with the menu myself.

The next day we are enlightened on the art of water conservation. Roger jumps to turn off the faucet when Rupert begins his morning wash–up. "We never let the water run. Also, use a cup filled with water to brush your teeth." Captain Brake specifies that no one showers with fresh water. (Sometimes he allows one shower a week as a treat.) Each day after swimming, we wash with a special salt-water soap we purchased, only by chance, at a boating store before leaving. We then rinse off with fresh water doled out meagerly, cup by cup, usually run-off from the air conditioner.

Shortly thereafter, I realize with a start that the water coming from the hose used to wash the dishes comes directly from the ocean. Sue adds a cupful of Clorox to the dishwater but it is still bay water. I ponder the philosophy of this hygienic enigma, since the toilets of our boat and any others in the bay, empty into this same water after being ground up by the macerator.

After delving deeper into the water dilemma and reducing the problem to its lowest level, the reason for all this rationing becomes apparent—Roger is cheap. The water tank holds eighty gallons. Water bought in the Bahamas is expensive and Roger refuses to pay the price. I sigh with relief. Fresh showers are on the way. *We* can pay for the water. But now Rupert becomes stubborn.

"No, I won't," he says. This being uncharacteristic I inquire, "But why not?"

"Because we brought presents for everyone. I'm paying my share of the gas. I gave Sue money for God only knows what, we brought food, wine, beer and liquor. I'll be damned if I'm paying for all the water." He looks me in the eye.

"Besides, he'll still keep his family rationed and if we use a lot of water, we'll look like assholes. I won't do it." I've heard that men's personalities change when they go to sea. Roger's identity has altered and now Rupert's temperament seems about to metamorphose. I decide not to push the issue at this time.

The days begin to follow a basic pattern—tidying up in the morning, proceeded by the men departing soon after lunch to fish for dinner.

Because Roger doesn't Scuba dive, " Rupert complains, "Jack and Jim and I haven't put our tanks on once. He only anchors the dinghy in a few feet of water and we all have to free dive to spear fish." He pouts.

"Then why don't you and Jack and Jim go alone in *Jack's* dinghy?" I ask. Rupert smiles and calls Jack on the radio who soon comes alongside to pick Rupert up. Roger casts off alone accompanied by the boys, and now Roger pouts.

Sue starts imbibing beer around noontime. The first few days she cooled the brew but now drinks it warm, directly out of the case she keeps on deck. I suggest a game of Scrabble but after spelling out a few words her mind wanders and she begins to complain about Roger: living on the boat, sailing every summer, all summer, and life in general. Later she retires to her cabin to sleep off her buzz. I read and do crossword puzzles. Katherine plays Barbie.

As the sun sets after dinner, we all sit on deck playing games or watching Rupert, Kevin and Joe fish for sharks. The boats anchored in the harbor throw out scraps every night after mealtime and sharks are scavengers. In the Bahamas bays we do not swim off the side of the boat. These monsters circle the boat snapping up skeletons of fish we served for dinner. The balance of nature at its finest.

It's exciting to hear the reel go ZZZZZZ as the creatures take the bait and run. We all jump to the edge of the boat to witness duplicates of the infamous "Jaws" before Rupert cuts the line. The boys are especially thrilled with this sport. Although Joe lives on the boat, he has never owned a fishing rod. Kevin's father, Danny, works as a charter captain and Kevin easily falls in beside Rupert attaching hooks, rigging and baiting lines. The ripening sunset overwhelms the vibrant horizon and suddenly today's petty dissentions become trivial.

Happily, the children have turned out to be a delight. Kevin and Joe entertain each other playing cards and games, swimming and jockeying around in the dinghy, then sleep on deck at night under the stars. Katherine is a solitary little girl who, when not clinging to her mother's shorts, sits quietly playing with her Barbie dolls and occasionally tries, without success, to join the boys at play. As with all children, they are all constantly hungry and food disappears as though by magic.

We are happy to hear that our next stop, Chubb Cay, will have a grocery store, a Laundromat and a club with a restaurant. I relish the idea of tying up to the dock, hooking up to fresh water, plugging in the electric, washing clothes, buying fresh meat and dining out. Next day before we travel, Sue drugs the kids and we set sail, quite literally, for the only time on our three-week trip. Flapping sails filling with wind, spray gushing across the bow as we slice through white-capped water, nothing but sea and sky surrounding us, creates a fantasy come true. My other fantasies, however, are short-lived.

Roger aborts my first daydream by anchoring the boat well away from land. I rush to Rupert's side and whisper desperately, "Aren't we going to dock? Plug in the electric? Hook up to fresh water." I gulp. "Go out to lunch?" I sense my eyes glaze over as he takes my hand and lowers me gently to a folding chair.

"Janet, I doubt that we will ever dock," he explains calmly through clenched teeth. "Don't forget, that would cost money."

A subliminal message of, *So near and yet so far,* floats between myself and the distant island community and for the first time in my life I wish to walk on water.

In due course, on the second run, Rupert and I dinghy to shore where we transform the gamy laundry to sweet smelling clothes once again. From there we hurry to the grocery where other surprises await us. There is no bread. The baker left the island yesterday to see a doctor in Nassau. He may be back tomorrow. 'Fresh' meat consists of hot dogs and square boxes of frozen chicken.

We console ourselves with a quickly eaten ice cream sandwich and head for the restaurant where we savor the absolutely most perfect lamb chops I have ever eaten. The boys play ping-pong and ride back to the boat with us. At dinner the kids devour the hot dogs as though they were steak. Roger, the great white hunter, has not purchased any food.

Our excursion will not extend to many islands. We up-anchor only twice more—once to another uninhabited island and then back to Chubb Cay where there is an airport. Petty annoyances crop up daily now. The Brake family, although they have always lived aboard ship, are a disorganized group. When they are finished with an object, it lies where they get done with it. The most prevalent sentence in the Brake family being, "Where is it?" This becomes so flagrant that Rupert and I, being very tidy souls, end up mocking them with, "Wherizzit? Wherizzit?" Their smiles are becoming stiff.

Rupert becomes protective of his possessions. No one washes out his Scuba masks after using them or returns them to his dive bag. His fishing rods have been left out of the holders. Tangled lines straggle across the already cluttered deck. He now locks his tackle box and stows his dive bag below deck.

Sue's mood swings are hard to follow. Most afternoons she bitches about Roger and eating fish but at the dinner table she oohs and aahs. "Oh Rog, this fish is sooo good!" Roger, coerced into playing Pictionary, runs true to form and reacts badly when he loses. Ice cubes are made only at night and squabbled over in the morning. On the bright side, I believe I have terminated the life of the gigantic cockroach that leaps out at me every night when I use the head. Thank you, RAID!

Although the high points of this adventure compensate for the adversities, we begin to anticipate our own homecoming. We also wonder what they are saying about us. Paranoia sets in. During the last week there begins to be talk of how Kevin will get home.

"Oh, why doesn't he just stay with us all summer?" asks Sue in her inimitable air-headed way. Roger appears less than happy about the idea. (Another mouth to spear for?)

Rupert suggests consulting Kevin. "Look Kevin, we're leaving soon and this is the last island with a shuttle to Fort Lauderdale. Do you want to spend all summer on the boat?"

Kevin's answer is an emphatic, "NO! Will someone please call my father?"

Now the 'passing the buck' interlude begins, the proverbial straw that fractures the now frail link between the Brakes and the Staudners. Roger, that old rogue Roger, calls Danny. Calling the United States from the islands requires patience and money. Since Jim, our friend on the other boat, is the only one with an AT&T credit card, ultimately, all calls will be charged to him. Roger will not pay even though he originally requested Kevin's presence as a companion to Joe.

Traversing like a downhill racer, in the next two days Captain Bly neatly sidesteps out of making the somewhat knotty arrangements for Kevin's return. Rupert becomes the designated travel agent. Hostility crackles in the air like heat lightning. All boat conversations become short and to the point. After two days of trips to shore, phone calls and other maneuvering, Rupert at last lines up *two* planes slated to arrive tomorrow that will ferry Jim, Kevin, Rupert and I together with tons of diving gear back to Fort Lauderdale for a reasonable fee. Danny will pay for the second plane.

That afternoon, those of us that are still speaking, Jim, Jack and Brigette and ourselves decide to eat at the club for lunch. We offer to treat but the Brake's beg off. Later they load the kids in the dinghy and head for shore. I jump into the shower and wallow in fresh water singing "na-na-na-na-na-na," like a misbehaving child.

The next day Sue and the children remain on board while Roger silently ferries us to shore. We stack our luggage, dive gear and fishing equipment beside the tiny airport runway and say our good-byes. Token hugs had accompanied our arrival, clipped thank-you's and brief handshakes signal our departure—living proof that within the confines of a boat at least, familiarity does indeed breed contempt.

THE ULTIMATE SIN

I remember he's dead the instant I wake. Valium makes my head fuzzy but I'm not likely to forget that. I slide out of bed and glance down at my wrinkled clothes. I've fallen asleep fully dressed. It's also very late. The old joke about being late for your own funeral pops into my head. Only it isn't my funeral, it's Jack's. I open the door a crack and call, "Mom?" She's here so quickly I think she camps outside my bedroom door.

"Please take the girls to the funeral home for me," I ask. "I've overslept and someone should be there early." She objects, as I knew she would, doesn't want me left alone. Alone sounds good right now. My children's eyes are asking too many questions. The answers can't be put off forever but they won't be resolved today. For now I'm only safe in a crowd.

I wear the gray dress I bought for his sister's wedding. It isn't black but I'm not playing the grieving widow—just the widow. Gray is a rather indecisive color and suits my mood. Besides, I'll get some wear out of the dress. I try on a hat then throw it back in the closet. It looks old fashioned and I'm a modern woman. I've proved it.

I lock the front door and glance over at Jack's bike leaning against the garage. It needs repairs. The car hasn't been starting well either. Jack promised to fix it but never did. Just like all his other promises. I turn the key hoping the engine won't catch but today it coughs and starts right up. I mutter under my breath, "Wouldn't want to miss your wake, would I Jack?"

As I drive, raindrops splash against the windshield. Shifting nervously in my seat, I reflect on the weather and what a perfect setting it is for a wake; clouds, rain and gloom. Ahead on the right a small roadside sign announces HILL'S FUNERAL HOME. I scan the row of cars and recognize every one of them. It's a small family.

The building appears as weather beaten as I feel. Both of us could use some sprucing up. The tires crunch against the gravel driveway and grate in my ears. I approach the entrance door warily. The funeral director recognizes me and grasps my elbow in a firm grip as though I might try to escape.

The cloying smell of flowers chokes me and I dig in my purse for a tissue. Actually this serves a dual purpose. Some of his family may think I'm crying, but that isn't true. I doubt if I'll ever cry again. My tears ran out ages ago. I finally realized that Jack would always be an unfaithful, thoughtless, self-centered bastard. There, it feels good to get that out.

Ahead of me, my teenage daughters stand to one side of the casket. They are unprepared for death and are dressed in dark cotton skirts. Their blouses hang limp and untucked from their slender waists. I notice their heads covered with squares of black lace. An added attraction by Jack's Catholic mother, no doubt. My heart twists and reaches out to them, the innocent victims of this tragedy. As I pass between the chairs, I hear Jack's father sobbing. He stretches out a withered hand to the passing priest, seeking comfort. I hear him whimper; "I say my prayers for my son in French, Father."

"God understands all languages," says the priest, brushing quickly by.

"That's good to know. That really helps," I mumble to myself. The fact is my father-in-law doesn't deserve sympathy. I know for a fact that Jack's flaws were fixed long ago in childhood by this unscrupulous man. It's only life's cycle out of sync.

The room stills as I walk to the open coffin and study the waxen face, the motionless body. Unconsciously I step back expecting him to grab me like he does when he's displeased. Repressing a smile I think how displeased he must be today. But he doesn't raise his fist or open his mouth to shout in drunken fury. I marvel at how silent death is.

I feel my mother standing guard beside me. She glowers at the small crowd, daring anyone to dispute the worth of her daughter. Hostility surrounds us like a shroud. She knows the story of those years with Jack. She's my friend.

Some of Jack's relatives are here to mourn his untimely demise. No one is all bad, I guess. The others came out of curiosity. I'm here to make sure he's dead.

I peer down at my husband's face and reminisce briefly about happier times. I owe him that much. In the beginning times were good. I make a mental note to remember that fact in the future when I talk to my daughters. He's dead and they'll need some happy memories. I can do that—for them.

But blackness consumes me. My memories go back only two nights ago as I stand horrified outside my little girl's bedroom door.

I wake that night knowing something is wrong. I hear strange sounds coming from her room. Jack isn't in bed. I fumble for the gun in the bedside stand and rush to her room.

She's crying, "No, Daddy! No!" She sees me and screams, "Mommy!"

My hand is steady as he leaps from her bed and faces me. He smirks as he walks toward me, his hand reaching out for the gun. "Go ahead," he taunts. "Shoot me!"

And I do.

A CASE OF PROCRASTINATION

Time: Mid Eighties

No one's sure when she hit town. Around Key West it's hard to tell when someone moves in for good. She drove a fancy car and wore trendy clothes the first time she visited. But after looking the situation over and being a with-it chick, she left pretty quick. When she came back she had a bike and an old pair of jeans, blending in with the regulars at SLOPPY JOE'S and the BULL, mingling with the crowd, going undercover, so to speak. Down here we're laid back. Don't generally travel too far north of Marathon Key. Sometimes we forget about the rest of the world. We just took her in, unsuspecting, gullible citizens that we are.

Now and then rumors circulated about her. She showed up in some strange places. Got caught sneaking out of a few back doors where she didn't belong. Never did find out where her money came from. It just seemed to keep slipping in, greasing the right palms, making a few changes here and there. Here in the Keys, we don't appreciate change too much. Some of us began to worry some when two big hotels started going up in town.

Well, time passed. We drank some more beer and watched a lot of sunsets. Finally decided they'd planted enough trees around the Pier House to disguise the new hotel. Blended it into the landscape so to speak. Down by County Beach they renovated the old hospital, made the inside pretty showy but the outside didn't change much. Just a facelift. She said change would be good for the economy and probably it was. So we drank another Pina Colada and sat back under our paddle fans.

When the first cruise ship docked we started the investigation. We'd never been on their route before. Why now? Tourists came pouring down the ramp of that ship, flooding every corner of town, not even leaving an empty bar stool for a late afternoon drink. She said, "Don't worry," she knew from a reliable source it would only happen twice a week. Brought a lot of money into town, helps the merchants. Everybody benefits she said. It seemed to make sense.

So we wandered over to Mallory Square catching the sunset, weaving through the masses gathered on the pier watching the entertainment, waiting for the sun to disappear below the horizon. Small boats buzzed back and forth in front of the pier, full of waving, happy folks. Everybody's soaking up the Key West atmosphere and loving it. So did we.

But what's that big building going up next to the pier? We amble over. The sign reads, "Time Share." She brushes it off too easy this time. Says they'll plant some more trees around this new building. Still, it looks pretty high for the keys, a little too modern for the Conch Republic. This needs checking out. It's crowding our sunset.

We should have suspected something was up when she disappeared last summer after making a big ruckus on the pier. Artists were being banned at night, a warrant issued for those that didn't observe the rule. Then the lowest of the low, they arrested the, "Cookie Lady!" The KEY WEST CITIZEN printed the whole story. She wants our pier and parking lot to build a dock for cruise ships! Wants to take over our sleepy little town. Make it a booming tourist trap, commercialize it, sully our quaint, old world charm. We've been had.

The time had come to smoke her out. Prove she's the villain behind the whole scheme. Make her own up to it. Run her out of town. We searched everywhere, the old conch houses, City Hall, the beaches and piano bars, stationed a guy out on A1A to watch for her in case she tried to sneak away. But she'd vanished. No doubt hiding out, waiting for just the right time to come creeping back. So, the case is still open. We haven't solved the mystery yet. Did find out her name though.

They said it was: PROGRESS.

Notes on the Short Stories:

Motivation behind a short story varies to such a degree it is difficult to pinpoint where a story originates. Often a personal experience or that of an acquaintance becomes the germ of an idea. Once embedded, springs to life. After painstaking nurturing, a touch of embellishment and skillful wordplay, the tale emerges and blooms.

VENGEANCE IS MINE

Standing slightly behind the stewardess at the open doorway of the jet, Jacob's brown eyes scanned the long line of oncoming passengers. Only a slight twitch of his dark mustache revealed the tension playing havoc with his mind.

Before coming to Miami Airport, Jacob had driven aimlessly in his rental car, savoring the warm sunshine, the brilliant scarlets and fuschias of the tropical foliage. He'd cruised east where the calm ocean sparkled, inhaling as he drove the perfume of gardenias and the fishy-salty scent of the sea. He'd absorbed the rhythm of the palms swaying in the warm spring breeze, and gazed in delight at the bright cerulean sky dotted by soft white clouds. He'd driven west to see the Everglades, the River of Grass--eternal, beckoning. And then, seeing it all, he returned to the immense terminal and parked the car.

Nothing in *his* life would be the same after today. So how could the world seem so peaceful? Was this how terrorists felt when they were about to perform their grisly deeds? But his aim was *justice.* His plan was not wrong. It was an eye for an eye. Nobody deserved death more than Chester A. Fairlane and he, Jacob, would be the instrument to make it happen.

Watching the passengers approach, Jacob's brown eyes suddenly widened. *Here he comes, the slime.* He felt euphoric as his target barreled down the crowded ramp towards him. *After 25 years of searching, he'd finally found his sister's rapist.*

Lincolnesque in a short beard and black suit, Jacob kept his gaze fastened on a shorter, pudgy man with a receding hairline and glasses. *An unlikely Romeo, but who could account for women's tastes.*

Pretending to look through the magazine rack on the wall outside the plane's tiny serving area, Jacob extracted from his wallet an old photo which he'd found in Liza's hand when she died. Yes, no doubt about it. This round-bellied guy in the tropical sport shirt and red shorts was definitely Chester Fairlane, but older. *Now, if his plan would only work.*

Jacob watched where Chester sat and followed him, pushing ahead of several passengers to climb into the empty seat beside his quarry. Had that seat been taken, he would have found a way to inveigle whoever was in it to move. As it was, he had to turn on his sweetest smile moments later to placate the lady whose boarding pass indicated he was sitting in her seat.

"I'm terribly sorry, Miss," he said. "I must have read it wrong. My seat is actually 14B. If you'll have the stewardess bring my crutch, I'll move." He made an exaggerated attempt to rise.

"A crutch? No, sit still. I'll take 14B," the lady said, moving away.

The pudgy man in the sports shirt grinned at him. "You lazy dude; you weren't limping when you sat down. I gotta remember that line. Hey, it's a nice May day for a trip, isn't it?"

Jacob's eyes narrowed. "Yes. Guess it'll be just as nice in Atlanta," he said. *But you're never going to make it, Chester*, he mused to himself.

"Hope the weather's even half as good when our city gets the Olympics this summer. Man, I'll be glad to be back home. You married?" Chester didn't wait for an answer. "Just had a visit with my third wife—ex-wife, that is—and the kids. Sure, I love my kids, but I never should have had them. I'm 49. Two by my first wife were enough, you know what I mean. These brats get on my nerves. She never disciplines 'em."

The cabin door was closed now and the flight attendant was going through his spiel about oxygen and flotation devices.

A feminine voice, the captain, announced they were waiting for takeoff.

A woman pilot. When Liza was alive, there probably weren't women pilots. Poor Liza never had a chance to do anything with her life, Jacob thought, as Chester rattled on about his wives and kids. Barely listening, Jacob said silently, *I know all about you, Chester Fairlane. I've been seeking you over half my life. Two years ago, the national phone directories and the internet led you right into my parlor.*

I know you're a computer programmer with a really bad ticker. I know you're somewhat superstitious and that you believe in dreams. I know you're on-line almost every night, at least when you aren't out chasing women, you sorry bit of detritus.

"I'll never marry again," Chester leaned back and cleaned his ear with his little finger. "There's too much sex around that a guy can get without being tied down, right?" He jabbed Jacob playfully in the ribs. "Like this hot little number on the Web. Ooooh, man! Her name's..."

...her name's "Azil"" which spells Liza backwards, idiot, Jacob said to himself. *And "Azi" is me: Jacob. And this Azil, who turns you on so much that your fingers can hardly work the keys, is how I knew you were coming to see your ex and kids. You told Azil everything; you didn't know you were wasting all that steamy sex talk on old Jacob, here.*

On and on Chester talked. Now, Jacob thought, it was time to start the plan. The plane was full, its engines warming up. Soon, they'd cruise down the runway.

"My friend," he interrupted Chester. "This plane is going to crash."

The pudgy man stopped talking and waited for the punch line. He was grinning. "Yeh?" he prompted.

"No, I'm telling you, this plane will go down."

Chester lost his smile. "Don't joke like that! It's not funny."

"No joke."

The computer ace frowned.   His hazel eyes looked troubled. He ran a hand through his thinning hair. "W-why do you think we're going to crash, man."

This was too easy. "Because I dreampt it. I dreampt it every night last week."

Jacob could see Chester's face fall. "Well now, you must not believe it or you wouldn't have gotten on the plane." Chester was trying to act indifferent but his skin looked gray.

"I'm like you," Jacob answered. "I need to go home, too. What flight I took wouldn't matter."

"Oh, sure.   Then what makes you think this flight will crash?"

"Because you were in my dream. When I came down the aisle just now and saw you sitting there beside me, I knew this was the flight."

Chester pulled a handkerchief from his pocket and mopped his brow. "Oh, Lord, why don't they turn the air on in this plane. Are you as hot as me? Geeze, it's hot."

Jacob could see his subject squirming. If Chester's heart killed him, nobody could say he, Jacob, was responsible. "Yes, it's this flight all right."

"Look, I'm stifling. I don't feel good. Can I still get off this plane? It' too damn crowded. Look at it. Every seat's filled." He unfastened his seatbelt. His eyes darted around the cabin.

Up front, a tiny bell gonged. Outside, the slam of the luggage compartment door sounded above the hum of the engines.

Sweat broke out on Chester's plump face; his upper lip and brow became drenched. "I don't believe you, you know," he said.

"And in my dreams, just as you went down you called a name: Liza."

Chester was gulping air now, one hand on his heart. "I don't know any Liza. Your dream's wrong."

"My dream showed a beautiful, very young, overly-protected dark-haired girl who adored you. But you were a hot-shot of 24; no marriage in your plans, just another "score." And she wouldn't go for one-night stands. In the guise of getting a ring, you took her out, drank a little, then raped her brutally, tearing her heart and virgin dreams to shreds."

Jacob remembered how he'd found his little sister beaten and bleeding. Berzerk with fury, he'd tried to find the attacker. She'd confided his name. But Chester Fairlane was long gone. The shame, the pain, the betrayal were more than Liza could bear and when she found she was pregnant, she killed herself. Jacob, in college, had nearly gone insane. When his heartbroken parents died within two years, Jacob became so determined to find Liza's rapist, he ruined his own happiness.

He remembered what his beautiful fiancée had told him when he arrived at their wedding two hours late after stopping to chase a clue: "Jacob, you were always the sweetest, gentlest man I ever knew. I adore you, but you're obsessed. You've put vengeance ahead of living. Goodbye." He'd been hurt, but he knew she was right. Still, he couldn't resist the search.

He never gave up hope of avenging Liza's death. When Fairlane finally re-emerged, Jacob hatched the plan.

Now, as the crowded jet revved up to depart, Jacob watched his sister's betrayer flail the air and gasp. No one else noticed Chester's death throes. People were looking out the windows, reading, talking as the big bird's engines came to life.

"My pills," the man begged before slumping in the seat with his eyes shut.

Suddenly a wave of pity and concomitant self-revulsion swept over Jacob. No way could he just sit here and watch Chester Fairlane die. Yet how could he possibly quit just as vengeance was within his grasp? Was it because the plan was working too well? All these years, the obsession, the complete ruination of his own life, of his romances...for what? He had thought Chester's death would be the ultimate closure. But no, there was no relief in this. *Let the scum go.*

Jacob threw off his seatbelt, climbed over his unconscious seatmate, and stood in the aisle. A stewardess was beside him at once. "Sir, get back in your seat, please. We're ready for take-off." Then, noticing Chester, she gasped.

"Bad heart, Miss. But I bet Mr. Fairlane carries nitro." In one swift movement, Jacob reached in Chester's shirt pocket and withdrew a packet. Extracting a pill, he slipped it under the man's tongue, then scrubbed his own hand on his jacket. "Tell him...tell him he was having a bad dream," he told the woman who softly called "Mr. Fairlane" over and over as she patted Chester's cheek.

"He's coming around!"

Yes, he'd come around. The Chester Fairlanes of the world usually made it. Jacob hurried to the cabin door. "I must depart the plane. Please let me out. And you better help your coworker back there."

After a brief hesitation, the male flight attendant opened the door, then rushed to help revive Chester. Jacob raced up the ramp seconds before it telescoped itself against the terminal.

Feeling drained and depressed, he went to a snack bar and ordered a cup of coffee. *Why had he given up his life's aim? Now there was nothing left.* He spent a long time supping the hot liquid.

Liza, I've failed you. I vowed I'd find him and see him pay, but you're dead and he's free to go on with his stupid way of life forever.

Jacob wasn't sure how long he sat at the table. When he finally dragged himself back to the concourse, he walked to the airline counter where he'd checked in over an hour before. The ticket agent had her back to him. He cleared his throat to get her attention. "Miss, my suitcase went up on your last flight but I didn't," he quipped. "Can you do something about getting it back."

Turning to Jacob, she smiled but her lip was trembling and tears clung to her cheeks. "Yes, sir. Of course we can. Which flight are you asking about, sir?"

"Let me re-check the number again, Miss." He pulled his ticket agenda from his jacket pocket and shoved it towards her.

"Here it is: *Flight #592*. I'm a pretty unlucky fellow. I didn't make my flight."

She stared at the paper Jacob gave her. "I-I'm sorry, sir. I'm afraid your luggage is lost, but if we can be of any other service...And sir, you're not unlucky. You're not unlucky at all! The Everglades...Dear God..." The young woman turned away, sobbing uncontrollably.

Puzzled, Jacob retrieved his flight agenda from the counter and stared at it. What was on that piece of paper to make her cry and say he was "lucky?" With a sigh, Jacob shrugged and walked away. After awhile, he'd ask another *ValuJet* agent. He was sorry this one was so sad.

(**Editor's note:** *At 2:04 p.m. on May 11, 1996, ValuJet Flight 592 left Miami International Airport and crashed into the Everglades killing all on board. It was an engineering disaster that some compare to the sinking of the Titanic.*)

THE FORGIVING

Katy Lester's knuckles paled as she leaned forward and clung to the dash of the small red seaplane which had taken off from Palm Beach International less than a half hour before. All above her, the blue and white magnificence of the Florida sky imbued her with freedom and omnipotence. Below, the feeling was challenged by the earthy beckoning of green sea and turquoise gulf split by a zipper line of keys. They were getting close to Perrito Key. She could sense it and was afraid.

The pilot of the amphibian, Ted Steele, was a young Tom Cruise type, clean-cut, capable, kind, and adventurous. Ted wanted her to marry him. He had asked her again, just now, playfully threatening to turn the plane upside down to help persuade her.

"Don't you dare, Teddy!" She laughed with a mirth she didn't feel. "But I do care for you, honey. Jackson did, too. I couldn't have made it after Jackson's death without you." Letting go of the dash, she brushed a strand of dark brown hair from her face and tried not to let Ted see she was also wiping her eyes.

"Katy, we're alone up here with God, the sky and the water. Tell me what keeps you tied so tightly, darling. You know Jackson'd want you to be happy." His blue eyes were soft and full of love.

Ted would be a great husband. Better, even than Jackson, with his keep-to-himself ways. But such an idea was disloyal.

She felt the tears well up in her eyes as they'd been doing so often since her husband died eight months ago. She barely heard Ted's sigh over the hum of the motor. She sensed his frustration. He should find a new woman. She was no good for him. She could never marry again.

"Look, Teddy," she said, "There's Perrito Key. Please fly to the left or right. I *can't* look at it." She pointed to a small isle far in the distance off the main chain, accessible only by boat. It belonged just to her now--a bitter reminder of her loss.

Once Perrito Key had been Eden. She and Jackson had reveled in their own private island with its little Spanish styled house, its boat landing, its beach, and its garden. Ah, its garden, her nemesis... She turned her head, refusing to allow the key into her vision.

"It's not on the charts," Steele said, banking into a slow curve that drew the plane to the right and over the gulf. "Hey, it *does* look like a little dog. That's what 'perrito' means, isn't it?" They were too far away to see more than its shape.

"Jackson named it when we first saw it from the air. Can you see what looks like a puppy's bushy tail sticking off the right? Jackson used that strip for his secret garden. He was a genius there. Planted hedges around it. Every year when we flew down to Perrito, we'd fly low over it and see what he'd planted the year before to surprise me with. Sometimes it was a rainbow arcing along the strip with red and pink hibiscus, purple flowers, yellow—all the colors. It was so gorgeous. I looked forward each visit to this treat. He loved that garden so."

"Then why don't we fly over and see it this year? It..."

"No!" She shouted.

He reacted as if she'd slapped him, then asked gently, "But why, Katy. Why? I bet he planted something there last year."

"No! There wouldn't be any...I mean..." She paused. How could she tell Ted the unforgivable thing she'd done to her husband. Trying to keep her voice light, she added, "I seldom went in his garden, anyway. It was his haven, his escape, a nook where he spent happy time alone, grafting gardenias, planting seeds, experimenting. I tried not to violate his privacy (*I was shut out.*) Oh, Teddy, *please* fly on to Key West."

Glancing at her, Steele's lips parted. He reached over and gently wiped her damp face with a finger. "You're a beautiful woman, my friend. You were good for that withdrawal fault of his. Look, don't worry. We'll be at Key West in a matter of minutes, honey." The plaintive look on his face moved her.

"You think I'm so perfect. Such a loving wife. Did it ever occur to you that I may have done something which caused your partner's death?"

"Only in your imagination, Katy. Jackson and I've known each other all our lives. We grew up together. Don't you think I'd have sensed it if you had? He'd have given it away."

"I don't want to talk about this. I'm sorry." She drew her full lips together tightly. What she'd done to Jackson, she'd done the day before he died, and Ted hadn't seen him afterwards. When Jackson found out, he scarcely spoke to her—just went off in his hidden garden. He never said, "I forgive you." If he had, she might be able to forgive herself now. But there hadn't been time. The accident. Those weeks that followed were so cruel, so full of sorrow and guilt. She'd suffered. She'd suffer till she died.

"Okay, kid, no more nagging from me. We came down to have a good time. So hang on. We're at the southernmost city in our country and here we go down." Ted nosed the plane towards the water. Despite her sadness, a sense of excitement and admiration engulfed her as she watched his strong hands twist dials and move the yoke and throttle.

They glided onto the water like a graceful egret. After docking and leaving the plane, she felt a weight lift from her shoulders. Teddy was such pleasant company and he didn't hold her attitude against her. Just for this trip she'd try to forget the past. They *would* have fun. For his sake.

"Today, Katy, we'll play tourist. We'll start with the pier, buy some souvenirs, go through the shark place, eat conch, go through Hemingway's house, buy some Key West t-shirts..."

"Stop." She laughed, feeling better already. "It sounds wonderful!" He looked the part of a vacationer in his bright sport shirt and white slacks. Before leaving the plane, he'd slung a camera around his neck. He snapped her picture as soon as she disembarked.

Following his agenda, they stopped at Key West's *southernmost point*, where a black and white sign said: "90 miles to Cuba." When a sailor offered to take the two of them together, Ted accepted. Just before the shutter snapped, he leaned close to her, placing his cheek against hers. She felt the slight roughness of his invisible beard and sensed the virile scent of his cologne. She experienced a warm, shivery sensation at the touch.

By the time they had completed all the sightseeing he'd promised, Katy had not felt so relaxed in months.

"Now, my beautiful lady, let's go find the motel rooms I phoned for, change, and go out to wine, dine, and dance."

A twinge of remorse hit her as she took his arm. She was enjoying herself too much. *Maybe I can pretend I'm someone else, she told herself. Then I won't have to feel guilty.*

After dressing in a soft blue knit gown with matching heels, she met Ted in the motel lobby. They took a cab to a restaurant overlooking the ocean. It was candlelit and romantic. The food was delicious. By the time they'd finished off the evening with wine and dancing, and headed back to the motel, Katy was spinning inside, as dizzy and elated as a teenager with her first crush.

Unlocking her door, Ted handed her the key. "It was wonderful." His voice was husky. In the dim hall light, his eyes had a sultry green look.

"Oh, yes, Teddy, so wonderful!" She reached out to hug him goodnight. His shoulders were so strong. She longed to be closer. Suddenly, his lips were on hers. Unable to help herself, she kissed him back with all the fiery passion she'd stifled for so long. Amazed, she sensed the ice of the long year break apart, deluge her with intensity, rush through her veins, erasing rational thought.   It was when Ted moaned and pulled away that she finally regained control.

"No, Katy, no!" His voice was hoarse. "I want you but not like this.   Not because I bought you too much wine."

She knew it wasn't the wine.   My Lord, she must have been in love with Ted Steele for months.   How could she feel this way so soon after Jackson?

Thinking of her husband brought Katy to reality.   Ted wanted to marry her, but... "I have to tell you what I did," she began.

"No. I love you," his voice was strained.   He almost ran to his room next to hers and shut the door.

Once in bed, Katy tossed and turned, too aware of Ted on the other side of the partition.

It was just before she finally dozed off that the memory of those last days with Jackson came back so intensely she could smell the sea air and hear the rusty-gate cries of the white gulls coasting above the surf on Perrito Key.   They had quarreled, she and Jackson.   Something silly no doubt, she couldn't recall. What she did remember was that they hadn't made love for weeks.   At first, she thought it was because of his flu, but he'd gotten over that, choosing to spend all his time in his garden, shutting her out as if she didn't count, ignoring her, taking her nowhere.   Other years they had spent much of their vacation making love so beautiful she sometimes wept.   This year, the vacation was ending and there'd been nothing.   On this next to the last day she'd tried every way she could think of to seduce him.   When nothing worked, she threw aside her pride and begged.

She could see him yet, standing in the living room looking at her, that eternal cigarette hanging out of his mouth. "Not today, Katy," he told her.   And she'd felt like a whore.   She ached to hurt him, to shake him out of his selfish complacency. She did it the cruelest way she could think of; when he went to the bedroom to take a nap, she took a hoe and mangled his stupid old garden.   Dug it all up—poinsettias, lilies, impatiens, everything—and left their dying green bodies slung in mucky piles. Now he would notice her, she told herself.

But even after he went out on the puppy's tail and saw the mayhem, he didn't let on. She knew she'd hurt him. The garden was his pride and joy. But he continued to work there even more than before, and he barely spoke to her the rest of the day and the following morning. She'd regretted her act immediately and told him so. But when he didn't respond, even with anger, she couldn't let it alone. He came back to the house at noon, perspiring and exhausted. The minute he sat down on a kitchen chair and lit a cigarette, she began on him, wanting a rise from him, a quarrel, anything except the silent treatment.

"You don't love me anymore, Jackson Lester," she screamed at him loud enough for tourists in Marathon to hear. "Well, just go on and play with your precious plants and flowers. Climb in that little chest you keep seeds and fertilizer in and sleep with them. I'm sure they'll give you all the love you need and I'll go get me a real man!"

She saw the hurt pour over Jackson's face, dousing the fire in his violet-blue eyes. "Oh, Jackson, I didn't mean that! Please forgive me." She hugged his too-thin frame. With a pang, she felt the prominence of his ribs and wondered at the virus causing him to melt away in front of her. He'd been losing weight ever since the flu last month. Fear clutched her with icy claws. After six years, she didn't know what she'd do without his strength and care.

"You think I don't love you, Katy?" A vein stood out on his pale skin, which used to be so swarthy. He took a drag on his cigarette and then continued. His voice was strained with emotion. "You think that I'm in the garden forgetting about you?" A sudden paroxysm of coughing convulsed him, frightening her. She ran to the sink and brought him back a paper cup of water. She spoke lightly, trying to make a joke while she held the cup to his lips. Beautiful lips, she thought. Was she imagining it or had they taken on a bluish cast? She wished he'd quit smoking.

He drank the water, said he wasn't hungry and returned to that dead, crushed garden. There was nothing there to tend. She'd ruined it for him. He hadn't forgiven her, obviously, and was spiting her by passing the day among the plants she'd killed rather than spend it with her. It rained, but he didn't come in.

That night, the night before they were to return home from their vacation, he took the boat over to Marathon to see about their flight the next morning. When the police arrived around ten to tell her he'd crashed into the bridge and been killed, she fainted. Guilt, grief, terror, and anger swept her out of the real world for what seemed eons. It had been agony.

Now as she lay in the motel bed she wept silently. Dear God, why did he have to die? He was such a good person. But of course she knew; *she* caused his death just as surely as if she'd fired a pistol into his beautiful blond head. How could she even think about marrying Ted Steele? If Jackson had lived, would he finally have forgiven her? Would he have ever understood she truly loved him in spite of the cruel thing she did? At last she slept, determined to tell Ted to forget her.

But next morning, Ted was so sweet and so happy, she postponed telling him. They left the motel and returned to the plane. Once in the air, he reached for her hand, squeezing it possessively. She closed her eyes as they soared, wishing they could stay aloft forever. But Ted called her name.

"I need to tell you something now. Something important," he said, shouting above the plane's motor. He leaned towards her. "Jackson had lung cancer. The 'flu' was part of it. The doctor only gave him a month or so to live. He told me to tell you when I thought the time was right, honey."

Wave after wave of shock hit her and for a moment she couldn't speak. So that was why he...Jackson had really been sick and couldn't...Why didn't he tell me?

"He couldn't bear your pity. Why did he tell *me*? He wasn't just my partner, Katy, he was my best friend. He knew I loved you. He knew I'd take care of you. He loved you so much."

Until I ruined it! Katy turned away, unable even to cry.

Suddenly Ted exclaimed, "Look, honey, look below. *Now!*"

Wondering, she stared out the window. There, below them was Perrito Key, and what she saw on it changed her life completely. The giant letters: "K, I LOVE U FOREVER. J" were white bordered in red with a green background and they were stretched the length and breadth of the puppy's tail— Jackson's beloved garden. The green was undoubtedly grass; the white and red were probably impatiens. Elation washed through her like a shot of wild turkey. He *had* forgiven her right along. That's what he'd been doing that final day in the rain. Making a garden and telling her in the only way he knew. He'd loved her that much. Oh, poor darling Jackson. He'd released her at last. She began to cry but the tears were joy. She reached over and squeezed Ted's hand. "I love you," she said. And she meant them both.

NIGHT OF THE WILD WIND

By early afternoon the wind began to whine. Later, around five, the encroaching super-storm had doubled in strength. Howling its power and sweeping along the beach in noisy gusts, it piled sand against the stilt-block supports beneath the Weston's two-year-old house. Now, hurricane bands roared in from the Gulf of Mexico, chopping the water's surface into mountainous, white-topped curls that thundered onto the sand of the little peninsula just off the Florida Panhandle.

High in her comfortable kitchen overlooking the tortured beach, Ann Weston made sandwiches for tonight's party beside her husband Dave. The slender brunette's emotions varied from fear to excitement. The hurricane party was strictly Dave's idea. Had the decision been up to her, she probably would have opted for security and evacuation. But Dave was determined and fearless. Of course, that was part of his charm, she thought; his complete confidence in anything he undertook. He was always in control and never afraid to face anything. She loved him for it.

Just for a moment, Ann shut her hazel eyes and listened to the eerie raging of the wind. It sounded like some tormented animal whose agonized shrieks heralded a painful birth—the birth of an evil entity. An entity named Ivan.

From the TV in the living room, Ann could hear the weather channel blaring news. In spite of the din outside, she caught snatches of Miami's National Hurricane Center making its five o'clock report with coordinates of the storm's location.

"Hurricane Ivan is a dangerous 135 mile per hour storm," the forecaster intoned. *"Ivan is centered about 135 miles south of the Alabama coastline and moving north at 14 miles per hour. Hurricane strength winds will be felt up to 105 miles away from the center as it hits land. Ivan is crashing ashore as weary Floridians still deal with destruction from Frances and Charley."* The director of the center said grimly, *"We're very concerned with the storm surge."* He added that land east of where the eye of the hurricane was passing could face storm surges of 10 to 16 feet, *"with some very dangerous breaking waves on top of that."*

A local announcer spoke further, *"Coastal areas east of the eye are already taking a pounding. We're asking everyone on barrier islands and near the beaches to evacuate. Do not wait. I repeat: this is a very dangerous storm."*

The announcement frightened Ann. They should have left this morning along with 98 percent of the peninsula's population, not stayed to host a stupid party. Dave claimed they'd be safe because their house and others in the area were "so well built." But was he merely echoing the hype they'd been using the last couple of years to sell this section of houses to prospective buyers? The newscaster was right. They should get off the peninsula. She shivered.

Still, she knew the sudden chill running up and down her spine was only partly caused by the weather. She glanced at her husband and sighed. Their marriage was eroding as surely as the beach in front of their dream home. Even worse, Dave's solution to cure that erosion—or "boredom" as he described it—was, to her, absolutely unspeakable. Nothing she could say would change his mind. What he planned to do hurt and terrified her as much as the storm.

Momentarily, he'd put down the sandwiches he'd been filling for tonight's festivities. She noted the rapt look on his ruddy face as he stood staring through the wide pane above the sink. His blue eyes, half-hidden below the tumbling locks of sun-bleached hair, were sparkling with excitement. In contrast to her devastating fear, the storm was obviously giving him a high.

"Wow! What an ultimate. Look at that surf, babe, it's halfway up the beach already. Lucky our home's up on pilings. You couldn't pay me to live in that Gonzales house." He indicated a flat bungalow hugging the sand a few hundred yards down the beach. "Oh, Annie, can you believe the power? Makes a man feel like a—I don't know—a stallion, maybe. You know, like the shots they always show—a horse rearing, pawing the air…" Dave laughed, his hips against the counter, the firm muscles of his bare chest accentuated by his stance. Without looking, his hand reached over and playfully squeezed her waist above the white shorts.

The gesture surprised her. It was the first time he'd touched her that way in six weeks. Sleeping on the couch because he was "tired," he was also too "busy" to pat or pinch. First she'd been relieved because she, too, was "tired," but then she developed a sick feeling in her chest; was she losing him?

Responding to the slight intimacy, she tossed her curly dark hair and, in mock bravado, straightened tanned shoulders above her white bikini top. "I've never seen a hurricane before," she said, and thought of their personal storm with equal trepidation. She loved him so much, why couldn't she think of something to improve their marriage?

"Neither have I, you know that. Oh man, this 'cane party's the best idea I ever had." He laughed again. "Another bonus of moving to Florida, babe. Hey, you better take advantage of my helping with the sandwiches, Ann. Don't quit on me, or I'll take off and go run on the beach, which incidentally sounds like a perfect idea. Want to run with me?"

She shook her head, wishing she could relax like Dave. He'd always been like that, rolling with whatever punch life offered. That's why he was Peninsula Properties' leading real estate agent, although she herself wasn't bad either, having closed a number of sales for the firm. Ann's full lips tightened into a line as she snatched up the knife and began to trim the edges from a stack of bread.

Outside, startling her, a palm frond hit the window with a slap and was held there for several minutes by a powerful gust.

The wind was getting stronger and this was just the beginning. Were they wrong not to leave?

"I wonder, Dave," she said, "Mr. Lewis at the store says everybody should evacuate. He says what happened to Punta Gorda the other day during Charley could happen to us. Maybe…"

"Hey, look," Dave snapped in a sarcastic mood reversal, "you want to follow that old coot's advice, leave. I understand how you feel. I'll just stay here alone and take care of the house. It's okay. You can take the car and drive to your Aunt Jean's in Tallahassee in a few hours. I know you're scared."

"No, I wouldn't want to leave you, Dave." She turned her head, hoping he couldn't see the expression on her face and realize that leaving him was definitely not an option. If she did, it might finish off whatever was left between them. But she didn't see how she could go along with tonight's plans. That might kill everything, too.

He'd promised a new sort of excitement with this party: *a couples' swap.* At first she'd argued intensely against it, feeling a deep revulsion. But Dave was a good salesman. He said how boring their marriage had become and she felt forced to agree, and thus, ultimately, to agree to his "game," as he called it. Would it backfire?   Would it blow their already faltering marriage apart? She definitely didn't want to swap. On the other hand, she didn't want to break with Dave. Their relationship had been so great once. So in this case it was *damned if she did and damned if she didn't.*

As they continued with the sandwich making, Ann's mind wandered back over their four years together. Funny, all she could think of were the hundreds of perfect nights they'd spent together—until the last six months.

When a friend first introduced her to Dave, it had only taken one date for her to realize that none of the other guys she'd been dating meant a thing. Dave didn't have a diploma, nor was he wealthy, but along with a great gift of gab and a rich uncle with Florida holdings and a construction company, he had exactly the right chemistry. Dave had charmed her into moving in with him and, before long, they decided to marry and give the uncle's business a go. When they first came to Florida, life was idyllic. They'd made wonderful friends with two other couples, the Bradfords and the Stoutenmillers. They'd all worked hard together as real estate agents for Peninsular Projects. Work became their life, but it was such fun.

It wasn't until the money started rolling in that trouble began. They all still worked, only now they could also play. With success, things had become easy. The struggle was gone. The six of them began drinking. That, too, had been fun at first. But Dave was right. Somewhere along the way, things became boring. They had too much. Maybe if they hadn't put off having children. She hadn't wanted any. Neither had Beth Bradford or Amy Stoutenmiller. But now... She swiped at a tear with the back of her hand.

Feeling suddenly tired, she sat down at the kitchen table, hating herself for not knowing how to cope, hating the day, hating the sandwiches she'd agreed to fix for the stupid fiasco tonight, but most of all hating Dave for not loving her as he had when they first got married—for wanting somebody else.

As if he'd read her mind, he said, "Hey, you're not changing your mind about tonight are you?"

"Yes, let's not play that, you know, that swap game. Why should we?"

His mouth dropped. "You admitted our marriage is boring."

"But why would you want to swap with our best friends?" Her voice was coming out wrong; it sounded strained, hoarse.

"Don't you ever want variety, Ann? It'll do our marriage good. I'm not a cheater and I'm not picking people up on the street. I'd never do that and bring AIDs to you, for cripes' sake. Our friends, they're like family. They're clean. This will be some new thing to share. It's just a fun game."

She groaned, sensing the vicious screaming of the wind as if it were part of his plan. The windows were humming. She heard a thump and knew that something else had hit the house, a piece of driftwood, perhaps, or even a small tree. Everything had turned into a nightmare. *If only she could awaken.*

"Come on. You're no fun these days. This would only be for tonight. I went down this morning and got some of the best Scotch you ever tasted. Take a little of that and you'll change your mind. The others are willing. Hey, you can even ask that new couple you're always talking about. The Gonzales, the couple who live down the beach in that little house. How'd you like to have him…"

"Stop it!" She shook her curly dark head and got up to leave.

Dave grabbed her wrist and pulled her against him. "How do I know you haven't already been out with that dude. They say Hispanics are great lovers and…" He released her. "No, you're just a scared little rabbit that won't leave her burrow. Not the live-wire you used to be. You use it all up on your job. There's nothing left for me. Well, babe, we're going to do this thing whether you want to or not because it's all set. You've got to grow up, Ann. Look, kid, it's only a game. We draw numbers. Ken goes for you. Let him get your number."

She could feel her face getting hot. *So they'd been talking it over about who wanted her.* "No, I…You're crazy, you know that?"

She saw his face darken, his fists clench. As he stepped closer to her, she knew he was furious. Her breath came faster, dreading his displeasure.

He shut his eyes for a moment. When he opened them to glare at her, he had gained control of his voice. "Admit it. We got one dull marriage. You're as bored as I am. All day at the project office we work together trying to talk suckers into buying lots on this god-forsaken Florida peninsula. At night, we play together and sleep together. The excitement's gone."

"No, you're wrong Dave." She turned away, whimpering.

His laugh was ugly. "Face it. You don't care that much for me. Don't think I didn't know you got the hots over district manager whats-his-name when he was down here last month. I heard you talking. Okay, it hurt my feelings, hurt them a lot. But then, I got to thinking and I understood. I'm fed up, too, and either you go through this deal tonight or I'm splitting."

She couldn't believe his words. Was the weather affecting him? She watched him as he stalked out of the kitchen, her stomach churning like the angry sea outside. At last, she started to work on the sandwiches again, filling them with cheese, cold cuts, or the ham salad she'd made earlier, adding lettuce, then wrapping the stack in plastic before placing the party food in the refrigerator—enough for ten hurricanes, she thought.

She didn't want to give Dave up—she *wouldn't,* but she'd be damned if she'd give in to every whim he had. She'd leave now, today, before the wind got worse. He could have Amy or Beth. See if they could put up with his nutty demands. She wondered what Ken and Jason, Beth and Amy's husbands, would say to that.

She picked up the mayonnaise jar and returned it to the fridge. She'd finished the stupid sandwiches. He could do the rest.

Through the window, she could see Dave on the beach below, braced against the wind. Amy Stoutenmiller was there, too, her long auburn hair fanning away from her face like a brilliant flag. She saw Amy reach up and touch his cheek and she wondered if he'd choose Amy's number in the game tonight. Because Jason and Ken were Amy's and Beth's husbands, she'd never considered them as anything but good friends. She couldn't possibly be romantic with Beth's nice, plain Ken even if, as Dave had said, Ken did want her.

Then, on her way to her room to pack, she thought of an idea. The new couple. Dave said she was always talking about them. The only reason she'd mentioned them was because the guy treated his wife so nice, always hand-in-hand. It was something a woman noticed. She'd assumed they were honeymooners.

David suggested she ask them to the party. Okay, she would, and Roberto Gonzales would be the one to get her number. Now there'd be a challenge. Thinking about it for the first time, she recalled how really good-looking the guy was with that black thick hair. He was not particularly tall, but he was built like an athlete. Ann smiled.

The sick fear abated and pleasant excitement took its place. Why not, if that's what it took to please her husband, she'd do it. In fact, she'd overdo it. Two could play at this game. She'd make Dave just as jealous as he was making her.

She ran to her dresser and put on lipstick. Then, for a moment, she lost her nerve about asking the couple. After all, she didn't know them other than to say hello. They were a cute couple who stayed to themselves. Both darkhaired, they were always together—Rosa and Roberto; Roberto and Rosa. Well, after tonight perhaps it would be different. She wondered if Roberto had ever noticed her. The thought made her cheeks warm.

Amy and Beth often asked about the Gonzales. "Y'all think those two have evah heard of the *Stepford Wives?*" Beth once asked in her syrupy Alabama drawl. The three of them laughed. Rosa so obviously adored her husband.

When Ann stepped outside moments later, the front door almost blew off its hinges. The wind was like nothing she'd ever known existed. It took her breath away. It was a swarm of insects as it stung her face and hands with sand and twisted her curly brown hair into unmanageable snarls. Leaning against the storm's force, she struggled from the high ridge on the west side of the house down the dune onto the beach, clinging for a moment to one of the sand-banked pilings beneath the east side of the house. There she took off her sash and made a headband to keep the strands of hair from slapping her face and eyes. Then she ran, ignoring the bits of shells, leaves and branches that whipped against her body.

The wind-urged water was ignoring the law of the tides. It should have been receding at this hour. Instead, it was far above the high tide mark already. The nest of some seabird rolled down the beach like a Mexican sombrero.

"Annie, what are you doing out in this storm?" Dave jogged towards her shouting through the clamor. He'd pulled his shirt up so only a small portion of his face was visible. "Amy came to say she was getting cold feet about staying out here on the peninsula for the 'cane. Said she wanted to drive east to Tallahassee while she still could, but I talked her out of leaving. I imagine parts of Highway 98 are already pretty wet." His blue eyes sparkled with exhilaration above the shirt-mask.

"I'm going over to the Gonzales' place." Ann's own voice sounded far away. "You told me to ask..." Sand was getting in her mouth. It gritted on her teeth.

"Sure, ask them. The girl's hot. I've watched them a time or two. Ask them."

He made no move to come with her, so Ann pushed through the wind to reach the small house. At first, no one seemed to be home. Water was lapping the stoop. Rosa and Roberto were smarter than all of them, she thought. *They'd evacuated.* That's what she and Dave should do, too. For a moment, the terror resurfaced and she swallowed hard to keep from crying out. Then, suddenly, the door opened, and a surprised young woman with clear, tan skin and dark hair and eyes looked out at her.

"Oh, come in, come in," Rosa said, stepping back. She had just enough accent to be appealing. "You're the lady from the big house that's up in the air, are you not?"

Ann smiled at the woman's description of their stilt home. The Gonzales home felt as if it were vibrating. "Yes, I'm Ann Weston. My husband's Dave. He's project manager for Peninsular Properties here." She met Rosa's proffered hand.

Before she could say more, Roberto came out of the bedroom, pulling his shirt around one of the most muscular torsos Ann had ever seen in person. Considering how she'd been thinking of him, Ann felt herself blushing. "I—we thought you might have taken off. Gone to Orlando or somewhere off of the Panhandle."

"No," Rosa said, as her husband pulled up a chair for Ann. "We know no one in Orlando, you see, and we don't have enough money to stay in a motel." Perhaps Rosa caught a signal from her husband for she hastily amended, "I mean, it's in the bank. We'll be fine here."

Ann felt nervous. Maybe to ask the couple was a mistake. On the other hand, she wondered about flooding. The little cottage was so low. All the other homes on the peninsula were built up like hers and Dave's. "We wondered if you'd like to come to a party tonight at our house. Beth and Ken Bradford, and Amy and Jason Stoutenmiller will be there. We're all connected with the Peninsular Properties projects, you know. Uh—we were a little worried about you two being so close to the water-line." She didn't mention how that idea had entered her head as an afterthought.

The couple exchanged glances. "Que bueno! That's very good of you, senora," Roberto told her with a wide white grin. "I was worried about my wife. Yes, I think we come, gracias. What time, please?"

They were coming. Ann beamed. Wait until she told Dave. "Around seven, I guess, unless the storm gets worse sooner, then come any time."

"Oh, thank you. Unless the world ends, we'll be there. We certainly will. Muchas gracias, senora."

They had their arms around each other and were both smiling when she left. Rosa was a pretty girl. Sweet. Well, maybe the two of them needed a little American indoctrination. Maybe Dave was right. Maybe a little mix would do everybody's marriage good.

Promptly at seven, the doorbell rang, and Dave, now dressed in new stonewashed jeans and a t-shirt reading "Party While It Blows" opened the front door and hurried the Bradfords and Stoutenmillers inside. Because 250 mile per hour wind-proof glass had been installed in these houses, they had no need for shutters. Nonetheless, the house felt snug and secure and completely impervious to the storm. Ann, who had already had a glass of Dave's Scotch to numb her nerves, laughed as the three men wrestled together to pull the front door shut. A hard rain blowing horizontally made the outside air cold. As she hung the visitors' damp jackets and scarves on hangers in the kitchen, she invited both couples to help themselves to the repast she and Dave had laid out on the dining room table. She wondered where the Gonzales couple were. They'd better get here soon or it would be too late to walk in the wind.

After each of the guests had a drink, they settled back on the circular, white leather couch in the large living room, making jokes and small talk about the storm, the residents who'd chickened out and departed the Panhandle, and the plans for the party this evening. In spite of the whiskey, there was a tenseness in the atmosphere that was nearly tangible. None of them had ever before experienced a hurricane.

Ann sensed that it wasn't the storm alone that had Ken chain-smoking and Jason cracking disgusting jokes. It was this wife-swapping game they were gearing up for. In spite of what Dave had told her, she wasn't sure if the women knew about it until she saw Amy wink at Dave and her heart squeezed together in her chest. Lord, her best friend wanted her husband as much as he wanted her. *Nice! Get the wife's blessing on the whole sick game.*

Upset, Ann rose quickly. Her hand brushed the glass off the end table beside her chair. The drink left a wet stain on the pale blue rug and splashed onto her jeans. She ran to the kitchen to get towels to mop up the damage. She stayed there for several minutes to pull her feelings together and calm the churning of her stomach. As if the storm weren't enough to face, the picture in her mind of Amy with her Dave made her sick. She and the other women had always been like sisters. What had happened? Was she to blame for what was going on? She felt like crying.

"You okay, Annie?" Ken's voice at the kitchen door made her jump. He approached her quickly, running an exploratory hand over her arm.

She felt awkward, not knowing how to act. They'd always been good friends, now she was expected to be something else. "Oh, I'm fine, Ken. Let's go back with the gang." She forced a smile.

He pulled her to him and showed her a card with the number "3" written on it in Dave's hand. "I got your number, kid." He winked.

"Oh, Ken, we shouldn't have drawn yet. The Gonzales— you know, that Latino couple down the beach—they're coming."

"I doubt that, Ann," Ken frowned down at her. "The damn wind's way too high by now. We barely made it here an hour ago. Bet any amount of money, those two took off this afternoon for a shelter or something. Probably when the gulf got too close to that squatty little house of theirs, they freaked out. You'll find, I'm sure, they didn't wait for our party, they split from the beach early on."

She mumbled, "You're probably right, Ken."

Ken added, "Why the hell did Dave ask *them?* The girl's pregnant, didn't he know? I thought we had this party all set up."

She drew in her breath. Then, not knowing what else to do, she grabbed up some paper towels and returned to the living room.

"I've already cleaned up your mess, babe," Dave greeted her. His voice was slurred and he had one arm around Amy whose auburn head rested on his broad shoulder.

Ann couldn't believe her own reaction. She wanted to grab that head and throw Amy off of her husband. *She would stop this game right now. They'd end up hating each other.*

Something heavy crashed into the house. Beth screamed. The lights dimmed. But Dave was undaunted. "Here, everybody, have some more drinks. Old Ivan can't get in here, kids." Her husband was a good host, Ann thought dryly. He let go of Amy long enough to fill everyone's glass. Amy, she noted, had drunk too much, already.

She watched as her red-haired friend climbed on the white leather couch with bare feet, her slim body bouncing up and down. "Catch me, Davie," she called as she climbed over the back. "I'll be the mouse and you be the cat." Amy hiccupped and giggled.

Ann seethed, ignoring Ken who was trying to talk to her. She downed her Scotch in one motion, welcoming the warmth that spread through her body. The drink relaxed her at last and she wondered if she were being a prude. After all, Ken was nice and he did like her. What difference did a little sex between friends make. She lifted her face to him. As his lips sought hers, she remembered the Gonzales couple again and wondered what had really happened to keep them away. Over his shoulder she could see Ken's cute wife, Beth, curled up in a chair with Jason.

Lord, that drink was knocking her out. She was scarcely aware when Ken lifted her in his arms. They were almost at the bedroom door when she heard Amy scream. Recognizing the genuine terror in the woman's voice, Ann slapped at Ken's arms until he put her down. She weaved her way to where Amy was staring through the picture window that faced the gulf.

"Look," the frightened woman said, "My God, I must be drunk. Where's the beach? Where is it?" She began to cry. "Oh, what shall we do? Jason, oh Jason, I need you!"

To Ann's horror, Amy was right. They may as well have been in a boat. Water was everywhere. Huge, frothy waves, as big as a house, pounded the block supports within a foot or two of the base of their floor. She felt the blood leave her head. She leaned against the wall, willing herself to sober up. They should have listened to old Mr. Lewis; they should have evacuated. For God's sake, they were all going to die.

Everything seemed to change at that point. She saw Jason Stoutenmiller run to his wife. Ken left her to embrace Beth who was becoming hysterical. "Kenny, do somethin', honey! We're all goin' to drown tonight, ah swear it."

The lights blinked and went out. Biting her lip, Ann groped her way to the table and lit the candelabra, thankful that Dave had placed candles and matches in every room in case of an electrical outage. As the group silently huddled around the flickering trio of lights, their shadows danced to the wild orchestration outside. It was a weird, macabre setting, something out of a horror movie, or a nightmare. Where was Dave? Didn't he want her at all? They shouldn't have stayed. They were all drunken fools.   Ann knew her teeth were chattering as fear consumed her.

When Dave came up behind her and put his arms around her waist, she felt tears roll down her cheeks. "There, there," he comforted. "We'll make it, babe. These homes are like steel."

In one hand he held a small portable radio.   He pulled back from her long enough to turn it on.   Over the crackling static, she heard a local announcer give Ivan's coordinates.   Way too close to their narrow peninsula.   Highways 98 and 10 are inundated," warned the voice. "Stay inside."

An ear-splitting bang made them all cry out, as part of a large pine tree crashed into their house, raking a large hole through the wall.   Hurricane force rain poured in, extinguishing the candles.   An increasing freight train sort of noise shattered their ears and sanity as its powerful sound burst into the dark room.   The super-strong windows crashed, sending glass all over the blue rug now drenched with Ivan's clear, cold blood.   As if with one mind, the group crawled under the table.   It afforded them some protection, and there they stayed.

Suddenly, the world seemed to end in a monstrous explosion and a deluge of sea water.   Ann screamed as she felt the house drop on the gulf side.   In the darkness, they grabbed table legs and each other, certain they were doomed.

"The stilts!" Dave rasped. "The blocks have given way. Oh, God, is everyone okay?"   His voice sounded strangely humble.   When no one replied, he whispered in Ann's ear, "Please, please forgive me."

Clinging to the table with one hand, she reached for him. She felt the others against her feet.   She held on, aching for the terror to end.   Some time in the night, they all slept.   Some time in the night, the rain stopped.   It was over.

A gray light awoke them early, accompanied by a knock on the door.   Looking around with shocked eyes, Ann saw that the badly tilted house was a shambles—glass, sandwiches, and an inch of water covered the saturated carpet with heaps and pools.   The pine tree segment, hung with seaweed, had made a giant yellowish mark on the white couch. It rested there, the focal point of what looked like a real-life Dali painting.

Dave rose to his feet and sloshed to the door. Two men in yellow plastic raincoats and wearing Red Cross armbands entered. "Well, we see you survived," the older of the pair said with a wide smile.

The younger, thinner man asked, "Anybody hurt? We've got a boat to take you back to dry—well, dry-er land—and a shelter. You fared good, considering. Your neighbors weren't so lucky."

"Why? Who? I thought all our neighbors out here evacuated." Ann held her breath.

"Not everybody. Gonzales was the name on the marriage license she was clutching. Married ten years, it said. Hispanic. Drowned slicker'n rats."

The group, now awake and extremely sober, moaned in unison.

"We figure they'd been fixin' to leave. You know, bag packed, purse on her shoulder, marriage license, passport. We think their house was breaking up from the 'cane. One end of a two by four must have come loose out of the ceiling and hit her. Her long hair got twisted in the nails and loose wires. Probably couldn't get free. Then the surge came. Water rose and drowned 'em."

"They were due here," Dave said.

"But why didn't he get out and get help?" Ann grabbed a chair and held on. *She hadn't caused the deaths. What made her feel so very guilty?*

For a moment no one spoke. Then the older man said sharply. "He wouldn't leave her, we figure. Found 'em with their arms around each other, his watch stopped at 6:45. Surge came later." The thinner man cleared his throat. "Sorry about it. Self-preservation's so strong, most guys would have finally saved themselves. He didn't. Okay, look, get your things together and we'll leave."

Ann looked at Beth and Amy, both sobbing silently. She touched their shoulders, wondering if they, like herself, felt relentless self-contempt. She wondered what Rosa possessed that inspired a man to die for her. How vapid her own marriage was by comparison.

"Gonzales was some man," Dave said softly as they stepped out the door to look at a watery unfamiliar world, "Lord, Annie, I'd give anything to have the balls he had. We've got to set up some sort of plaque, some honor, in their name." He took her hand. "Don't hate me, Annie. Let's start again, please." His kiss was tender; his eyes penitent.

Maybe, just maybe, she thought, the Gonzales' tragic death had taught them something. She wasn't exactly sure what it was but she'd start by forgiving Dave. Maybe herself, too, though it might take a while to feel right about any of their gang. She was a good real estate person. She could make her living anywhere. Maybe that's what she'd do. Get a new perspective. Start over, away from memories.

As she stepped into the rescue boat, the sun broke through a cloud. The blue sky reflected in Dave's hopeful eyes. Ann smiled.

The Forgiving. I wrote this story after taking a fast boat ride through the little unmarked keys near Marathon. As we sped along through the waves of the Gulf of Mexico with the Atlantic Ocean in view, I wondered how many stories existed on these small patches of existence.

Vengeance Is Mine. I was very moved, back in the nineties, by the tragedy of ValuJet 592. I wondered how many stories died with the senseless crash, and decided that some day I would make up one of my own. I also believe in the strong meaning of the title. I do not believe it's up to us to dole out justice.

Night of the Wild Wind was inspired by the four hurricanes we went through this summer in Florida. Although I was in Tampa and Delray Beach, at one time, I had spent a year on the Florida Panhandle. I knew the area. In September, 2004, Hurricane Ivan caused tremendous devastation there. I also recall Hurricane Camille of 1969, and how a group of party goers died along that strip of beach when they did not evacuate.

This is my personal memoir of growing up with a mother who has paranoid schizophrenia. In Chapter Three, my mother has been committed to a mental hospital in Jacksonville, Ill., and my little brother, Stevie, my Dad and I visit her for the first time.

CHAPTER THREE

Growing Up Crazy

Mom has been gone for over a month and soon it will be the fourth of July. Our house is so quiet that I can lie on the couch and read a book or watch TV or just sit and think.

But that night at supper Dad says, "We're going to see Mom tomorrow."

Stevie cheers, but he is only three. I don't say anything.

The next morning I stay in bed, even though I can hear Dad and Stevie, until Dad yells up at me, "Mary Kay, we're leaving. Hurry up and get down here."

Slowly I get dressed. Dad and Stevie are sitting in the car waiting for me when I go outside. I take baby steps as I walk towards the car.

"Hurry up or you're not going," Dad yells. "You can just stay home."

Begrudgingly I climb into Dad's dark, blue 1953 Buick. It has three holes on both front fenders. When Dad first brought it home, I said, "Dad, does it have those holes so the water can run out when it rains?"

He laughed and said, "I don't think so."

Illinois is a big state, and Dad told me that is over 100 miles to Jacksonville from Galesburg. It will be a long ride, and before we even go a block, Stevie starts to fake cry. He has purposely untied his shoes and doesn't know how to tie them. I refuse to help him and think how dopey he acts until my dad yells at me again. "For crying out loud, help him tie his shoes. You're nine years old. Act your age."

I know Stevie is excited to see Mom, and for some reason that makes me angry. "It's not going to be fun," I say.

"Young lady, I am going to pull this car over and spank you if you say one more word," Dad warns me.

I stick my tongue out at my brother and give him the ugliest look possible. He fake cries again and says, "She stuck her tongue out at me."

Dad just keeps driving and doesn't say anything.

"Shut up," I mouth to Stevie, but I know I better not say anything else.

We drive past cornfield after cornfield. My favorite song, "How Much is that Doggie in the Window," is playing on the radio, and before it ends, I am asleep and stay that way until I feel the car slowing down.

"Dad, are we there?"

"Yes, we are. You slept for almost two hours," he says.

Dad pulls in to Tootsie's Café. "We'll eat before we go to the hospital," he says.

I plan to say, "I'm not hungry," but Stevie starts to cry and throws a fit so anything I say will be ignored. Stevie wants to go see Mom right now.

I sit on the grass waiting for my brother to act normal again instead of like a goof. I pretend like I am a princess, but I don't get to be a princess very long because Dad somehow convinces Stevie to calm down.

Before we even walk inside, I can smell the grease from the many hamburgers that have been cooked in this restaurant over the years. A real princess would not eat here.

We sit down at a booth. A fat blond waitress in a pink dress with a white apron and little white hat that looks like a small nurse's hat walks over very slowly and smiles a large smile only at my Dad. "You sure have cute kids," she says.

I know she doesn't mean it because she didn't even look at us.

She stretches her red lipsticked mouth as far as it can go so she can smile even more at my Dad, and her face becomes almost all teeth. I think she looks like a Halloween mask.

"I don't want anything to eat," I say and afterward I hold my lips together so tightly it probably looks like I don't have any and I wrap my arms around myself.

Dad ignores me and says, "We'll each have a hamburger and I'll have a chocolate shake and they'll split one."

"Coming right up," she says.

Stevie kicks me under the table so I kick him back.

"Owie. She kicked me."

"Will you two stop it?"

Stevie kicks me again so I pinch him.

"Daddy, Mary…"

Dad ignores him and says, "Your Mom has a present for both of you."

"What?" Stevie asks forgetting about the kicking game he started.

"I'll let her show you when we get there."

The waitress comes back and gives us our lunch. "Can I get you *a-n-y-t-h-i-n-g* else?" she says.

Before my Dad can say anything, I say **"No,"** as loud as I can and everyone in the restaurant looks over at us.

I look at my Dad. He has turned his head, and I think he is laughing because his body is shaking. The waitress throws the check on our table and doesn't look back as she walks away.

I guess we were all hungry because our food quickly disappears. "Let's go," Dad says. "Mom is waiting for us."

It seems to me that it takes a long time to get from the restaurant to the hospital, which is not in town but in the country. When the car finally pulls through the large metal gate I say, "Dad, my stomach doesn't feel good."

He doesn't answer me.

Stevie bounces out of the car and is jumping up and down and holds Dad's hand as we walk towards the biggest house I've ever seen. I know it's supposed to be a hospital, but it looks like a beautiful white mansion to me.   There are lots of trees and I can hear the birds singing and flower gardens are everywhere. Maybe Mom likes living here.

I run up to the tall wooden door and try to open it, but it is locked even though it's daytime. Dad rings the doorbell, and a nurse lets us inside. "Good afternoon, Mr. Thurman," she says.

Dad must have been here before since she recognized him.

Inside, it is huge and makes me feel very small. I am a little afraid. The nurse is as white as white can be. Her dress is white, her hat is white her legs are white and even her shoes are white. She wears a bunch of keys at her waist. Every door has big locks, and I've never seen a place with so many doors. "Follow me upstairs," she says.

But I don't want to follow her because next to the stairs, there is a door. And a woman behind that door is screaming the most awful screams I've ever heard...even worse than my Mom's. She sounds like someone in a horror movie.

Stevie doesn't move so Dad picks him up. My legs and hands are shaking so hard, I can barely walk and I can't make them stop. I grab Dad's hand as we walk past the door. "Dad, why is she screaming like that?"

"I don't know. But don't tell anyone."

"Okay Dad," I say but I don't understand why I shouldn't tell anyone.

At the top of the stairs another nurse is sitting at a desk in front of another locked door. She is also all white and has a lot of keys attached to her waist. Neither nurse smiles, not even at Stevie, and they don't talk very much either. The second nurse speaks as she takes a key from the many she has so she can unlock the door. "I'll take you to Mrs. Thurman's room," she says.

We walk down a long, bright hallway where there are many locked doors only these have large windows in them. Nearly every room has a sad looking person sitting there, but at least they are not screaming.

The nurse stops when we get to my Mom's room, and I see her sitting on her bed. Stevie is too short and can't see, but when the nurse opens the door and he catches a glimpse of her, he bolts and runs in and hugs Mom and won't let go of her. They both cry. "I love you. I love you," she says.

Mom is wearing a white blouse and a blue skirt. Her long, brown hair looks the way it did when I was little and with her arms around Stevie I can see that her fingernails are painted red...the way they used to be. When I was a little girl, my Mom had the most beautiful fingernails in the world. She told me that if I stopped chewing on mine, she would paint them any color I wanted.

Next, she hugs my Dad. It seems like Dad has tears falling down his face, but I know that's not so because Dad's don't cry.

Then Mom looks at me and holds out her arms. Slowly I walk over to her. She hugs me, and she smells like the flowers that grow in our yard. "I've missed you all so much," she says.

I don't know what to say.

Like everything else here, Mom's room is white. I know they don't want my Dad to stay here because her bed is only big enough for her.

I wonder how she combs her hair because I don't see a mirror. And I don't see a bathroom either. I wonder what she does if she wakes up in the night and has to go really bad and her door is locked.

A soft, white, ruffled curtain covers her window, and although I can see through them and see the beautiful yard, I don't wonder anymore if she likes it here or not.

"Would you like to go outside," Mom asks us still wiping her nose.

"Where's my present?" Stevie asks.

I don't think I should be asking for a present, but Mom smiles. She opens her closet. It is not locked.

She takes out a little statue of a dog that she has painted. It is black and white like Spotty, and she gives it to Stevie. Then she hands me a cat that kind of looks like Cacky. It is tan and white and black.

I start to say, "Cacky has to live in the garage because she bit Auntie Eloise," but instead I swallow my words because Dad is giving me a funny look.

Mom smiles a lot once we are outside. There are lots of other people here, and I can't tell who lives here and who doesn't, but I don't see any other kids. There are two nurses out here, and they have cookies and lemonade and, although they don't talk or smile very much either, they give us as much lemonade as we want.

In what seems like no time, we have to leave and Mom has to go back inside.

"Art, I want to go home," Mom says and she grabs my Dad and holds on tight to him.

He hugs her back but then pulls away. "Not yet, Kay," and his face looks like it did when my Grandma died.

Stevie hugs Mom and starts to cry. "You look pretty Mom," I say before I hug her.

One of the nurses walks over and locks her arm in my Mom's. Crying, Mom waves goodbye to us.

It is getting dark as we drive back, and my Dad doesn't talk very much. Before I fall asleep, I think about my Mom. *Maybe she does like my Dad and me a little bit. But I'm not sure. If she'd said she was sorry, I'd be sure. But she didn't.*

The three of us visit Mom about once a month. The second time Mom leaves the hospital with us for the afternoon, and she laughs and smiles as we drive through the big gate. Our family goes out to eat, but not to Tootsie's Café. I am glad because I bet Mom wouldn't like that waitress with the big smile either.

The third time we visit Mom, we go to a motel. "Your Dad and I are very tired," she says.

Stevie falls asleep, but I am bored. "Mary Kay, why don't you take a shower?"

At first I say, "I already took one."

But the more I think about it, the more it sounds like a good idea because Mom says I can sing in the shower as loud as I want. And I sing lots of songs.

This time when we leave the hospital, we wait in front of Mom's window so she can wave goodbye to us. She smiles and waves, but Stevie starts to cry and yell. He screams, "I want my Mommy," and screams it over and over again.

Mom presses her face so hard against the window that I think she might come through it.

Stevie has planted himself in front of her window so Dad and I have to grab his hands very tightly and pull him to the car. He cries and cries and there is nothing we can say to make him happy. Finally he falls asleep but the entire trip back home he still cries out in his sleep from time to time and says, "Mommy."

The next day I am very tired and sleep late. When I awaken no one is in the house, but I can hear voices outside.

Still wearing my shorty nightgown, I join them.

"Morning Sleepy Head," my dad says.

"Dad, why are you home?"

"I'm taking you school shopping today. Did you forget that school starts next week? Go get dressed, and we'll go."

School, clothes and shopping are not at the top of my list of fun things to do. "Can we get breakfast at the drug store first, *p-l-e-a-s- e*?"

He scrunches his eyes and mouth like he's thinking about it. "All right. Hurry up and go dressed because I'm going to work afterwards."

"Is Stevie going?"

"No, he'll stay here with Eloise."

That was all I needed to hear. Just Dad and me...I almost fly up the stairs. We used to go to the drug store every Saturday morning while Mom cleaned the house, and Dad always let me have a Coke and a chocolate pastry. I throw off my pj's and put on a pair of shorts and a top and quickly run a comb over the top of my dark hair. In two minutes I'm dressed and running back outside shouting, "I'm ready."

"What took you so long?" Dad asks.

For some reason my Auntie Eloise, and the neighbors who are also outside standing around talking, think that is hilariously funny and laugh and laugh.

We live ten blocks from downtown Galesburg. Grown-ups never walk there, but kids do. So of course, Dad and I ride in the car.

I look out at the big elm trees that line both sides of Kellogg Street where I live. Like giant guards they silently stand and protect everyone from the sun and rain. Their huge branches stretch across the old, red brick road and it seems like they are trying to touch one another but can't quite make it.

We drive past the houses, which are almost all white. They all have large yards and most of them have a big porch in the front with a swing. In the summer, neighbors walk by every night to get cool and stop and talk to anyone who is sitting on the porch, even a kid. It takes a long time to walk anywhere because of all of that talking.

As Dad and I pull onto Main Street, I stick my hand out the car window so I can feel the cool breeze, and I can't imagine why anyone wouldn't love living here.

It is nearly lunchtime as we walk into the drug store but I still want a chocolate pastry. I can have a cherry Coke or a lemon Coke or a plain Coke. "I'll have a lemon coke," I say to the waitress.

I watch the waitress as she pours the syrup into the glass from the big red Coke machine and then adds just a splash of lemon. Lastly she adds the fizzy water, and it spills all over. I don't get to have pop very often and want the glass to be as filled with as much of the sweet potion that I love and that every kid I know loves. "Don't put too much ice in my glass," I say.

When she sets my drink on the counter, I slurp the fizz on top really fast before it disappears. Then I drink the rest of it slowly with a straw so I don't look piggish and besides it burns my throat if I drink it too quickly.

Resting on the counter in front of me is a little jukebox. Looking down the counter, I see there are a lot of them. Inside are pages that can be turned. Written on each page are the names of songs with a number beside them. For a nickel, it will play any song I choose. If I had a nickel, I would have played *Mr. Sandman.*

When my roll finally comes, I lick the chocolate off of the roll before I eat it. My Dad doesn't like me to do that and makes a face. "Don't do that," he says.

I like sitting on the cherry red stools because I can rock back and forth while I watch everyone. There are mirrors on the wall behind the soda fountain so not only can I see myself in it, I can see everyone else who is sitting there.

There is a lady with red hair sitting two stools away from my dad. I can see her looking at him in the mirror but pretending like she isn't, so I look at her and pretend like I'm not. When she leaves, she smiles at me and says, "Hi."

"Are you glad you're going to go back to school," Dad asks.

"No, not really," I say as I twist back and forth on my stool.

"Are you ready to go get your school pants," he says and he gives me a little punch on my arm.

I laugh because everybody knows that boys wear pants to school and girls wear dresses. We can only wear pants under our dresses when it is very, very cold and then we have to take them off as soon as we are inside the building. "Dress nice and you'll behave nice," our teachers say.

Dad says, "When I was a boy, I had only one pair of pants. When my Mom washed them, I had to stay in bed under the covers until they were dry."

"Gosh, Dad."

"And when I was a boy, I went to school in a one-room schoolhouse in the country, and I took the first grade and second grade in one year."

"I wish I could do that because now I'd be in the fifth grade instead of the fourth."

Dad smiles at me and says, "Let's go shop."

We walk to the store. It is only a block away. *O. T. Johnson's* is the biggest department store in Galesburg. They have racks and racks and racks of clothes for girls. Dad isn't sure what size I wear, and I'm not either. A clerk walks over to help us. "Hello there you two. May I help you?"

"We're looking for some school dresses for her. What size do you think she'd wear?"

She looks at me and says, "She's not very big. Where's your Mom?"

I just look at her because I don't want to talk about my Mom.

She looks at both of us and waits for an answer but quickly gives up and says, "I think a size 10. They're right over here."

As we follow her, Dad says, "We can manage now."

Dad looks at all of the dresses. The bright colors all hanging together look like a rainbow made out of clothes. Unbelievably my Dad finds a brown one and pulls it out. Even more unbelievable, he finds another brown one and then a gray one. Proudly holding them up in front of me he asks, "What do you think?"

Yuck I think while making a face, but I don't want to hurt his feelings so I say, "Okay."

If I count my Brownie dress, with these I will have three brown dresses and one gray one. The gray dress is shiny and has ruffles on the front of it. It ties in the back with a bow so it is a little pretty…but not very.

Dad sure is a fast shopper, and he must not have seen all of the pretty dresses although I don't know how he could have missed them.

Pleased with himself, Dad says, "That didn't take long, did it? Now we've got to get you some shoes."

Looking down at my feet, I can't see anything wrong with the ones I'm wearing but Dad says, "I don't want you wearing those to school."

After Dad pays for my clothes, we go to the shoe department. "I have only five dollars left so we'll have to watch how much we spend," he says.

We sit down in the shoe department and another lady comes to help us. She measures my foot and brings out two boxes of shoes. Even to my nine-year old eyes, the first pair are ugly and that is the pair my Dad likes. I try them on and he says, "Those are great."

"No Dad. I don't like these."

They are big, black shoes and look like witch shoes. Even the shoelaces are black. I hate them. When I put them on, my feet feel like they are in cement and I won't be able to run or jump rope in them.

The sales clerk looks at me sympathetically. She is young and I like her. Pulling out the next pair she asks, "How about these?"

They are perfect. I love them. They are girl shoes, and they look like the shoes that Dorothy wears in the Wizard of Oz and they even have straps. Smiling at my Dad I say, "I want these."

Dad isn't convinced. "The other ones will keep your feet warm and dry and these skimpy things won't," he says.

"All of the girls are wearing them this year," the salesclerk says.

It's two against one so Dad doesn't have much of a chance. And as I walk out of the store wearing my beautiful new shoes and hanging on to my Dad's hand I say, "Thanks Dad."

"Dad. Is your favorite color brown?"

"No. Why'd you ask that?"

"I dunno."

"Do you like your new dresses?"

"Yes," I lie. But someday when I grow-up I will have a beautiful dress and it will be as blue as the sky and shiny like the stars. *Brown is good only for chocolate*, I think to myself.

Dad walks and I skip back to the car.

"You know what, Mary Kay. You were right. Those shoes were ugly."

I look at him and say, "Wanna race?"

And even with his arms full of packages, he races me back to the car. And I win.

There are still a few days left before school starts. One afternoon Barb and Cheryl and I play King on the Mountain. We use the picnic table in my back yard as the mountain and I get to be King. Barb and Cheryl try to pull me off of the table and pull so hard that the whole table tips over and I do a somersault and plop on the ground.

Laughing, I stand up, but Barb and Cheryl scream, "Run Mary Kay. Run."

So I run, but I don't know why I am running until I feel their fury. It feels as if I am being jabbed by darts of fire over and over again. As I run even faster I turn my head and now I see them…zillions of black hornets and they are all aimed at me.

Screaming as loud as I can all of the way to the house, I finally reach the back door and slam it shut. Auntie Eloise hears all of the noise and comes to see what is going on, and through the screen door we see them swooping through the air just waiting for me.

Auntie Eloise wraps her arms around me and says, "Poor little girl."

I cry and shake my head in agreement with her.

Cheryl and Barb aren't stung but they run home crying anyway.

The hornets swarm near our door for a long time. Auntie Eloise tells me to take a warm bath with baking soda, and she gives me some pink lotion to rub on the stings. She brings my pillow downstairs and I lie on the floor and watch TV.

Baby Judy is in bed so Auntie Eloise lies down beside me and shares my pillow and we watch *Queen for a Day* on TV. On this show, all of the ladies tell their sad stories, and the one who has the saddest story gets to be queen for a day, and she gets lots of presents.

"Auntie Eloise, if I were on *Queen for a Day*, I bet I could be the queen today.

Auntie Eloise looks at me at laughs. "I bet you could too," she says.

For the rest of the afternoon and even that night, I stay inside just in case the hornets are looking for me. Dad and

Uncle Chuck won't be home tonight to help with the hornets, but when it's almost dark my Uncle George shows up. He is my Mom's brother and one of my favorite uncles.

Standing at the front door, he says, "Knock. Knock," before he lets himself inside.

He sits down and talks to Auntie Eloise, Stevie and me for a while. " Mary Kay, how ya doin' honey?" he asks. "I heard them hornets came after you. They're nasty things."

"She sure knows," says Auntie Eloise.

"The tomaters are really good this year," he says as he hands us a bag of the large, delicious ruby-red jewels that grew in his garden.

Uncle George probably has the best garden in Galesburg. One day I helped him pull off the big, fat green tomato worms from his plants. I hated touching them, and I knew they were going to die and I hated that, too. Uncle George threw them in a bag and tied it shut before he threw it in the burning fire pit.

"Couldn't we just put the worms far from your tomatoes?" I asked.

Uncle George didn't say anything. He just smiled and rubbed the top of my head.

Uncle George goes froggin' too and brings home huge frogs for us to eat although we just eat the legs. Sometimes he digs dandelions from the yard and cooks them but I don't like the bitter greens.

When it is dark, Uncle George goes out to hunt the hornets and he's not a bit scared. I watch from behind the safety of the screen door.

He is only out there for a couple of minutes before he comes back and says, "Mary Kay, they won't ever hurt you again but don't pick any more fights with hornets." And he waves good bye to the three of us.

The stings burn and itch for about three days. And I don't play *King on the Mountain* again for a long time.

A few days later school starts. And a few weeks after that when I come home from school, Dad says, "Mom is coming home in a few days." That means that Auntie Eloise and Uncle Chuck and Baby Judy will leave, and I will miss them so much.

The leaves are beginning to change and fall. They cover the sidewalk. When I walk home from school I walk very carefully so I don't step on any cracks even when the leaves are covering them. And I say, "If you step on a crack, you break your mother's back."

"Everything is changing," I say to myself. *I don't want things to change.*

It is 1956 and Stevie is 5 and I am 12 and in the 6ᵗʰ grade.

CHAPTER EIGHT

Growing Up Crazy

Christmas vacation is behind us now and afterwards everything seems a little boring. Especially school. I love my teacher and I love the sixth grade, but I wish we could have a day when we could just play all day long.

Barb and I are at recess, and even though it's cold I am glad to be outside. We are jumping rope, and I haven't missed for over 150 times. Then the whistle blows, and because of that we have to stop and go back indoors. It's not fair.

"Let's not go back inside, Barb. Let's stay out here," I say.

"Okay."

We continue to play until we are the only two kids left on the playground. Mrs. Case, my teacher sees us and blows her whistle hard. "You girls get in here right now," she yells in a deep, loud voice that I've never heard her use before today.

"I think she's mad."

"Me too," says Barb, and we both take off running towards her as fast as we can.

Three faces very close to mine…so close that they could be a three-headed person. "She's awake," says one of the faces, and they all seem to smile. Then the faces move back a little.

I am in a foggy place. The fog lifts for a moment and then returns and lifts again, only to immediately return before it leaves and does not come back. I look around. *This is very strange.* I realize I am lying on a cot in the nurse's office, and the faces are Mrs. Case, the school nurse and the principal.

I open my mouth to talk, but at first the words don't come out. But just like the fog disappeared, my voice returns. "Why am I here?"

"You slipped on the ice when you were running," Mrs. Case says. "At first I thought you had hurt your leg because you didn't get up."

After she says that, I notice that my leg does hurt. I probably hadn't noticed because my head feels like a hammer is pounding in it.

The principal walks out and says, "She'll be fine."

"Can you sit up?" the nurse asks.

"I guess," I say as I try to sit up without moving my head, "But it feels like I'm in outer space or something."

"You need to just lie here for a while," the nurse says.

"I'm going back to class," says Mrs. Case. "Mary Kay, you come back when you feel like it."

"Okay."

Mrs. Case leaves and so does the nurse. I lie back down but I don't like lying here alone in the large, gray room that is far away from everyone else so I decide to go back to class.

Slowly I walk down the big flight of stairs, still feeling like I am in outer space. When I walk into my classroom, all of the kids turn around and look at me.

"I know you won't believe this," I say to one of my friends, "but I can't remember where I sit."

She points to an empty chair.

I walk over and sit down and ask another girl, "Who sits next to me?"

"Leslie."

"Oh. Where is she?"

"She's sick today."

I don't seem to have forgotten anything else, but now my head feels like it might explode and I wish I hadn't come back to class.

When it's noon the bell rings, and I go into the coatroom and grab my coat so I can walk home for the lunch hour. Barb is outside waiting for me and she says, "I thought you were dead."

"You did? Why?"

"You fell, and you just laid there. You didn't even move. Mrs. Case came running over, and she thought you were dead, too, because she put her head on your chest to see if she could hear your heart."

"She did?"

"Yeow."

"And then the janitor came outside and carried you to the nurse's office. Your arm was hanging down by your side. I tried to come with them, but they told me go to my room. I cried, and Mrs. Case said, "Don't worry. She'll be okay.""

The more Barb talks, the more my head hurts, and I am glad when we get home. Surprisingly, Mom and Stevie are gone so the house is quiet. My stomach feels a little sick so instead of making a sandwich, I just lie on the couch until Barb knocks on the door and it is time to go back to school.

For the next three days, my head hurts, and I don't talk very much. Dad is out of town so I tell Mom that I fell on the ice.

"It'll get better," she says.

Mom was right, because three days later when I wake up, my head doesn't hurt at all. I run over to Barb's a little early before we leave for school to tell her the good news, and we celebrate by jumping rope at recess.

The following week is more good news because when I come home from school, my mom says she has a job. I can hardly believe it, but I am so happy because that means she'll be gone every day.

"I'm going to be an executive secretary and be around important people," she tells us. The next day she leaves for work. My brother has to go stay with a neighbor until Mom finds a babysitter for him.

A few days later when I come home from school, Mom is home. She is screaming and hollering and drunk. "I was fired," she screams. "He said I'm incompetent. No one ever said I'm incompetent."

"Stupid! Incompetent!" she screams as she speaks for the voices in her head and then she laughs and cries and screams all at the same time.

It's still too cold for Stevie and I to go outside so we go upstairs. Pretty soon Dad comes home and he talks to Mom, but it doesn't help. She screams at him, "I hate you. I hate you, you dumb bastard. I don't need you, and I don't need anyone."

She starts throwing dishes. Dad says, "Just stop it."

Then I hear more breaking dishes. I'm surprised we have any dishes left.

Dad comes upstairs. His shoulders are drooping and his lips seem to barely part as he says, "Let's go get something to eat."

Steve and I vote to go to our favorite diner that is in downtown Galesburg, and the three of us each have a hamburger and french fries. Afterwards we walk around and window shop. I love to look at the many treasures that are sealed behind the large windows of the closed department stores.

" I wish I had those skates," I tell my Dad. "Stevie would love that red wagon."

After I've made about one hundred wishes as we walk past store after store, Stevie starts walking slower and slower and slower until he is barely moving. "I'm cold, Dad," he says.

Dad looks down at him and picks him up, and Stevie falls asleep almost as soon as his head is on Dad's shoulder.

Dad and I walk back to the car. It is a starry night, and the warm glow from the streetlights and the brightly lit store windows make me feel warm inside despite the cold weather that is biting at my nose and toes and fingers.

In the soft light, with my brother draped over him, Dad looks like he is carrying a little sack of potatoes, but I know it's my brother. "I love you Dad," I say.

"I know Toots." I love you, too."

When we come home, Mom is still screaming. I am really sad that she got fired and when I go to bed that night I pray really hard that she finds another job.

God must have listened because a few days later, she has one. She is going to work for the government, and she will start working the next day. And I pray again only this time I ask, "Please God. Don't let her get fired from this job. Please. Please. Please."

She has found a babysitter, too. Mary shows up the following morning before I leave for school. She smiles and says, "Hi there," and the smile in her blue eyes shines right through her glasses.

Mary is about twenty and has straight, blond hair that is probably even blonder when it's clean. Her dark slacks have many spots on them that are most likely from the various meals she's eaten over the past few days. And when she sits down on the couch to talk to my mom, she rests her hands on her large stomach, which Stevie seems to think is a living pillow because as soon as he comes downstairs he jumps on the couch beside her and nuzzles his head in it. As he does, she rubs his little head with her large, gentle hands.

"It was nice to meet you, but I gotta go. Bye Mary. Bye Stevie. I'll see you at lunch," I shout as I dash out the door to school.

Today I have to walk alone to school as Barb is sick and isn't going, but it doesn't matter because for some reason I hum a happy song all of the way there.

When I return home for lunch and walk through the door, a wonderful smell greets my nose. "My favorite, Mary," I say. "Vegetable soup. How'd you know?"

"A little birdie named Stevie told me"

"Thanks a lot," I say smiling as I sit down to my scrumptious feast.

And when I come home from school, she says, "We've been waiting for you to get home. Do you want to play Monopoly?"

"Sure. Should I call Barb to see if she's over being sick and can come play?"

"The more the merrier, I always say," she says.

I pick up the phone to call, but our teenager neighbor is on it. We have a party line, which our family shares with three other families on our block. Sometimes when I am bored, I listen to other people when they are talking on it...especially our teenage neighbor who talks all of the time about her boyfriends and what clothes she is wearing on a date. I have to be really quiet when I listen to her because if she hears me, she says, "Get off the phone you little brat."

But today I don't want to hear her conversation and if I wait to call Barb until the girl gets off the phone, my mom will be home. You're supposed to be polite and get off of the phone when you hear a click and know that someone else is trying to use it, but she never does. So I just run next door and get Barb.

It becomes an after school ritual that we play a game every afternoon when I get home. Stevie always plays with us too even though he doesn't really understand what we're doing.

Mary makes sure we follow all of the rules and doesn't let anybody cheat although one time when we were playing cards I could have sworn I saw her pull a card out of her pocket.

Happily Mom doesn't get fired, and Mary is at our house everyday. Sometimes she even makes dinner for us although she doesn't stay so Stevie and I can eat before mom gets home and starts screaming.

The days are growing longer, and soon I will be out of the sixth grade. I am kind of sad about that, but I am excited to go to junior high.

Dad is out of town and after supper, Mom says, "Let's go for a ride." Dad takes us for rides in the summer when it's hot so we can cool off, but Mom never does.

"Okay. Where are we going?" I ask.

"Just get in the car."

Steve and I climb into the back seat, and in no time we are in the country. We keep driving, and from the sour smell I know where we are.

"Are we going to the old coal mine?" I ask my mom.

She doesn't say anything but by then the smell is very strong, and as we drive closer I can see the smoke. It is starting to grow dark, and I don't like it out here.

I heard that a long time ago there was a big fire in the mine one time, and it never stopped burning and just keeps smoking.

Mom pulls the car as close as she can to the old mine. "Get out," she says.

I suddenly feel very cold and start to shiver. I take Stevie's hand as we climb out and hold it tightly.

Mom looks at me and her eyes narrow as she smiles at me with a smile that's not really a smile.

"Are you scared?"

"Yes. I wanna go home."

Mom starts to laugh and then I start to cry. Then Stevie cries and says, "Mommy, I want to go home."

It is dark, and the only light on this moonless night is what is coming from the burning coals. Their red light shines into my mother's eyes making her eyes seem as if they are red too.

Stevie starts screaming, "Mommy, I want to go home. I want to go home."

I stand there and hold on to my brother as tightly as a deep sea diver holds on to a life line.

The sickening stench of the coal mine grows stronger, and I think I might throw up. It is dead quiet, and we are not around any other houses.

Stevie is too heavy for me to pick up and run with, and I wonder if I grab his hand if I can pull him and we can run really fast.

I look for a big rock and I see one.

Mom steps towards us, and Stevie sits down and screeches, *"Mommy, I want to go home!"* and buries his little face in his hands.

I run over and pick up the rock and know that I am going to have to hit her in the head as hard as I can and I pray, "Please God, help me."

But Mom stops and then looks like someone who just woke up. The eyes that were slits just a second ago grow round, and she stops laughing. She stands there for a little bit. "Get back in the car. Yeow. Yeow."

She drives back home really fast. Stevie is still crying a little and says, "I didn't like that. Why'd we . . ."

I put my hand over his mouth before he can finish the sentence and whisper in his ear, "Shh."

He tries to speak again and once more I put my hand over his mouth and put my finger to my lips and shake my head back and forth.

When we are home, I run in the house as fast as I can dragging Stevie behind me. "Go to the bathroom," I tell him.

"I don't have ta," he says.

"Go to the bathroom," I scream at him and he starts to cry again. But he goes.

I use the bathroom too because I want to be sure we don't have to come back downstairs.

Then we go up to Stevie's and play trucks in his bedroom for a little bit.

"Put your jammys on," I tell him, "And then I will tell you a story."

"Okay," he says. As he jumps in bed, he asks me, "Mary, why'd we go out there? I didn't like it."

"I know. Don't worry about it, okay? If you lie down, I'll tell you a story that Mom used to tell me when I was five just like you. Only you have to keep your eyes closed"

He closes his eyes and smiles as he pulls the covers up to his neck.

I tickle his eyelashes so he has to keep his eyes closed and tell him a story Mom used to tell me. "If they lined up all of